Feral Terra
By Steven Bazydlo

Feral Terra

Feral Terra

Steven Bazydlo

Published by Steven Bazydlo, 2023.

This is a work of fiction. Similarities to real people, places, or events are entirely coincidental.

FERAL TERRA

First edition. October 29, 2023.

Copyright © 2023 Steven Bazydlo.

ISBN: 979-8223138747

Written by Steven Bazydlo.

Table of Contents

Little thought

Chaos and turmoil will make a parent do crazy things to protect their children. How far they go though, can be scarier than the hell that surrounds them.

FERAL TERRA

Credits

Editor- Tasha Schiedel

Cover art- Matt Seff Barnes

STEVEN BAZYDLO

Chapter 1 Emergency Broadcast

~ Chris

"Get the contingency plan in place, we have a full facility wide breach! We need to start evacuating... " The line went dead. I stood there very confused, "Must have just been someone pulling a prank."

Hanging up the phone, I felt an odd sense of unease at the seriousness in the man's voice, but pushed the thought aside while fastening my tie.

"Hey hun, come get breakfast. You don't want to be late!"

Hearing my wife's voice, I looked down at my watch and realized she was right. Rushing down the stairs I pecked her cheek with a kiss. The kids weren't awake yet, but I knew Beth would explain. I had to stay focused for my interview.

"Hun, at least grab something to go. No employers are going to listen to your mouth when your stomach is grumbling over it now will they? " A big beautiful smile formed as she shoved a bag with a sandwich and a mug of coffee into my hands.

"Thanks babe, but I gotta go. I'll call you after and let you know how it goes."

"Oh, you better." A suggestive look in her eye caught my interest. "And if you do get the job, maybe I'll do a little something special for you to celebrate," she said playfully biting her tongue.

"Guess I better be on my best behavior then, shouldn't I?"

"Maybe you should," she said with a wink. "Now take your sack and get that job."

We shared a laugh and I walked out the door. The neighborhood was not surprising at all. I waved at my neighbor who was also leaving for work, but he seemed a bit rushed.

"I know I was on call, however, no one fucking called me. So if you don't mind, let us focus on how we can fix this." He complained into the phone as he ignored my wave and slammed his car door.

Huh, something must have happened at the lab, I thought while ducking in through the car door.

Driving into the city the radio was nothing but talk shows. For the life of me I couldn't find a good music station, and I was feeling the cold sweats starting to creep in. My grip on the steering wheel tightened with each closing mile. I *really need this job to work out. The rent is behind and I still haven't told Beth yet that we are dangerously close to an eviction.*

"Okay Chris, we got this. It's only a quick interview and we can save this whole situation. We can call the landlord and let him know once I start I can begin making payments again and I won't have to worry about the kids and us being on the street." Repeating this throughout the ride into the parking lot, I couldn't help but have a sinking feeling of possible failure. "No Chris, stay focused, just keep your eyes on the prize."

Stepping on the welcome mat, the doors opened to the grocery store and I felt a feeling of dread as all the anxiety I had been holding in on the trip here suddenly rushed to the pit of my stomach.

It's okay Chris, just relax. Focus on just answering the questions and all of this will be fine.

Finding a worker, I was led to where the interview would be held. I waited in the quiet room with only the sound of the ticking clock to keep me company. Sitting there I felt my mind start to wander and the thought of the phone call started to creep its way back into my brain.

The sound of panic in his voice and the urgency in which he spoke seemed almost genuine. Maybe there really was an emergency. *Should I call someone? Who would I call, what would I say?* "Oh yes, hi Mr. Police, some strange person called my house talking about escaping and activating some kind of contingency plan." *Yeah, that shit wouldn't fly, at least not without me being given pills in a cup for the rest of my life.*

Before the intrusive thought could take over, the door swung open and a well dressed man in a suit walked in.

"Sam, great to see you could come in for the interview!" His voice, a boisterous and inviting tone.

"Chris, sir."

A confused look came over him. "What was that?"

"My name sir... It's Chris."

His demeanor changed and his voice was almost monotone now. "I'm sorry, I must have mistaken you for a colleague of mine's son."

"Oh it's okay, can we still do the interview or...?"

"I'm sorry to say my boy, but that won't be necessary." He walked to his desk sitting down now very formal. "See, we here believe in... hiring from within and making sure the business stays in a small circle of ... ownership."

I knew exactly what that meant. *Guess someone else was already slated for this job.* "So I take it we won't be discussing my possible employment here?"

"Again, I don't think that will be needed. Now if you don't mind I believe my next meeting is waiting." He gestured behind me and some weasley looking prick was standing waving through the office window.

Well shit, now what am I going to tell Beth?

The air in the room became very tense as reality set in and I squeezed past the embodiment of nepotism.

"Sam my boy, you look like you are ready to take the world by storm!" That joy filled laugh the manager had as he embraced the rat faced little kid, killed me as I walked out.

I know it was just a retail job, but I still felt like I was just kicked in the nuts. The drive home I felt horrible, I literally just got cuckolded by some snot nosed kid for a job that I desperately needed. I felt my stomach grumble, making me feel sick, but also reminding me I hadn't eaten yet.

Slowing to a stop at a red light, I grabbed the brown bag and found the sandwich. I knew this would probably be my last meal because no way was Beth going to believe nepotism was to blame for me not getting a basic management position at a goddamn grocery store.

Come on Chris, don't let this little setback ruin your day. Just take a deep breath and relax. Something will turn up soon and you guys will be okay... yeah... fuck!

The rest of the ride home I felt nothing but my stomach lurch and tighten up knowing that Beth was going to kill me, or worse, leave me.

Pulling into the driveway, I didn't know whether or not I should go in or just pull out and keep driving... *eh but the kids... fine... shit! I gotta figure this out.*

Opening the car door I noticed that the neighbor's wife seemed distraught while rushing out the door to their other car. We made eye contact briefly before she peeled off down the street.

Wonder what's got her so scared.

Stepping into the house I caught my wife getting lunch ready. I guess my face said it all because when she turned her smile faded away.

"Seeing as you're home earlier than expected, that's a good sign?" her voice seemed to tremble with a little worry as she tried to cover it with a smile.

"Uh yeah, about the job babe... I don't think I got it."

"Chris! God damn it, it's a freaking retail job. High schoolers are qualified to work there. How can you be so incompetent that even an entry level job is out of your reach."

"Babe, I wasn't even supposed to be there. See the manager there..."

"No! You have no excuse for this one!"

I sat down knowing that this was going to be a long one. We argued for hours about how useless I apparently was and that her family was right. I was about as useful as a dead cat, blah blah blah. It only stopped when the kids finally got home from school. Needless to say, dinner was pretty quiet.

Laying there on the couch, I couldn't help but feel she was right. I tossed and turned all night just thinking about the whole day. Not like I did much, but everything leading up to this just could not get any worse.

The sound of my phone's alarm exploding and vibrating startled me awake. It was sometime in the morning and through blurry eyes I made out the text about a natural or national disaster or something and that they were evacuating Boston along with all surrounding areas. Beth came running down the stairs with the kids. Saying something about people reporting strange attacks popping up.

I was still half asleep while we rushed to the car. The alarm was followed by a mass text telling everyone to evacuate to some quarantine zone in the city, but there are smaller ones throughout the suburbs. We were almost an hour's drive from there and we had no clues to go off of, or what was going on?

It wasn't long before the kids were asleep in the back seat. Traffic was a nightmare, but at least it wasn't dangerous, just slow.

"Apparently we were not the only ones to get the message."

I reached down to turn on the radio, but I felt a sharp slap on my wrist.

"Ow, what was that for?"

"We just got them back to sleep and you wanna go and wake them up with some shitty music."

"We literally just got a national emergency text and alarm and I figured maybe someone was talking about it."

"Chris, what's going on?"

"How should I know?"

"I don't know, you know a lot of dumb shit, maybe say something because I am not sitting in this car in silence." I was astounded by her train of logic. I had never seen her this nervous before.

"Hun, I understand how confusing this is, but I know just as much as you do. So if you don't mind, maybe we can just turn on the radio and maybe we can learn something."

"Don't talk to me like I'm an idiot."

"Well currently I'm trying to find out what happened, but you just slapped my hand away."

Fumbling her phone she snapped at me again "Whatever, turn the damn thing on, but if it wakes up the kids you are taking care of it."

I wish I knew what was going on with Beth. There is no way this is all about the interview thing. *Why is she checking her phone so much though? Oh I don't know Chris, maybe for the same reason you wanna listen to the radio.*

I turned down the volume on the radio, hoping it wouldn't wake the kids. Slowly, I raised it until I could hear what sounded like a recording on a loop.

"All civilians are to be evacuated from the surrounding areas around Boston. Please be advised medical examinations will be implemented at the quarantine zones. All medical personnel are to be advised of a possible viral outbreak and all CDC guidelines are to be followed. Please identify yourself at the checkpoint and report to where you are directed."

"The phone call?"

Beth turned to me with a very confused look. "What phone call?"

"The other day I got a phone call from some guy. I thought he was trying to prank us or something."

"Well? What the hell was it about?"

"I don't know. It was frantic and he said there was a breach or something."

"And you didn't think to mention this odd phone call?"

"I was being rushed out the door, I didn't..."

"Oh so it's my fault now that you didn't mention something important."

"Where is this coming from? I thought it was some kid. There is no reason you should be this mad at something. I'm sure you would have thought the same thing, had you been me."

"No, I would have called the police to report it."

"Who the fu..."

It happened so fast. One minute we were arguing and the next thing I knew, I was upside down in the middle of the road. I could taste blood and my vision was blurry. "What... what the hell happened?" Unbuckling the seat-belt I felt the jolt of pain as I fell from where I was now partially restrained.

"Beth... Derrick... Tyler... you guys okay?"

"Dad, Tyler's not moving!"

Looking around I saw Beth was knocked out and it looked like Tyler was as well.

"D, I'm going to need you to do me a favor, alright?"

Wiping the tears from his eyes he looked at me with such a scared look I knew I had to try and keep him calm. "Bud, you're going to have to unbuckle your seat-belt and then I'm going to need you to help get your brother out of his. I'm going to help mommy and then we can climb out of here, okay?"

"Okay." Through his scared sniffles, he undid his seat-belt and I helped him down so he wouldn't drop and get hurt. "Okay, now I'm gonna help mommy and I'll come back to help you with your brother."

After nodding in understanding, I had to cut Beth free and managed to work our way out of the car. I took a quick look around and saw what the cause was. Someone decided they didn't want to wait in traffic so they drove through it with a plow. They were stopped maybe a hundred yards down the way and people were swarming all over it. The screams of pain seemed to drown out the commotion though.

I turned back and heard Derrick struggling with getting his brother loose when the gunshots erupted from the plow. The people scattered like rats as a man emerged from the truck's driver's side door. He didn't look too good and he appeared to be wearing some kind of camouflage.

"What the hell is..."

"Dad, help!"

My son's voice tore me away from the graphic scene. The man stumbled from the door and into the now screaming and disorganized crowd of people attacking anyone who got in his way with what looked like a whip.

"I'm coming, be careful when you get out here. Stay down and be as quiet as possible."

"Dad, what's happening?"

"I don't know, but that man seems very bad and I don't think we are safe anymore on the highway."

Grabbing my pocket knife, I was able to cut Tyler free and pull him from the car. Beth started to groan as she regained consciousness.

"Chr... Chris... What happened?"

"Babe! Okay good, are you okay?"

"My... my head hurts..."

"We were in an accident, Tyler is hurt and we aren't safe. Can you move?"

"Yeah... I.. I think so."

The screams were getting closer and the deranged man was now heading in our direction. I didn't know if he had seen us or not, but I knew we had to move now.

Scooping Tyler into my arms, Beth staggered to her feet and grabbed Derrick's hand. I didn't know where we were going to go, but I knew we had to go somewhere.

Taking cover behind a car, I could hear Derrick crying. I did my best to try and keep him calm when something caught my attention. All the screaming had stopped.

Hesitantly, I raised my head above the trunk of the car. My view was obscured by the lights of the vehicles flipped from the plow, leaving only a large, thin, hunched over figure. It suddenly jolted forward, shadowed tendrils waving around it. I could see them pulling something heavy, back towards its thicker limbs, and a massive mouth split from its chest.

I dropped down as sweat poured down my face, back against the cold car.

"Babe... what did you see?"

I didn't even need to look at her to see the worry in her eyes. Her tone said it all.

She started to put her head up when I grabbed her arm.

"We have to go, we have to go now. Grab one of the boys and..."

Before I could finish, a blood curdling scream came from where the boys were. I shot a glance in their direction and Tyler was sitting bolt upright, his eyes glued to whatever that shadowy creature was.

Looking back towards it, its body turned slowly and began lumbering into a stampede as it headed in our direction. Its heavy frame crushing into the concrete, sounding almost like bombs smashing down with every step.

I grabbed the boys and ran as hard and as fast as I could. I felt Beth's grip on my arm tighten as she struggled to keep up. Its bulky tank of a body crushed the car we were hiding behind, adding to the thunderous noise.

A split second later and I felt my body lifted into the air followed by a sharp pain in my shoulder. The whole world seemed to slow down as I looked to whatever caused my sudden stop. The world drained out as the site I saw became clear.

The jerk of my body being ripped back freed my son from my grip, but it was clear he was hurt as blood splattered from a wound on his face with the violent motion.

I felt my body tense as I was yanked through the air. The light from the fires illuminating just enough for me to see two giant leaf-like mandibles open to a mouth filled with what looked like venus fly traps snapping open and closed — like rabid starving dogs awaiting a steak.

I closed my eyes just hoping it would be a quick death, but another sudden jerk and I felt the sharp pain tear free and my body spun through the air before crashing onto the concrete divider and falling behind it.

As the world went black, I could hear only what I assumed was gunfire followed by an explosion. The silence was deafening as my vision funneled into nothing.

~Zack

It was finally my day to have Tabitha, her mother was being a cunt, but at least I was able to get some custody. I'm annoyed though, getting called in for an extra shift isn't what I wanted to deal with, but if I drop her off at my moms I'm sure she will understand and then I can make it up to her tomorrow.

The smell of cheap coffee brought me downstairs to where I saw my little angel attempting to pour herself some cereal. She must have seen me because her smile lit up like a flood lamp.

"Daddy! What are we going to do today?" Her smile faded slightly when she saw my uniform.

"I'm sorry baby girl, but daddy has to work today."

It killed me to see her look down and her smile completely gone as she went back to trying to shake out some of the sugary bullshit they called breakfast nowadays.

"Don't worry, I know I've let you down, but you're going to see grandma today and tomorrow I promise I'll take you for ice cream and we can do whatever you want so I can make it up to you."

"You always say that and then you're always too tired to do anything."

Pouring myself a coffee, I knew she was right. Even though she was still a kid she was old enough to know I was always exhausted after a long day, especially a bad one.

Walking over and grabbing the box, I filled a bowl and poured some milk in. She sat there pouting and I know I had promised her a lot, but it was just hard sometimes to make it line up with work.

"Tell ya what, how about even if I am tired we can go to the mall and you can get whatever you want, would that be a fair trade off?"

She looked up to me with her little blue eyes and a small smile started to appear.

"Can we go to the stuffed animal store!" Her voice now back to happy and excited.

"Of course sweetie, now hurry up and eat. I have to get you to grandma's."

"Okay daddy." she gave me a big hug as that seemed to satisfy her.

We finished our breakfasts and headed out the door. I heard the ring of my phone and already knew who it was from the tone. "Great... here we go." Closing the car door and pulling out the driveway, I answered the call.

I didn't even have the phone to my ear and Sarah's voice was already yelling at me about how I was abandoning "her" daughter with my bitch of a mother. Honestly, I had no clue where she was getting that from because my mom has been nothing but a loving grandmother to our daughter.

"If you like child support you have to understand I have to work for the money."

"Figure out a way so you aren't such a deadbeat son of a bi.... Click!"

I hung up the phone and saw that Tabitha was looking out the window and even at her age she understood her mom wasn't right in the head.

"Daddy?"

"Yes hun?"

"Why is mommy so mean to you?"

I was kind of taken aback at her question and had no idea how to answer.

"I..uh... don't know baby girl. But, I don't want you to think any of this is about you, okay?"

There was a moment of silence as I was hoping what I said would suffice. This wasn't the first time she's mentioned it, but I thought the last time would have been the end of it.

"When can I live with you?"

I felt horrible when I heard the words, but I had to tell her the truth. "That's not up to me. I love you very much, but I... I have to listen to what the courts say and they think your mother is a better caretaker."

"But mommy is always drinking and yelling."

"Honey I know, I'm doing all I can to try and fix that."

My phone started to go off with an emergency broadcast and I asked Tabby to look at the notification.

"What's it say hun?"

"E... evacu..nation order?"

It took me a second, but my eyes widened and I pulled over to the side of the road. Grabbing my phone I read the mass text and instantly began speeding to my mothers house.

Turning on the radio, I listened to the emergency broadcast in its robotic tone repeat on a loop that this was not a drill and that all non-essential personnel were to evacuate out of the state.

"Daddy slow down, you're scaring me."

"It's okay baby, just try to relax. We just have to get to grandmas' and then she will get you to safety."

Weaving in and out of traffic, I searched through my phone for my moms number and was frustrated she didn't answer when I called. I didn't catch what the evacuation was for, but understood that if it was to clear the state. It must have been nuclear or war. Maybe the power plant was going to melt down, or worse.

Pulling onto my mothers street, I was confused by the pandemonium. People were going insane. Some were even attacking each other with what looked like branches or thorned vines. I didn't have time to look. I screeched to a halt in front of my mothers, and I felt a sudden sense of worry. Her front door wasn't just open, but kicked to pieces like someone had taken an ax and smashed their way in.

"Baby, I need you to stay here okay, I'm going to go make sure grandma is safe."

I could see the fear in her eyes as she turned to watch the carnage in front of her.

"Close your eyes and stay out of sight. I'll be right back."

Stepping into the street, I pulled my baton and made sure the door was secured behind me.

Luckily all the fighting seemed to be taking place down the street. However, I had an ever increasing feeling that something happened to my mom.

Approaching the splintered door, I could see that the inside of the house was a mess. I felt my pulse race understanding that there had been a struggle.

Maybe she was able to fight off her attacker?

"Ma!" I shouted out for her not caring that the culprit could still be in the house.

I searched downstairs and when I got to the kitchen I started to see what looked like a thick almost black-green substance smeared on the floor along with what I was hoping wasn't my mothers blood. I heard a heavy thump come from above my head, and it made me jump.

I ran upstairs hoping that she was safe and just locked in her room or that maybe it was her dog and they were just trying to get my attention to come help her.

Reaching the room I heard the thump again and I started pounding on the door. Something rustled on the other side. I grabbed the handle, but the door was locked.

"Mom let me in, it's me... Zack!"

The only response I heard was the sound of a window shattering. Taking a few steps back, I didn't know what to expect, but I ran my shoulder into the door several times before it finally gave way, swinging open to a horrifically bloody scene.

My mother's dog was sprawled out and attached to the wall by what looked like vines protruding out of its chest. Its head twisted around at an unnerving angle with more of the rope like tendrils sprouting out of its mouth. Its chest still heaving as if struggling to breath with a painful whimper, each time, he vines would tighten as it strangled the defenseless animal.

I couldn't bear to watch the old dog suffer, but I was powerless to do anything to end its pain. She began to convulse and I shut the door, not able to watch any longer. A sickening, tearing sound followed by a sharp yelp forced me to cover my ears. A few seconds passed and I heard a muffled scream, but knew right away who it was.

"Grandma, no!" Followed by a blood chilling scream.

I was on my feet in an instant, almost falling down the stairs before running out the front door to see my daughter being lifted into the air by whatever monstrosity was now my mother. Her little legs kicking at a spiny appendage starting to pull its way out of the old woman's chest. Her head tilted back, starting to peel open. Her arms were covered in thorns and I could see the blood running down my little girl's arm.

Everything went quiet and I felt my body move as if out of instinct as I watched. Beating away the spiked tongue like growth, I just kept swinging each connection feeling like I was hitting a garbage bag full of meat.

I don't know how long this went on for, but I remember grabbing Tabitha and getting her into the car. She was screaming, but all I could hear was the sound of my heart beating as blood rushed through my ears.

"Daddy, it hurts!"

Finally snapping out of my stupor, I looked down and saw a large thorn with a pulsating sack sticking out of her little wrist. Cuts and scratches littered her arms and legs from where she had been held. Tears ran down her face and I didn't know where to even start.

"I know it does, I'll get you someplace safe and we can get you feeling better okay? Just stay calm and when we get to daddy's work, we can have one of the doctors there take care of that."

Through all the tears and sniffles she was able to muster up a nod and winced with every turn or bounce.

Pulling into the parking lot, I was overwhelmed at the sight of military trucks and lines of people trying to get into the prison. Turning off the vehicle, I sat watching as soldiers were flashing these lights into people's eyes before letting them enter. A man on a gurney was rolled in as a woman and her children were separated from him after one or the other failed to pass the test.

"Daddy."

"It's okay honey, here put this on and if those people ask if you were hurt or anything I need you to lie and say you aren't. If you don't, they will take you away from me."

Wrapping her arm and putting a long sleeve shirt on her to cover the protrusion, I picked her up and carried her to the door. Passing through the crowd of people, I showed my badge letting the soldier know I worked there. He quickly scanned my eyes with the bright blue light and let us pass. I guess he figured since I passed whatever test they were administering that Tabs must be fine, too.

We were ushered into the main cafeteria area through the halls lined with people. All of their faces show a story of how they got there. I watched a man comforting his wife as she clutched a photo of what I could only guess was their son. A child wandered around calling out for his parents not too far from the grieving couple, only for them to look up with hope before a wave of tears again, not recognizing the child. A man began punching the wall, screaming for the loss of his lover. It was absolutely heartbreaking.

When we reached the wide open area, I saw the nurses already doing secondary scans of those that made it inside. I was happy to see that Zoe had made it. Ever since the divorce I kind of have been admiring her from afar, but I knew that one day I would eventually work up the guts to ask her out on a date.

Looking over the room it seemed to me they had the whole place blocked into sections for each nurse to have a set amount of people in a rotation. Waiting for a few minutes, I made my way over to Zoe's section and placed Tabitha down, telling her to stay put while I went to get a doctor to look at her arm.

I didn't know how long it would be, but I understood that whatever was going on, they were separating people who I'm guessing had contact with whatever the hell happened to mom and Tabby.

Looking myself over, I saw a few scratches and a greenish purple substance covering my clothes. I knew what it was, but I couldn't bring myself to accept that yet. *Had I failed the screening and been sent to be with the infected?*

Dipping into the locker room, I changed into a cleaner uniform. All the morning's events replayed in my head. I wanted to tell someone and find out what was going on, but if I did that, then I'd be putting Tabitha in danger.

Exiting out the back door, it was eerily quiet. I knew there was at least one person in medical I could trust, but leaving the cordoned off area in the front, I'm sure there would be more showing up that I couldn't.

Taking the long way around it was so weird, seeing this hallway so deserted, especially at this time in the morning.

I started watching my steps when I began hearing voices and radios make their way down the halls. Following them, I could hear people talking about a virus or something that had escaped containment, all infected had a hundred percent mortality rate." Dispose at all costs to keep from spreading" was the line that caught my attention and made me not want to listen any longer.

Backing away, I knew I had to save my daughter. Turning to run I stopped, seeing shadows approaching from the way I came. I didn't want to be caught, but I couldn't stay in the open like this. Looking around I saw a bio-waste bag filled with old disposable lab coats. Not seeing any other option I grabbed one and threw it on before sneaking inside the isolation wing.

I was shocked at all the activity, but was horrified at what I was seeing being held in the cells. Walking over to the mostly soundproof rooms, I looked in through the little windows and saw people like mom in various degrees of whatever the hell they were now. Their skin, all leathery with the texture of various plants. Little stems and flower bulbs popping with pus, grew from their bodies. For some, whole limbs were gone, replaced with parts that would have been more at home on trees.

I found myself looking in several, stopping at one where the occupants looked vaguely familiar. The woman's neck seemed to be stretched to an unimaginable length around the room creating a kind of blockade. Her face was peeling back revealing needle-like teeth protruding from a stretched vertical lip pulling back, revealing a spike filled gullet — like a snake with a flytrap for a head, poised to strike any who came too close. Her elongated fingers gripping onto what I was guessing were her children, both covered in spike-like teeth. Long dried up sacks dangled as their glazed over eyes began to split open like roses. A stem antenna extended up towards the fluorescent lights. Their mouths opened in silent screams as roots sprouted from what I could only guess were the pores in their skin. Locking them to the floor and to each other in one last embrace of twisted love. The air was filled with leaf-like skin as their bodies pulsed and appeared to breathe through their purplish-green muscles.

I stepped back collecting my thoughts when a group of people, a mixture of doctors and soldiers, walked over and began to talk about something they finally had delivered to take care of the infected.

I couldn't understand much, but from what I could understand it was essentially some kind of weed killer on steroids. One of the men dressed in a more military style hazmat suit walked over with what looked like an exterminator's backpack. A thick liquid sloshing back and forth in the semi-transparent plastic tanks.

One of the scientists gestured to the soldier with his hand and spoke in a relatively blunt and nonchalant tone like it was business as usual.

"This is for a small demonstration. This is what we use at the lab to destroy any potential problems. We have modified the nozzle to fit into the feeding slit in the door for this particular situation. However, the end result is all the same."

With that, the man nodded and the soldier sprayed the inside of the chamber. Almost instantly, a shrieking howl of pain escaped from the gap as the cell door began to bend from the force of the pounding from the creature within. A furiously knotted hand burst through the bulletproof glass opening and thrashed around to grab onto whatever it could. The fingers unfurled, revealing a screeching slit like a mouth, spitting a thick liquid over the plastic shielded group, before it started to flake apart and shrivel. Finally, breaking down into a mush and falling to the floor in a muddy clump.

When everything was silent again, the same scientist looked in and turned back to the rest of the group.

"We have already rerouted the sprinkler system and charged the lines with our mix. We have completed a few test runs and it has been very successful. We already have the first full batch of subjects ready for disposal. If you will follow me, our head of staff Dr. Ian Michaels will be there. His office has made it clear he will supervise each use to verify every instance of the infection is properly destroyed.

Chapter 2 Quarantine

~Chris

I woke up in bed to my alarm going off. My body heaving with the feeling of fear rushing through it. I was relieved that it had all just been a dream.
The annoying ringing sound wouldn't shut up until I hit the top of the clock. The sun was shining through the window and I could hear the dump truck driving by. The smell of burnt toast was in the air and I had a sudden burst of energy as I felt an overwhelming need to rush downstairs.
Rounding the corner, I saw my wife at the stove scrambling eggs and hash-browns. I couldn't see her face, but was relieved that she was okay.
"Hey hun, whatcha cookin?"
Her silence was only blocked out from the sound of the scraping of the spatula against the pan.
"Babe?"
Approaching her and placing a hand on her shoulder, she suddenly stopped cooking and the scraping stopped. An eerie quiet filled the room and I stepped back.
"Is everything..."
The sound of frantic footsteps from above stampeded to the top of the stairs and descended them with inhuman speed. Turning back to face my wife, her neck stretched up as her arms began to writhe under her shirt, her hands splitting at the webs into fleshy plant-like tendrils, her nails becoming jagged thorns. Turning her head she looked over her shoulder towards me, her eyes becoming a sickly shade of yellow mucus. Her head began to crack apart at her ears, her mouth and jaw dropping down as her eyes and forehead reared back revealing needled teeth and a long fleshy vine like tongue working its way up her throat, bulging it as it creeped up.
Stumbling back I felt my hands being gripped. Looking down I saw my sons, their faces equally as disfigured, wrapped around my hands and their thorny appendages beginning to twirl around and sink deep into my skin. Try as I did to escape, it was pointless to struggle.
Looking back to Beth, she was now standing, her head in the shape of leathery petals surrounding her voracious maw. Her neck snaked back and forth before in an instant striking forward and the world went dark.

The sound of gunfire and shouting woke me up. Before my eyes could even focus, someone was shining a light in my eyes.

"Sir, sir! Can you hear me?"

Groggy, my vision slowly adjusted and the blur of a face and light formed into a nurse with a flashlight.

"What... what happened?"

"Oh good, I thought we were losing you. Take a second to get your bearings, but we are going to move you with the others to a different cell block. You took a nasty hit, but should be fine."

Before I could even ask a question, she was off to help another patient. Sitting there, I saw that I was surrounded by people in varying degrees of pain. Those not screaming or huddled up were locked with a thousand-yard stare or dead. Armed guards were patrolling what I could only guess was a cafeteria of some sort that had been turned into a makeshift triage center.

Rubbing my head, I felt a headache starting to become more evident. I felt tears welling up as I noticed I couldn't see my family. I reached over and grabbed the arm of the nearest nurse and started demanding to know where my wife and kids were.

"Sir, I have no clue. If I had to guess they are probably in quarantine which is where you will be going when you do what I asked you to do and go over there and wait with the rest of those cleared to be admitted." The annoyance in her voice and her straight answer made it clear she had no clue what had happened to my family. The feeling of hope though that maybe they are in the next area made me relax my grip.

It took a moment for me to notice her looking, not at me, but behind me, to someone over my shoulder and I realized that what I was doing was wrong.

Pulling her arm free of the grip, the nurse's stern expression softened. "Listen, I'm sorry for the confusion sir, but if you can't tell, something major is going on. I wish you the best of luck finding your family. However, I do not have any knowledge of even who your family is. In the last hour or so, all of these people, including yourself, were just pulled in here and now the military has set up a perimeter and shooting at whatever they see that did this."

"What was that thing out there, what's going on?" The feeling of defeat started to set in.

"I don't know sir, like I said, once the shit hit the fan communication with the outside kind of stopped. I was given this flashlight and told to scan incoming civilians' eyes by the soldiers. Something about the UV function lighting up indications of exposure. Please wait over there. If your family is here they are in there." With that she turned back to her duties.

As I walked away, I heard her call out for a soldier in a biohazard suit, and the woman she was examining was led out to a separate plastic chamber. The woman seemed to resign herself to the situation, but her husband stood up to rush the guard only to sit back down when another soldier raised his weapon. The nurse looked at the soldier and then tried to comfort the distraught man. I couldn't hear what was said, but she seemed to sympathize with him for a moment before shining the light in his eyes.

I was still a little groggy from being unconscious. I stumbled and swayed through the crowd of people all being sorted by a handful of medical staff. As I got closer to the doorway, I noticed the uniforms weren't police, but corrections officers uniforms. I must be in the prison. Soldiers were patrolling the room as well as the halls beyond the barred doors.

I can only hope my family is safe in here, wherever they may be. I just had to keep telling myself that. They must have been taken while I slept. I'm sure they made it. They were hurt, but still alive.

I waited where I was directed for a few minutes before several others joined me. When the soldiers came, we were only told to follow them and where we were led to, we could hear the prisoners shouting in protest.

They marched us along the catwalks before placing us together into small cells.

I looked in every one that we passed and was disappointed that all of them were filled, but none looked to be my family. Closing the doors behind us, the guards went off to do whatever, while we tried not to rub against each other like sardines.

I managed to work my way over to the toilet and sat down. The shouting and banging of angry, confused adults and the crying of scared children eventually died down as the night progressed.

The sobbing silence is only broken by the popping sound of gunfire occasionally breaking through from outside. I sat with the thought that somewhere in here my family was probably worried sick and I couldn't even be there to help comfort them.

I have no clue what that creature was on the road, but I know it wasn't human. That... monster was something out of a nightmare. I just hope they made it to a safe place if they aren't here.

I don't remember falling asleep, I must have had a concussion, but the sounds of gunfire and screaming woke us all up. It was not long after the sounds of distant explosions were getting closer.

An alarm began to blare as the whole building erupted in violence.

~Zoe

She knew she had said more than she should have, but that guy seemed just overly concerned. He needed some sort of reassurance.

"Hey Zoe!" One of the guards exited the quarantine area waving to her to come over. She had seen him a few times creeping around and watching her, but couldn't remember his name.

Great, what does this asshole want, can't he see I'm a bit busy? I shined the light over the eyes of the child sitting in front of me to act like I was busy, her irises glowing an emerald green with golden veins pulsating with a strange aura.

She felt her stomach knot, knowing that whoever goes into that quartered off part of the prison hasn't been seen since.

"Zoe, get over here now! I need to talk to you."

The little girl looked up to her while extending out her arm. Tears started to well up in her eyes, as she showed a large spike like tooth sticking out from her wrist.

In her best bedside voice. "It's okay sweetie." I patted the young girl's shoulder and fixed a few strands of hair away from her watery eyes. Smearing the tears into the girl's cheeks, Zoe looked around, but couldn't see any adults near her. "Hey hunny, do you know where your parents are?"

Pulling her hand away, the little girl shook her head no, and hid her hand away. Suddenly Zoe felt a hand on her shoulder and she closed her eyes, just praying whoever was there didn't see the spike.

"Well hey there darlin, I know the pretty nurse here is helping you, but I need to steal her away for a minute, okay? Here, maybe this will make up for it."

Zoe already knew who it was and she knew that this was just a facade. She watched as a gloved hand held out a candy bar over her shoulder and the little girl reached out to grasp it.

"Oh, what's that deary? Are you hurt?"

The girl looked reluctantly at me, but I couldn't look her in the eyes knowing what was about to happen. A soldier appeared and that asshole's voice was just so damn friendly, but filled with false concern. "Listen, my friend here, he's here to help people like you. See the little patch here on his shoulder?"

The little girl looked up, her expression relaxing into that of hope. "If you are ever hurt by whatever those scary monsters are, go straight to anyone wearing one of these. They will make you all better."

The little girl smiled and took the soldier's hand while holding her injured wrist to her chest. As she walked away, I lowered my head.

"Nurse... Zoe is it?"

Standing up to face him, he was putting a clipboard under his arm. I had to put on my best fake smile just to keep from hitting him. "Dr. Michaels."

"Zoe, you understand that we are dealing with a very unorthodox situation, correct?"

"Yes."

"Then do you mind telling me why, when you saw that girl's injury, you did not automatically call over one of these fine soldiers here, to assist?"

I stood there in silence as his smug face just looked like a punching bag while he continued talking. "It is paramount that we keep the infected people away from those lucky enough to have not been exposed. Now were you planning on reporting that girl?"

"Yes I was, I just wanted to find her parents first."

He adjusted his stance and a look of annoyance took over his face. "She will be reunited with them in the quarantine cells. I'm sure they will be more than happy to see her."

His tone was very direct, almost as if it was a parroted line that he has been saying a lot. "Now next time you find an infected, notify my men and we will take care of it, we wouldn't want to have to remove you from your duty for aiding the spread of a deadly pathogen now would we? That would more than certainly hamper any further career aspirations, have I made myself clear?"

"Understood sir." I felt my stomach churn as I said the words, but I knew it was the only way to get him to go away.

"Good, now carry on. We have lots to process." A smug smile of superiority formed on his face before gesturing to a guard and walking away. Only turning to look back at him as I slid down into a chair to breathe and scoff at the audacity of that prick.

I felt tears starting to form, but I managed to keep them contained. I couldn't have these scared people seeing me breakdown. I couldn't stand the thought that something bad might be happening to those who weren't so lucky to not be showing signs of infection.

I felt a warm hand on my shoulder and a voice whispered in my ear. "We need to talk."

Turning to look, it was the C.O. from before. I never did learn his name.

"Excuse me, do I know you?" I said, pushing his hand away.

A little put off and looking around, he lowered his head and whispered again, "Zoe, we work together, but I don't think we were ever introduced. I need you to listen to me though."

I didn't know what to say, but the panic in his voice made me listen. "What's wrong?"

Leaning in he looked around to be sure we were the only ones in the conversation. "They are killing those people."

"What?"

"The people being sent in there are being rounded up into these... these pens and being sprayed with some kind of chemical. I didn't stay to watch, but I heard the screams... That psycho is killing them."

The thought of the little girl flashed into my head. "Oh my God, are you sure they were dead? Maybe they were just having a reaction or something?"

Looking around again he pulled out his phone and started swiping." I took a few pictures, these are the same cells before and the ones that had already been sprayed... whatever they were being covered in was doing something to them and all that was left was this ... this dried out husk and melted sludge."

The pictures with each swipe got more and more disturbing before the final swipe dropped my stomach. It was the little girl from before. "Who's that?"

Tilting the phone back he had a sad look in his eyes. "That's my daughter, I brought her here but we were attacked by one of those things. I managed to pull my daughter free and we got here, but I've been pulled away so much I lost track of her. I was coming in here to find her so we could sneak out of here. That doctor or whoever he is is fucking nuts and I don't want to risk if they decide to just kill all of us."

"Why come to me though? I don't mean to be rude, but I don't even know your name."

His shoulders dropped a little. "We may not interact, but since you've been doing all the scans I figured you should know so you can keep an eye out for her. My name is Zack, her name is Tabitha."

I didn't know what to say, but he needed to know that psycho just took his daughter.

"Zack... Please don't do anything rash, but I saw your daughter earlier being escorted into the back by soldiers."

His head shot up and his eyes flared open. "What! I have to get her, they're going to kill her!"

Covering his mouth I looked around, only a few people turned to look at us. I had to think of something, the last thing we needed was a panic worse than what was already going on.

Leaning in close I had to think of something."Shush, I will help you find her but you need to relax, okay?"

His eyes closed and I felt a sad exhale blow threw my hand as he nodded in agreement. Pulling my hand away he seemed to relax knowing he wasn't alone now.

Turning away I started to gather my things. "Give me a minute here and we can come up with a plan to get your daughter out of there."

Looking back over my shoulder I saw he was already gone. Surveying the area I saw him looking back at me right before heading into the back rooms. "Shit!"

~ Michaels

Sitting as I went through the reports, the spread throughout the surrounding towns has been an unprecedented outcome. Even at their current rate of disposal of infected, they were facing an ever growing threat as the people kept coming in. Those infected were as good as dead and their only option was to dispose of as many as possible, as soon as possible. If he had it his way, he would just have the whole lot exterminated and call in an air strike. At least that's what I have to say to the higher ups.

Why waste time trying to save a doomed populous? The whole state was already quarantined. The military was erecting a massive fence and all who tried to escape were shot on sight. The cover up for this was going to be a clusterfuck. At least if we bombed the area we could claim terrorist attacks or a transport of a nuke gone horribly wrong. Anything was better than sitting here wasting time giving these people false hope while scrambling to try and contain this mess.

Picking up the paper with his continuation orders he crumpled it up. "Bureaucratic pussies!" *This isn't about containment anymore. This is about survival. It's been less than a day and already this virus has spread to the suburbs. Luckily the few experiments that managed to escape the area weren't killed. However, given the organisms nature that will only slow the inevitable. We must burn this state to the ground and salt the earth they fell upon just to be sure. But, the plan is already in action.*

"Sir, the next group is ready for disposal. We need your signature to proceed." I had been so deep in thought I hadn't noticed the soldier had entered the office. *Even they have realized the hopelessness of the current predicament. On last count, some have already deserted. Again, less than a day and even the "brave" men and women have abandoned their post forcing us all to pull double duty. I'm not even a soldier.*

Dawning my hazard suits helmet, I took a deep breath and sighed. "Very well, lead the way."

Walking down the deceptively calm blue hallway, we passed the plastic-walled rooms marked with the varying colors of biohazard symbols. The victims in yellow still had some time before the physical effects started to manifest. These were those who we sorted from the hoard of the unending people flowing into this hellish place.

The orange was for those already showing symptoms with minor mutations. These people are scared and don't understand this was not our intention with our research. Looking down I saw the little girl from earlier, the tiny spike in her wrist having now spread into a green leaf like sprouts were growing from the wound, wrapping their way up her arm and down between her fingers. Her face is already starting to show signs as well, with a dark gray green color forming in splotches against her skin — like mold on an old piece of bread. If only she could understand that had this been in the lab, she would have been an excellent test subject to monitor. Healthy children were hard to gather for tests. The best we could usually get had some kind of drug addiction or disease that would always skew our results, but looking at her I felt both joy and sadness that in all respects our experiment was a success and did exactly what it was created to do. But, the fact it was on American soil was disappointing. Sure releasing a controlled amount in some no name third world country is one thing. No one would miss a small village being burned down, especially when that is commonplace there, but you have to destroy a city or some suburb here and all eyes are on the situation like stink on shit. *Perfect.*

Pulling my gaze away from the sad child, we made our way into the red zone. The second to final stage. The people here have lost a majority of their humanity. The mutation has spread to the nervous system and the people have begun transforming completely. Their physical appearance is disturbing and contorted, we have to move them to their own isolation to avoid scaring the others. The fact none of the others have caught on just goes to show how much like sheep the general population is. The beauty in their tormented bodies is only something I will understand.

"We've had to increase our disposal times due to the rising numbers, and the infection appears to be starting to show its mutagenic properties of the sprouted much sooner after exposure." The soldier spoke with a dead tone in his resignation to his duty.

"I understand this is difficult, soldier, but please don't fret too much, this is only temporary. We have a cure in the works and it is only a matter of time before we get our first shipment."

At this the soldier let a small weak smile slip out as if knowing some hope of an end would get him through. I knew this was complete bullshit though. Even in our testing phase we only managed to make a small batch and even then if you didn't get the antidote into your system within a few minutes of exposure, you were too late. The only thing we had to offer those too far gone was a flamethrower or the weed killer, which we luckily did have in spades. If only the sprinklers had turned on at the lab all of this could have been avoided. My main concern though now, is if the infection is mutating faster, then it is only a matter of time before we need a black hazard room, at that point even I will be abandoning this shit hole. I did like the name the military personnel have given the infected. *The sprouted... I like the sound of that.*

Entering what used to be the isolation cells, the sprinkler system had been cut off and filled with the toxin. The doors were all opened and a lure was placed into the middle of the cell block. By the red stage infection, most have lost their cognitive abilities and were relying on their baser instincts. We found a small injured cat or whining dog would usually suffice for drawing them out. Once the cells were cleared, the doors were closed and sealed as the sprinklers were activated. Hundreds laid dead from the previous batches in various degrees of decay on the ground. Their bodies turned into an infectious mulch after they were killed off. We would eventually have to clear out the remnants. However, that might not be our problem. There were several of these locations chosen throughout the state, all of which were never meant to last.

Watching as the process was carried out, I felt hurt that after all my team's work, this was what it was turned into. A death camp for possibly the next step in human evolution. Evolution not by a god or nature, but from man itself fixing the imperfection of both their failures.

Reaching down and signing the tablet to request another shipment of toxin, and the report of whatever number disposal we were on, the power shut down causing complete darkness. Before the emergency power turned on, I heard something undeniable. I heard the containment cells opening, followed by the flashing of rifles firing in all directions.

~Zack

I knew I couldn't wait for Zoe, I was stupid to think she would understand the gravity, especially now knowing my daughter was in one of those psychos gas chambers. I also knew I couldn't go in guns blazing. Yeah I had some weapons training, but I wasn't a soldier by any definition. I knew where the holding cells were and that if I could get in there I might be able to find her pretty easily. Then it dawned on me. There was a fail safe measure in the power, that in case of a fire and the emergency power didn't turn on, the cells would open in order to allow the prisoners to escape to the yard.

The generators were downstairs and I'm no genius, but I do know how to break stuff. Then it's just a matter of cutting the main power which is not far from the generator room. From there it was only a flight of stairs to the isolation wing where I can find my daughter, cut the plastic barrier and then they can figure out a way out from there.

Flashing my badge and telling the guard that I have to go check on a few things, the extra use of the power and utilities might be overpowering the facilities breakers. He didn't seem to know any better and allowed me to pass.

It didn't take long for me to locate the generators and even less to pull a few wires and dislodge a part or two that looked important.

"That should do the trick. Now where is the breaker."

Going through the old basement room, I found a door with an unlit exit sign above it. I had heard rumors of tunnels under the prison, but figured they were all sealed off.

"I'll have to keep that in mind."

A few minutes of searching and I managed to find the breaker box for isolation. "No sense in cutting all the power."

Looking around, I found a rusted bar and placed it behind the insulated cable before prying as hard as I could. I felt my muscles strain before the wires tore free with a massive spark, causing me to fall back driving the hunk of steel into another power box causing an explosion of electrical arcs and the lights dimmed.

"Shit! Okay, gotta go!"

The amount of noise I had made was way louder than I had wanted, and I was scared that I would bring unneeded attention. I had made it halfway up the stairs before I heard the familiar sound of gunfire. The sudden worry rushed into my feet, driving me to run faster.

"Daddies coming baby, hold on."

Lowering my shoulder, I slammed through the door. The guard from before whipping around seeing me run out, he raised his weapon ready to fire.

"Don't shoot, one of those things is down there!"

Grabbing his radio he requested backup, but in the static you could hear the barrage of bullets being fired, followed by shouting.

"Did you have any contact with the creature?"

"No,thankfully not."

After a long second the soldier looked at the door then to me and told me to bar the door and that he would be back with his squad to clear out the creature and to get the power back up. He spun on his heel and started to run down the hall disappearing around a corner.

Pulling my baton from its holster, I ran down the hall towards the gunfire. Turning down the corridor, I had to stop at the hell I saw before me. The hallway was filled with people tearing each other apart. A brutal melee of the infected and the losing guards. I mustered all my strength to force out a shout.

"Tabitha!"

Taking out my flashlight, in all the carnage I could see the mangled mass of bodies thrown around the floor. Ragged corpses were pinned to the walls by spike-like appendages or tangled and wrapped in vines. Some of the mummified bodies were still squirming as the vines tightened with every breath they took.

Stepping over and around the bodies, I strafed my light and felt a wave of relief wash over me as my daughter was there. She seemed shell shocked, kneeling there over the body of a dead soldier. I could hear the gunfire now erupting in other parts of the facility. Small explosions from what I guessed were grenades. I ran to her swinging in the maelstrom of violence. I didn't care who I had to hurt to get to her, they were simply in my way.

In my frenzied state, I managed to smash my way through the crowded masses and found myself standing over my little girl. Leaning down, I touched her shoulder. "Tabitha, daddies here. Come now, we have to get out of here."

Without hesitation I felt her turn and buried her head into my chest with a painful hug.

Wincing at the sudden sharp feeling in my ribs, I had to ignore the pain and be strong for her. "It's okay babygirl, I'm here."

Scooping her up, I felt her little arms grip me tight and I started running for the exit. Entering the hall I started making my way back to the basement. We were almost out of here. I won't let these horrible people do anything to hurt you.

~ Chris

The darkness of the cell block was only contrasted by what little moonlight could enter from the windows along the roof. The sudden deafening screams and hundreds of moving shadows was enough to scare anyone. Shoving through the people, I managed to make it to the cell door just as it opened. I felt those behind me trampling forward and forcing me to the ground. I felt them stepping and tripping over those of us who fell. I managed to crawl to a railing and dragged myself to my feet.

In all the darkened chaos, I did what I could to follow the flow of people. It wasn't long before flashes of light flickered all around us and we saw horrific creatures in the quick illuminations. And that's when I learned what we were running from. I tried to stop myself from being forced closer to the fighting, but again found myself shoved to the side. I couldn't go forward and going back was impossible. Before I could even make a decision I found myself lifted up and over the railing. The feeling of my weightless body and the rushing air in the dark suddenly stopped as a sharp pain shot into my back. Then again with another sudden stop and all the air rushed from my body, when what felt like a pipe hit my stomach.

Rolling to my side, my adrenaline kicked in again and even in the limited light I made out the faint sign for "The Yard" and I could see a few people almost secretly running through the door beside it. Everyone else seemed to be preoccupied with the stampede of the others that they didn't see the exit right there. Even in the low light, I could make out that the figures I saw were a woman and her children. I felt a glimmer of hope. That had to have been them.

Using a table to lift myself up again, I knew something wasn't right, my left arm was limp at my side and I had a sharp pain in my chest as I breathed. Struggling through the door, the sounds of terror behind me and seeing my wife and sons drove me to try and push through the pain. If nothing else, I could at least be with them.

Feeling my way along the wall, with each agonizing step, I could hear the fighting fading into the distance replaced with the desperate panting of the few people who also must have seen the door. I saw through the next set of gates, my wife's blond hair in the flash of light as she ran out the building. I tried to shout for her, but it was too painful. My chest was heaving and in all the confusion I had forgotten how injured I was.

Falling through the next set of barred doors, I managed to crawl the rest of the way. I could see the yard was bright with search lights and knew it was only a little further.

I felt an arm wrap around me as I was struggling to get through the door and I was blinded as the search light lit up the doorway. Looking at my savior I didn't know this person, but I saw the bright orange of his jumpsuit.

"Th...thank you." I managed to struggle out.

He looked over at me and it became clear this wasn't a kind gesture.

"Don't be thanking me yet homeboy, I don't wanna be shot."

As the light filled the area, it became clear to me the tower guards were shooting anyone wearing orange as they scattered across the yard. The pop sounds followed by the wizzing sound rushing past me kicked up dirt all around us. He was using me as a human shield.

In my pain filled delirious state, I went from being blinded by the dark to blinding light barely able to make out the few shadowy figures desperately climbing the razor wire topped fences. We reached the base of the fence and

I felt the man drop me to the side, another sharp pain rushed through me as I felt my arm pop back into place. Lying there, I watched the large inmate ascend the fence, ahead of him I could see my wife and sons almost to the top. They stopped and with the lights in my eyes, I could see the shadow of Beth pulling off her jacket to lay it across the razor wire so they could climb over. I smiled knowing at least they would be safe. Then I saw the large inmate grab one of my sons, pushing and pulling him until he grabbed him off the fence before violently throwing him onto the wire. Screams of pain followed by blood being sprayed as the blades sank deep. I couldn't see who it was, but I could see Beth fighting the large man as he raked my son against the wire.

I tried to get to my feet, I was shouting Beth's name while trying to drag myself up to save them, but I was too late. I heard her scream as she lost her grip and I watched almost as if it was in slow motion as she fell from the top of the fence, before speeding up just before hitting the ground face first. A sickening crack followed the impact. Several gunshots echoed out and the inmate fell over the fence getting caught on the wire as the bullets ripped through him. He stopped suddenly as the wire synced tight, slicing deep into his leg leaving him hanging there. The sudden shaking of the fence caused the other boy to fall with another crack as his legs and arm fractured in all directions.

Pulling myself to the boy that was now howling in pain, I had no idea how I would even save him. Turning him over, I fell back as the wide eyed child just screamed not knowing how to process the pain, but I felt a new terror as I looked at him. This wasn't my son.

Looking over at the mother, I could see her eyes wide like her child and her chest was heaving as she struggled to breath. Her eyes darted back and forth, but she couldn't move. Try as she may, her broken limbs left her only able to attempt to get up, but the broken bones simply rubbed underneath the skin, unable to control her arms or legs. She could only thrash around like a turtle on its back.

I could hear the other boy on the fence still moaning in pain, but also unable to release himself. I heard him crying for his mother as his brother was going into shock.

I felt what little life I had in me got sucked away. Not knowing what to do. I felt someone grab my arm again, thinking it was another attempt to use me as a human shield. I turned, balling up my fist. I wasn't going to be used like that again. I brought my hand up to push away whoever was holding my arm away. I went to swing when I saw it was a guard and I stopped.

His hands went up in a defensive stance as if to claim he wasn't going to hurt me. "Come on, we gotta go!"

I reached out to try and grab the broken woman's son, but I didn't have the strength to hold on. Looking the mother in her eyes as I was pulled away, I saw beyond her, several of the infected were making their way out the door. Their leathery plant-like bodies in various horrific transformations. Some were running, others galloped like animals as they charged out like ants running from a burning hive. All the sound seemed to drain away as a high pitch tone seemed to replace everything. Her son's screams reduced to nothing but mouth movements, but her unflinching gaze staring into my eyes. I tried to scream I was sorry, but I couldn't find the words before I was dragged back inside to a lit up section of hallway.

The man that grabbed me laid me down against the wall next to a little girl. He barred the door with a chair before turning back to me. I couldn't hear what he was saying and I felt a small slap to my cheek. "Hey, buddy, you with me?"

All of a sudden, everything hit me and I started scrambling and screaming, swinging my arms before the man restrained me.

"Hey, hey, calm down, relax! I know whats going on is fucked up, but I need you to focus. I need help getting my daughter out of here."

"Where's my family?" I shouted at the stranger.

"I don't know man, but if they were in that cell block, then I'm sorry but they are probably gone. Not many made it past the doors and the few who made it to the yard are next."

Curling up at the man's words, I felt an emptiness form in me. Like a cavity slowly destroying the nerve.

"I know this is hard man, but we need to move. Those things are coming this way next."

Feeling the man reach his arm down to help me up, I did my best to steady myself. "Wh... where are we going to go?"

The man gave a small smile. "The basement, there is a tunnel that leads out of here, but I need help moving something out of the way so we can fit through. I felt an enormous amount of guilt as I took one last glimpse out the window where I saw those creatures attacking the mother and her children. I had to force myself to look away. "Please lead the way, I can't be here anymore."

~Zoe

In all the confusion and delirium of pain, time had passed and not knowing if what Zack said was true, I had to at least prepare for whatever stupid ass plan he had in mind. Gathering my things was pretty simple and I told one of the other people giving the tests that I needed a break. It had been hours since everything went to hell so no one really questioned it, we were all drained.
I wasn't allowed in the temporarily restricted area, but I was able to get into the break room where I could at least get some coffee, or get a nap in. I knew Zack was upset, hell if I had kids I would be doing everything I could to get them back, but there is no way he could get to where they have her, not with all the guards. He was lucky to have seen what he saw.
Going to my locker, I checked my phone and there were several missed calls from my parents. I guess in all the mess I hadn't had a chance to respond. "They must be worried sick."
Hitting the call button, the phone only rang once before I heard my mothers panicked voice. "Oh my god, are you alright? We saw on the news about some kind of quarantine and..."
"Mom, I'm okay... I don't really know what I can tell you, but everything is very touch and go at the moment. Please don't worry too much about me though, I'm safe and there are plenty of military guys here."
"They are saying something about some kind of animal attacks. The news is acting like this is no big thing, but the military is putting up walls all around the state. What the hell kind of animal needs to be contained like this?"
"Putting up walls?" I was confused. I knew they were planning on quarantining the state, but that seemed a bit excessive.
"Yes hunny, and the governor already called for martial law to be enacted. Please tell me you found a way out of the city."

I didn't want her to worry, but I couldn't tell her the truth. I was stuck here, at least until we find a way out of here. Besides, it's best if they think it's just some wild animals and not mutant plant creatures like some of these people have been freaking out about. I hadn't seen one myself yet though. "'I'm fine mom, but listen, if we lose contact I will be fine, it just might take me a little bit to get to you guys, okay?"

"Please let us know, we worry about you and ..."

"Mom... mom? What the hell?"

Looking at my phone the signal was gone. "That's weird, I usually have full bars." If what she was saying is even remotely true though, would they really block the cell signals? "I need to get out of here."

Peeking out from the door, I saw everyone was busy so I decided to make my move. If I take the back hallway here I just need to get past the guards out front. I hadn't seen too many patrolling back there and it would wrap around for a quick exit.

Grabbing my stuff from my locker, I changed my clothes. Just as I was about to head out the back door, I heard the front entry open and one of the officers walked in. We caught each other's eyes and I felt a sense of dread. I felt like a mouse caught by a cat and the only thought was, what would happen to me if I was caught with my self preservation plan in mind? But, he didn't do anything, no words, no angry disappointed dad face. He simply nodded as if to say he understood and simply mouthed the words "be safe." He then looked to be sure no one was coming and gave me a head bob to let me know it was clear to go.

We all knew things were getting bad, and I felt horrible leaving, knowing that all those people might not have a clue what's going on, but if we all get locked in here, we are as good as dead.

Moving as quietly as possible, there didn't seem to be many soldiers, but I still stayed close to the walls and kept as quiet as possible.

Where is everyone? I know I heard rumors that some of the soldiers had been going AWOL, but it seems like they knew something was up and just vanished. I gotta keep moving though, I don't have time to worry about others doing exactly what I'm doing.

Making my way down another two halls, I finally saw the front door, but there were a couple of soldiers posted as guards. *I wonder at this point if they were keeping whatever was outside, outside, or keeping us in here. If they had been the guards I'm sure they would have understood, but would these guys?*

Before I could finish my thought the lights dimmed and the sound of gunfire erupted from someplace else in the building. I froze when the guards looked at each other and back down the hall at me.

"Hey! What are you doing over here?"

"Uh... going for a walk?"

The shots rang out again and this time was constant and getting closer. The guard's radio static came to life with people begging for reinforcements. The guards looked at each other then back at me before they took off down the hall leaving the door wide open.

Looking around and now slightly terrified of the fact something has really gone wrong, the only thing that popped into my head was that Zack did something very stupid, but I also saw a wide open door that made all of this not my problem.

A flurry of gunshots followed by a wet splashing sound paralyzed me. It wasn't far and I knew there was another hall paralleling this one just out of sight.

I must have been standing there longer than I thought, because I started hearing something. Like something heavy and wet being dragged across the floor, an acrid smell of some sort lingered in the air and muffled screams strained to echo off the walls. I didn't want to be here for whatever it was that I was hearing, so I took off down the hall.

Approaching the door, I kept an eye on the corner of the hallway. Pressing myself up to it and ready to run at the first sign of trouble. Leaning out just enough to see what might be waiting. I gasped at what I saw.

The two guards had run straight into some horrifying creature. She had heard people talk about the monsters, but this was her first time seeing one in full. It held both men with arms made of tentacle like vines, a third was swaying behind as if it was saving it as it walked the halls. The tendrils wrapped around them pinning one to the ceiling completely entombed like a plant mummy and the other was still trying to scream on the floor as more of the roots and vines forced their way down his throat causing it to bulge and split open, bursting all over the floor like blood covered snakes.

Its multicolored torso made of fleshy petals was spread open with a tongue of thorns protruding from it. A bulb of pulsating sinew dripped with gelatinous fluids with black seed-like chunks suspended within, dripped from the thorny appendage. Its legs were squatted and seemed to be dug into the floor to stabilize its heavy body.

I watched the gruesome scene as the vines separated around the soldier's face that was pinned to the ceiling. His body was limp as it tilted his head back to open his mouth. Slowly it drove its tongue down his throat and a spasm later tore itself free. The bulb, now missing from the tip. It then whipped the bleeding unconscious body back towards me and I dipped back behind the wall just as his head impacted the floor.

Pressing my back against the wall, I stared at the crumpled body now jerking and twisting as it tried to pull itself to its feet. *Oh fuck! Oh fuck! Oh fuck! What the hell is that thing?*

A blood curdling scream brought my attention back around the corner, the creature was now repeating the process with the final soldier it had bound. I closed my eyes retreating back covering my ears to drown out the pain filled gurgling.

I screamed as the soldier's body seemed to spring to life mid flight as they were also thrown in my direction. His body sprouted from the cracks of the tightly wound vines. His eyes locked with mine and he began grabbing and pleading trying to get me to help him, but all that came out was blood frothing from his torn out throat.

His distorted and mutating hand reached out to me, his pleading gurgles of pain the only sound in that moment that I could hear. I could no longer hold it in when the soldier's hand finally got ahold of my leg. I screamed as the feeling of his fingers tightening around my ankle made this crazy nightmare situation that much more real.

Kicking his grasp away, I heard the falling of heavy footsteps, moving in my direction fast. I knew what was coming and I wasn't going to stick around to be forced to deepthroat that creature's seed sack.

Scrambling to my feet, I ran as fast as I could back the way I came, diving back into the break room only to have a gun pointed in my face.

"Don't shoot! Don't shoot!" I waved my hands in the air shouting and hoping he wouldn't pull the trigger.

As he lowered his gun he reached down to help me up only for a thick bundle of vines to grab and lift the man up into the air smashing him to the ground causing him to drop his gun.

The beast then slammed his lifeless body into the lockers before pulling him in close to do only what I already knew was coming. I grabbed the gun and dodged the creature's other vine-like appendages trying to snatch at me before escaping down the hall.

This is it I thought, home free I just gotta get through the door and... what the fuck?

Plant-like stalks began to sprout from the dead bodies as the others were rolling around the floor tearing at their chests. Several tendrils then violently burst from the bodies blocking my exit in the pulsating muscle and gore.

I could hear the thunderous steps again and I just ran as fast as I could down the hall that was now empty. Knowing it was taking me to the quarantine area. *I might be able to get to a way out from there.*

Rounding corner after corner, I was blasted with the smell from earlier as I passed by the countless bodies that thing must have killed its way through. When out of nowhere I saw Zack and the man from before. Zach's daughter tightly gripped onto her father's shoulder, her head dug in like a scared puppy.

"Hey! Wait!" I shouted and both men stopped in their tracks to look in my direction.

I was so happy to see someone familiar still alive in this mess. I just felt some kind of relief and a renewed hope.

"We need a way out, this way is blocked!" I shouted.

Zack hefted his daughter and looked at Chris, then back to me.

"You can come with us, we're heading to an old tunnel under the building. It leads out of here, but I need help getting through the gate blocking it. This is Chris, he's hurt but not infected."

I recognized Chris from earlier and he clearly had had a rough go since I last saw him. He seemed kind of out of it, but focused enough to keep moving. I couldn't see the little girl's face, but from what little skin was showing, it looked like it was peeling and cracking like bark on a tree.

"How's your daughter? Is she..."

"She's fine! She just needs to get out of here and get cleaned up."

The look in Zack's eyes told me not to press the subject any further, but I tightened my grip on the pistol though. I don't know if he saw me do it. However, I saw his eyes dart down to my hand and back up to mine. His tone changed after seeing I was armed.

"Listen we all need to get out of here, help me get her to safety and we will go our separate ways, okay?"

I didn't know what to say, but I could hear the thumps of the infected stomping its way back in this direction.

"Fine, let's go, we don't have time to argue! Something dangerous is coming this way and I don't feel like being here when it arrives. So, can we put a pin in this?"

Looking down and nodding in agreement, Zack started moving again and I walked over putting Chris's arm around my shoulder and helping follow along.

~ Zack

It wasn't too much further, but running into Zoe might have just screwed up our escape. I know my little angel is infected, but she still has time. Who knows, maybe she will recover, maybe she's building up an immunity now and will be fine in a few days. I mean it's just her skin that's a weird color, and some growths, she doesn't look anywhere near as bad as some of those beasts. Maybe she'll be lucky. Maybe it won't be too bad though, now that I have Zoe to pick up the dead weight. I honestly thought that this would be a lot easier than whatever this has turned out to be. At least I have Tabitha in my arms now. I just need to get her gun now and we can escape in peace. Maybe two corpses should keep those bastards preoccupied long enough so they don't follow us.

The screaming seems to have died down now, I guess the escaped infected have either made short work of the few survivors or people were able to escape. I clutched my baton at every corner knowing that at any moment we could run into more... obstacles. Now that the prisoners were out, it wasn't just those plant fuckers we had to worry about.

It wasn't long before we managed to make it to the hallway with the door we needed. Peeking around the corner I could see the coast was clear. Sliding back fast, I motioned for Zoe and Chris to get up against the wall and gestured that there was something around the corner.

Looking down at my baton I had to think of something. I made a walking sign pointing to myself then around the corner. They looked at each other and shook their heads. I put my daughter down, I had to make this look as real as possible and this was a risk I had to take.

Motioning for them to stay back, I readied myself and snuck around the corner, a second later I smashed the door with the metal stick making a cracking sound. I jumped back to the corner while calling the others.

My grip tightened and I could feel the sweat of my anxiety rushing out of my pores. As soon as I saw Zoe come around the corner I smacked her hand forcing her to drop the gun, I followed up with an uppercut knocking her back and Chris fell to the floor unable to do anything. Scooping up the gun I held them both at bay as I grabbed my daughters hand, lifting her up again.

"I'm really sorry about this, but I have to save my daughter. She's all I have left."

"Da... daddy"

"Yes hunny?"

Her little head rolled back, her eyes struggling to open as her skin seemed to be melding together and tearing as they stretched open. Her little voice sounded so lethargic and she was having trouble breathing.

"It's okay baby girl, don't worry about anything, daddy's got you. Rest now okay? Save your strength." I hugged her tighter and started to run. I had to get her someplace safe, away from everyone who will try to hurt her now.

I stared back at Zoe and felt enormous guilt at what I was doing, but it had to be done this way.

~ Zoe

I jumped at the sound of metal hitting metal as Zack disappeared around the corner. I didn't know what to expect. I followed him after he called the all clear. Whatever was there sounded big, but just as I was about to come around the corner, I felt a sharp pain in my wrist causing my only protection to drop to the floor. Another sudden shock hit me in the face, sending me stumbling back and to the floor. My vision blurry, fading in and out for a few seconds, I saw a shadowy figure standing over me, holding the gun now aimed at my face. I heard mumbled words saying "sorry" about something before bending down to cradle the little girl in its arms, that's when I realized, this shadow was Zack.

Sitting in shocked disbelief, I stayed down so he wouldn't shoot me. I looked over to Chris and he had his hands up in surrender. I couldn't blame him, he was in no condition to fight back.

When I finally could focus again the now armed Zack seemed upset at what he was doing, but in a flash his face went from sad to serious, as if he was thinking of shooting us.

Finally able to come to my senses, I tried to talk him out of whatever he was about to do.

"Please don't do this. We didn't do anything to you. Please just go and..."

"Shut up! I'm not going to kill you, I'll need the bullets. Please understand I didn't want to do this, but I have to. I have to keep her safe and you know what those animals are going to do to her if I don't take her someplace to rest and get better. If you are with us though I'll have to worry you'll just hand her off to one of those nazi ass scientists, who will just melt her like she was nothing more than a fucking candle. You may not have known what they were doing, but you didn't stop them from sending who knows how many to their deaths. These people are just sick. In a few days or weeks they'll have a cure or some kind of antidote and everything will be back to normal, but you'll have to live with those deaths on your mind. I'm not willing to risk you as a liability." His voice cracked as tears started to run down his cheeks. "If you have kids you will understand."

He backed away slowly, until reaching and opening the door. "Please if you stay quiet and give me ten minutes to get ahead of you, I promise I won't hurt you and you will never have to see us again."
With those final words he ducked into the darkness and I could hear his footsteps fade as he descended the stairs.
"Your friend is kind of a prick." Chris tiredly weezed out. "But I think we should take him up on his offer."
I was so confused by the whole situation that I just agreed with him. We both pulled ourselves up and sat against the hall walls opposite each other. The fighting now almost completely silent except for the occasional burst of gunfire or scream. I felt my heart pounding and I put my head on my knees to try and calm down.
How did this go so wrong so fast?

~ Chris

This is such bullshit. I thought as we limped our way towards whatever hallway this officer was taking me. I wonder if he was regretting helping me now. I have no clue what made me look like I could help him, but I needed to get out of here and find my family. As warped as the situation was, I still had to hold onto hope that they were still alive.
We managed to keep a good enough speed that we kept a decent distance between us and those things. Everything was happening so fast and I must have been hurt worse than I thought. I kept fading in and out, but my body seemed to be moving on instinct, just to get away. That poor woman's face from the yard, forever burned into my vision everytime I started to black out. I could see the replay in my mind, her son's screams were the only thing I could hear.
One of the times I faded back into something major must have happened, because the next thing I knew the nurse from earlier was helping carry me. Then another black out and next thing I knew I was falling to the ground and was begging for my life. The sudden burst of adrenaline woke me up for good

for the time being. I felt beyond confused and scared at the events playing out in such a surreal situation. Being saved just to be abandoned so close to our goal. There were no words for everything going wrong.

After Zack left us to fend for ourselves, I almost felt like giving up. But I knew my wife and kids were out there somewhere and they were probably petrified. Leaning up against the cool wall. My body was killing me.

"Did you ever find your family?" I heard the nurse whisper.

"I..., " sighing, "No, I thought I did but they were..." The woman's face flashed across my vision again. "No, I didn't see them. They must be out there somewhere still."

The sounds of dragging footsteps broke the awkward silence between us and we both shot a look down the hall and saw some kind of giant flower petal from hell marching towards us.

"Looks like we need to go." I was still in pain, but this wasn't a choice situation.

"Where are we going to go?" She said with a sarcastic defeated tone. "If we go down there that asshole might shoot us. If we stay here those things are going to get us eventually and from what I can tell, no matter where we go, we are going to be running into those things here."

"Well given our choices I'll choose being shot over being one of those things. Or whatever the fuck that thing plans on doing to us."

Using the wall as leverage, I forced myself up and began making my way towards the door. I kept stumbling, but about halfway there I felt the nurse's arms slide under mine and we rushed through the door. We know he said give him ten minutes, but he'll have to settle for five.

We made it halfway down the stairs before a series of gunshots echoed all around us.

~ Zack

I knew it was a risk leaving them alive, but I just couldn't bring myself to kill them in cold blood. All that mattered now was we were going to be safe, nothing and no one was going to stand in my way.

It took me longer than I had hoped to find my way through the dark, but I finally found my way to the room with the tunnel.

"Don't move!"

A flashlight beamed into my eyes and I instantly wrapped myself around my daughter. "Don't shoot! We're just trying to get out of here. Those things are right behind us!"

"Yeah sure buddy just like there was one of those things down here right?"

I felt defeated when I recognized the voice.

"Put your hands up!"

"I cant."

"don't fuck with me pal!"

"No, you don't understand. I'm holding my daughter. Please I don't care what happens to me, but please take my daughter far away from here. She's scared." The soldier's light grew brighter as he got closer. "Hand her over gently and stay there."

I felt his gloved hand on my shoulder and I knew I didn't have a choice now. Squeezing the trigger I felt the recoil and the spray of blood across my face as the bullets ripped into the man's body. The smell of gunpowder filling my nostrils. He fell back pulling the trigger on his rifle and a spray of automatic fire lit up the small room.

I just held my girl as tight as I could until everything was still again. Only the cone of light illuminating the otherwise dark room. Wavering a bit from the ringing in my ears, I made my way to the old rusted tunnel entrance and shot the cheap padlock that held the doors closed.

Looking back at the man that I just murdered, I knew there was no going back now.

Running my hand over my daughter's hair, I felt a clump slide off and tangle in my fingers. I closed my eyes and prayed that she would be okay and make it through this. I could see a faint light at the end of the tunnel. Gathering what strength I had left I started running.

~ Zoe

"What the fuck was that!" Standing up from where we dove down the stairs to. We realized that it wasn't coming from around us. Wherever it came from was deeper in the basement. Our gun worries were cut short by a flurry of blows smashing against the door, cracks of light splitting larger with each successive hit.

"Run!" Chris shouted from somewhere in the dark.

I managed to move just in time as the door crumpled off its hinges and came barreling down the stairs.

The slimy clicking sound of the creature began to stomp down after us as we began feeling our way through the darkened maze. Our only hope now was barely lit by the strobed light from the door above as the beast made its way down the stairs faster now than before.

I could barely make out Chris' shadow in front of me, but eventually was able to grab ahold of his arm. Out of blind luck we came across the body of a soldier. His light, a welcome sight to see in a morbid kind of way.

We could still hear the creature behind us. We took what we could gather. Shining the light in the direction we came from we could see the leathery mass moving faster as if the light was attracting it.

A few gunshots rang out. Chris had found the soldier's sidearm and was holding something else in his other hand. I saw him make a jerking hand motion and he threw whatever he was holding before grabbing me and we hobbled behind the old metal gate. Seconds later a loud explosion resonated in the room deafening us. The crazy bastard had thrown a grenade.

When the smoke cleared, we could still hear some movement and shined the light over the now decimated remains of the plant monster. Some of the chunks — in an attempt to survive — began crawling towards the dead soldier and rooted themselves into the corpse.

Holding his head, "That is way louder than the movies make it seem." Looking up, he saw that the creatures newly found host was beginning to convulse as the roots spread out through its limbs

"We uh... we need to go."

With that shared thought, we turned and ran, we ran as fast and as far as we could down the dark damp corridor. We heard a loud clang echo back our way and the feeling of a cool breeze could be felt against our sweat covered skin. A subtle sense of ease started to flush over us knowing escape was only a small distance away. We could only hope that asshole didn't block wherever the exit was.

FERAL TERRA

Chapter 3 ruined town

~ Zack

The grip his little angel was giving was as if holding on for dear life in the cold night air rushing through the damp musty hallway. The moon was so big and bright that it lit up our escape. I found a piece of pipe and managed to break the chain holding the rusted doors shut. The hinges screaming as they moved for the first time in who knows how many years.

Tabitha made a small sound of discomfort as I managed to pry the gate to move just enough for us to get through. I knew our time was slim, I heard a loud explosion echo down the hall. It must have been the soldiers.

"It's okay baby, we're safe now. Daddy has you."

I knew I had to get somewhere inside that wasn't here, but with those things everywhere and Tabitha not getting any better, I had to hurry. The rapid footsteps heading our way coming from the tunnel were only getting closer.

Where is someplace that might be evacuated by now?

Another moan escaped her little body, this time though I noticed it seemed more labored and phlegmy. Not having much time, I had to choose someplace. That's when it hit me. If I was going to lose my daughter, I would keep my promise.

"Come on baby, I know where we will be safe."

It might be big, but there are enough places for us to hide in there, that no one will ever bother us.

He could hear voices now and was shocked to recognize them. Sliding down into a small ditch he hid behind a bush and watched the two people emerge. He couldn't believe it. Zoe and the other guy came hobbling out and after a few seconds of struggling, managed to pull themselves through the tiny gap I had made.

Stupid Zack, you should have barred the gate.

Watching them, they seemed to hesitate on choosing a direction, but I felt a wave of relief when they took off in the opposite direction of where we were going.

With a sigh, I knew I had the gun. there was always that potential and I knew I was going to need the bullets. Looking down at my girl, I also knew I couldn't put her in harm's way. Holding her tight I stayed low and started to move.

~ Zoe

"If I ever find that asshole I'm going to kick him so hard in the dick he will never walk right again."

"I didn't know he was using us as bait. I thought he was trying to help."

Stepping up and grabbing another tree root, I knew this was not where we wanted to be.

"Hey, what's your name again? I know you helped me before, but I don't think I ever caught your name, and who was that cop?" He had definitely seen better days and was limping along, slowly, but he seemed to be driven to try and push past the obvious pain he was dealing with.

Turning to look at the guy, he stopped once he seemed to stabilize himself on the steep hill waiting for my answer. "I'm Zoe, and that asshole from earlier was Zack. He wasn't a cop, he was just another one of those C.O.'s that was more action than thought. That little girl was his daughter and... she was infected."

The look on the guy's face seemed to drop a bit, but it was hard to tell in the very little moonlight whether it was sadness or understanding. He was a dad himself after all. Grabbing another branch, she pulled herself up a little more and planted her foot on a rock.

Sensing the mood she tried to brighten the topic. "What's your name again? I know Zack mentioned it earlier, but I forgot. I mean if we are going to be escaping together I can't just call you dude or whatever."

The man's face looked up at her again. "My name is Chris."

Reaching for another branch, I looked back over my shoulder to look at him again. "Well Chris, it's nice to meet you, but I would have hoped it would have been under better circumstances."

I could hear a small laugh come from him as he was trying to find his footing again. "Yeah, this was not an ideal situation." He seemed to struggle a bit and had a slight limp.

"So, how did you end up at the prison? I mean I know when you showed up you were unconscious, but you said something about your family also being there."

There was a moment of long silence before she heard a small sniffle. " I..I didn't mean to... I mean..."

"It's fine... I'm sure they are okay and were able to escape.... "

"I mean when... when we were trying to escape the town, one of those plant things attacked the highway we were on. There was an explosion and the last thing I remember after flying through the air was seeing them huddled together, before the darkness hit suddenly. Then the next thing I knew I was waking up in the prison. I know my family is alive, but I don't think they ever even made it to the safe zone. I would have seen them or found them. So I'm going to just keep searching until I find them."

Managing to make it to the top of the steep wooded incline, I held out my hand to help him up the rest of the way. "Well, I will do my best to help you find them."

"Thank you, it's probably best we stick together anyways."

Even though I couldn't see him too well in the moonlight, I hoped he was at least smiling. It had been such a dark day that I couldn't bear to tell him his family was more than likely gone. If what Zack had said was true then they were probably in one of those death cells Zack was rambling on about.

"So Chris, where do you think they would go if not to the prison?"

"Honestly, the only place I can think of is maybe Beth's parents' condo only a few miles from where we are. I mean it's a long shot, but it's been hours. So it's at least a destination and someplace out of the open. Plus if she didn't go to the prison, that's the only other place she would feel safe enough to take the boys."

With his confidence reborn a little, it was easy to see that he didn't seem to lose faith in the love of his family and how he was so sure they would be there. "Well then, which way from here?"

I couldn't tell in the dark, but the shadow I could make out of him seemed to be looking around in confusion.

"I have no clue. I mean if the prison is there then maybe if we head east we might find a road that I'll recognize."

"okay Mr. Compass, which way is that?"

"Well, do you know where route 2 is from here?"

"Yeah, it's on the other side of the prison. You know where all the fire and gunshots are coming from."

"Well then that's east and where we need to go."

The sarcasm in his voice brought a welcome little laugh given the hell we were possibly going to face. If what happened in the prison was anything to go off of though, then God only knows what we will face out here.

It took some time to make our way through the dark wooded area, but we managed to make it to the edge of the small forest only to be stopped by the silence of the open road. The only sounds we heard were from the flames that randomly whipped from abandoned cars, barely lighting our way for maybe half a mile before the night settled back in beyond. Standing there for as long as we had, we were not sure if we should be glad or terrified at the now quiet scene. Only a few muffled gunshots and screams came from behind the tall prison walls.

~ Chris

Pushing the thoughts out of my mind, I had to stay focused and knew that my family was counting on me to find them as well. "Zoe, we have to go that way about two miles and take a right." The small light from my watch showed it was 4am. "If we manage to keep going at a decent pace, we should be there in maybe two hours or so."

The empty darkness of the highway instilled more fear in me than whatever those monsters were. I don't know what we will see when we get to the apartment complex, but maybe we'll find someplace safe along the way.

She seemed to be still staring at the carnage that replaced the once peaceful street. She must have just been in that depressive penitentiary since the attack started. I mean I know I wasn't much better off, but I saw that beast that attacked mine as well as other families trying to escape.

Walking over to where I could remember that creature throwing me. I searched for any signs of where Sarah and the boys might have been hiding when I had passed out. I don't know if it was my hope or fear that maybe they hadn't made it, but I felt my stomach knotting at the prospect. I checked the car that I struggled to remember seeing them huddled behind. Large claw marks gouged through the door and roof of it, the shadows dancing in the firelight. As I drew closer, I saw what looked like thorns embedded into the asphalt and metal alike. I felt tears well up in my eyes as I came around the trunk of the car to a torn bloody piece of fabric. I recognized it and I felt the tears starting to roll down my cheek.

I felt a hand on my shoulder and turned to see Zoe standing beside me. A look of understanding, but urgency on her face. She pointed to the front doors of the prison. In the flickering lights of the destroyed vestibule, the silhouettes of strange beings were waving in an unseen wind. Thin stem-like bodies topped with bulbous heads of teeth, began splitting open and beating against the glass as one of the larger monstrosities lumbered in the distance from behind them.

Looking around for anything we could use as transportation, we were stopped by the scene inside of a school bus. Cupping my hands, I tried to see whatever might be inside. I didn't know what I expected to see through the smeared and cracked glass, but I felt sick seeing several mid changed children in various disfigured forms. Some of their bodies suspended or twisted in ways that were no longer even human shaped. The closer I looked at the undulating masses of flesh and plant, the more the creatures moved and became more agitated.

A mangled, half-melted face of a child popped up to stare me in the eyes. The skin rolled and peeled off from half of it as a series of leaves pulled away from the muscle in a scream of hatred. I fell backwards and Zoe managed to stop me from going to the ground. It repeatedly smacked its head against the window and in an instant the whole bus began to rock back and forth before a series of shattering glass followed by a flood of those thin bodied things and oddly proportioned shapes fell to the pavement, and began crawling towards us with their root like appendages. Their heads swayed back and forth as they moved slowly through the debris.

Zoe grabbed my arm and pulled me away from where I was. I don't know where she was dragging me to, but my body felt weak and my anxiety was spiking. I followed her while keeping an eye on our pursuers. Seeing that even though they were slow, they were still gaining on us by just crawling over obstacles like ants about to swarm their prey. My beaten and battered body didn't help the situation either.

"Over here," Zoe shouted pointing to an old car and hopping inside.

Dodging through the cars, I kept stealing looks over my shoulder and saw that some of the head sprouted creatures were now frothing green saliva, dripping down to the ground. Wherever it landed began to dissolve and mutate.

I heard the engine roar to life and the one unbroken headlight lit up the small hoard of variously changed monsters, now blocking where we had just been. Opening the door, I fell into the seat and heard gurgling. I slammed the door closed only, for it to bounce open. The gurgling was replaced by the sound of bones cracking and the tearing sound like shucked corn.

A splash of the green excretion squirted up from the floor and coated the inside of the door. One of the smaller creatures' heads had lifted from under the beat up sedan and had been crushed in the door. Viscera splattered against the asphalt, followed by several smaller minion-like beasts scurrying to eat and smudge the disgusting filth that the now headless body was spraying as it tried to find its way, covering the car in the slimy innards.

We looked at each other before Zoe got a real serious look on her face and hit the gas. she weaved through the now filling lot, crashing into cars and creatures alike. The sounds of metal scraping mixed with splintering bone and wood filled the car as we screamed for the monsters to get out of the way. As we neared the exit, one of the larger things came around the corner of our escape route and I heard Zoe scream. "Hang on!" as she floored it. We slammed into the creature and its insides exploded across the windshield. We bounced over some more of the smaller sprout-headed creatures before we felt the somewhat smoothness of the road.

We drove almost completely blind, save for a small blurry portion of the front window giving ourselves some distance before swerving to a stop. I felt my body shaking from the adrenaline and I knew she must have been feeling the same way. We stared in silence at each other for some kind of confirmation that what just happened, had happened, before staring straight ahead.

"Do you think your insurance will cover that?" I didn't know what else to say, but it was way too tense.

The look on her face as she stared at me could have killed me had her eyes been guns. "Are you seriously trying to make a joke?"

"Sorry, I use humor when I'm scared. It's a coping mechanism."

Shaking her head, she started the windshield wipers – which smeared the entrails back and forth. "Maybe use the wiper fluid?"

"Chris, I swear to god I will kick you out of this car if you say one more..." before she could finish the back window smashed in and a petal-like mouth peeled back as if about to strike like a snake. Zoe lunged into my lap as it struck out, tearing a chunk out of the driver's seat effortlessly.

I scrambled trying to find the door handle, but in all the panic and Zoe now holding me down, it was impossible. I couldn't see, but I felt the creature bite down on the head rest and yank the seat back and in an instant I was now staring up at a vaguely human face. I knew this was it for me as it split open again. As it reared back, I closed my eyes just hoping for it to be quick before feeling my body being pulled back up to a sitting position and hearing three gunshots in quick succession.

Opening my eyes with the ringing in my ears I saw the creature thrashing in pain in the backseat. Half of its head now missing, and bleeding a white milky substance all over where my head was just at.

Zoe rolled back into the driver's seat, opening the door and falling out. I followed behind her, staggering to my feet and helping her to hers. We could still hear that thing trying to get free from the car, but it appeared to be stuck. I looked back and it was struggling as its bulbous body was pinned in place and it was trying to lift the car up to smash it off itself.

Zoe managed to regain her footing and we just ran off as best we could. I only hoped we wouldn't run into too many more surprises along the way. I just knew we would be relatively safe at my in-laws apartment building, and I hoped Beth and the boys were there.

~ Zack

My poor baby girl clung to me so tightly, yet I haven't heard her make a sound in a while. I guess that's for the best as we make our way through this new hellbound world. Making our way through this disaster of a town, I found that our escape was going to be more challenging than I thought. It seemed to be no matter where we turned there were infected searching for their next victims.

Ducking down behind a car, I couldn't tear my eyes away from the people screaming down the street trying their best to escape. As they ran I saw blurs of whipping vines tangling them up and dropping them to the ground followed by darker masses launching themselves onto them sinking teeth deep into the fallen. I wasn't close enough to see any more detail than that, but the creatures appeared to move almost cat-like.

Lowering my head down, I tried to figure out the next course of action when I heard a deep growl so low that even the glass of the cars started to vibrate. A loud distorted howl followed it like a warning. I looked up over the trunk of the car to see a gigantic mutant dog standing on top of one of the buildings and the smaller cat creature hissed in defiance until the hellish hound dropped down. Its massive frame crushing the cab of a truck. The street lights only showed enough for me to know I had to do everything to avoid it. The cat lunged at the beast, but was caught in the giant's jaws and throttled before being tossed through the window of a storefront, another ground shaking howl being bellowed out in its assertion of clear dominance.

Fuck me. Was all I could think to myself. I mean, maybe if I was alone I could sneak past that thing, but not if I have to worry about Tabby.

The feeling in my stomach was only getting worse, as the thought of this was my only way to keep my promise and I didn't have time to think too much about it, was killing me. Checking the clip in the pistol I saw that I had only a few shots left, but I don't think they would be enough to bring that monster down. I don't even think it would feel them to be honest.

"Well... better than nothing I guess." I whispered to myself as I mentally prepared for what I was about to do.

Looking over my cover again, I could see the creature was distracted by the fresh corpse lying in front of its now split open back. Several spike tipped tendrils stabbed into the motionless body, pulling shredded chunks into the maw that was gnashing in anticipation along its spine. I couldn't make out much from this vantage point, but it looked to be pumping something into the body as it reared back swallowing an arm.

Sitting here I knew I had to make a move. With those things sizes, it was bound to finish in just a few minutes. I could see a door leading into a small seafood shop. The lights were off, but it was my best bet to get us off the street and hopefully cover our scent.

Sneaking over, I peaked in through the window and was relieved to see that the backroom the door led to appeared to be empty. A small feeling of relief was nice given the situation, but I knew it wasn't time to let my guard down. Cracking the door, I slid inside and my senses were instantly bombarded by the smell of fish. *"Oh Christ"* I forgot how long it must have been since the power was knocked out in town. *I guess some of the coolers were starting to thaw.*

Staying low I walked over to the register and managed to steal a glance over the counter, to see that the wolf-like beast was now patrolling the area and joined by its now reanimated meal. The cat-creature was starting to grow roots down into the asphalt. Its upper torso swaying on its thin stalk of spine wrapped in woody vines. A fleshy bulb, almost like the head of a flower where their arms once were. The eyes stared vacantly in every direction as its body seemed to be constantly shifting to keep its balance. It took everything I had not to puke again at the sight.

Ducking back down, I took in my surroundings and was able to see another door possibly leading to the back alley, which would give us a better chance at not being seen, but I know if I went back there that there was no way out if something decided to wander back through. As is, I was lucky that the door to get in here was unlocked. No telling if I'll get that lucky again. Not knowing what else to do, I found a small office to hide in. At least in here we were out of sight – and hopefully out of mind of those things. Looking down at my baby girl, I knew she didn't have much time left, but I felt the day's action finally catching up to me.

I don't know how long I was asleep, but I was awoken by the sound of helicopters overhead and a roar from the monster outside. I couldn't see anything from inside the little office, but I heard and felt the ground shake as something heavy crashed down onto a car outside setting off its alarm. Bursts of gunfire and the sounds of carnage were deafening as whatever I was hearing fought the wolf. I held Tabby close as another burst of gunfire ripped through the store and the office. In an instant, there was chaos. As fast as it happened, it was done.

Scrambling for the door, I could hear the crashing of glass and crunching of metal. Opening it a crack I felt both relief and dread as I saw one of the military mech divisions had been dropped into the town to try and reclaim it. I had to take this opportunity to escape while I could. With how they were fighting, it was only a matter of time before they smashed through here, or worse, discovered us and tried to take Tabitha from me.

Slamming through the rear exit, I felt light headed trying to sprint down the still dark alleyway. Only a few sparse street lamps lit our way before the shadows of my vision began to tunnel. Falling to my knees I stared off seeing a clear path laid out in front of me, but for some reason had no energy to lift myself up.

"Wha...what's happening... to me?"

In my delirium, I could see a figure drop down from the rooftop. Its slender figure, obscured by my blurry vision. I didn't know what to do as the creature seemed to slink closer before the light finally revealed it to be the cat abomination from before. Its head splitting all the way back as it readied to pounce. Closing my eyes I felt a sharp pain in my chest as the beast lept towards us.

"I'm sorry baby."

I sat there waiting for the inevitable, but opened my eyes when the feeling of claws never came. I felt no teeth sinking into my neck. Confused, I opened my eyes and I fell back at the sight of a mouth full of jagged branch-like teeth only a few inches away from my face. As I fell, I saw Tabitha's body stay in place, pulling free from my chest. A long tongue tendril, barbed like that of a rose stem, emerging from her face. Her hand gripped tight around the creature's throat, her body started to heave, draining the trapped monstrosity of its blood. Each gulp followed by a sudden feeling of energy flowing into me. Not understanding why, I followed her other arm and I saw what had caused me the sharp pain. Her other hand was deeply embedded into my chest. A thick, dark fluid pulsating directly into my heart with each of her convulsions.

I stared in awe at this disturbing visual only to cry tears of joy that we were now closer than ever. Only a few moments had passed before she discarded the dried husk of the creature to the ground, its body crumbling and breaking like dried timber. I felt a rejuvenation surge through me as she curled back into my chest. I stood up and with this new found strength, began to run. Suddenly, my eyes adjusted to the brighter night, allowing me to see as if it were daylight. I felt my body tense and my senses sharpen as I approached a chain link fence. With no effort, I jumped and landed on the other side.
"I don't know what gifts you have given me, baby girl, but I will use them any way I can to protect you."

~ Chris

We could hear the helicopters overhead. Their lights flooded the street and we were slightly blinded. I was about to try and wave to try and get one of their attention, but Zoe quickly grabbed my arm and put a hand over my mouth. I followed the direction of her eyes and saw why she was so worried. In the gliding brightness we saw a field of staggering monsters. Some embedded into the concrete, others roaming the streets in an endless search for something.
We quickly dropped down behind a car. Looking out from behind our hiding spot it was pretty clear that we could not make a run for it to get through the town. However, looking back up to the helicopters, some had vehicles dangling from beneath them.
"Are those what I think they are?" I whispered to Zoe, her eyes still wide in amazement at the sea of plant people before us. "Zoe!" her focus finally seemed to snap back to me as I grabbed her shoulder to shake her a little.
"Sorry Chris, it's just... how the hell are we supposed to get through all of these things?"

Searching the area, I knew our time was short, but we needed to get those flyboys attention. There was just no way we were going to make it to my in-laws without their help. That's when something caught my eye. An old tow behind camper was flipped over on the side of the road. The truck towing it was totaled, its driver and passenger long since turned into some strange entangled amalgamation growing out of the front windshield. The mangled mass tormented by wanting to be free, but that wasn't what I saw that was important. What I saw was a propane tank laying on the ground not too far from a small fire.

"Zoe, I need the gun. I have a plan to get one of those choppers' attention." She gave me a puzzled look before handing me the weapon. Fumbling with the pistol, I managed to find the release and checked the magazine. I felt a knot when I saw we only had three shots left. Weighing our options and seeing that the cavalry overhead was starting to thin out, I made a choice.

"Hey Zoe, I have an idea but I need you to trust me okay?" She turned back to look at me and with a small nod and a confused look I took as understanding, I told her my plan.

"I'm going to get a little closer to that tank over there and then try and get it to explode. If it explodes I need you to run back down the way we came waving your arms and do whatever you can to show them you aren't one of those things. Hopefully they will see us and take us somewhere safe."

Not waiting for her reaction, I took off hiding behind whatever I could to get a better shot. The whole time keeping an eye out for our possible salvation. Finding a turned over motorcycle, I took aim at the cylinder. Taking a deep breath I squeezed the trigger, only an audible click was what followed. Frantically, I looked over the weapon and couldn't find why it wasn't shooting. I had never shot a gun before today, but I figured, *pull the trigger and it should go boom, right?*

As I tried to figure out how the damn thing worked, I hadn't noticed the hand flowering up from the other side of the downed bike. Its fingers bending back with a barbed nail-like protrusion emerging from its palm. So lost in thought, I finally had an epiphany and the image of every action movie popped into my head and I pulled back the slidey part and saw a round go into the chamber. "Ah ha!"

Looking back at the tank, I saw the deformed appendage rearing back and a sack underneath the blood-red spike appeared to be filling with something. "Oh shit!" I managed to drop down out of the way as the barb launched out of the palm missing my face by mere inches. Looking back at it, one of the fingers cracked into place, another jagged bone tearing through the tip, slowly, as it migrated to the center of the palm, readying itself for another shot.

I didn't have time to think and aimed as close as I could to the propane tank. I fired and heard it ricochet off something in the distance. The hand creature inflating again, I had no choice. Taking aim I shot the engorged section just as it ejected the makeshift flechet. I fell back in time again for it to miss me, but my hand tensed firing the last round up into the air. I felt my hope dwindle much like the life from the dying hand plant.

Knowing my cover was blown, I started to run back to Zoe. I saw the creatures that were able to move beginning to twitch to life. Some started to run in their strange almost galloping motions. One leapt onto a car that had hit a light pole, its body splitting lengthwise like a banana peeling itself open – more tendrils sprouting out from its crooked trunk like legs. I threw the empty pistol at it in a sad attempt to distract it. It jumped towards me and it was as if life had slowed down. My vision focused on its twisting body, preparing to whip one of its many limbs to end my pitiful life. The intricate weave of the vine-like muscles seemed to almost glow as they stretched with frightening power. I raised my arms and closed my eyes as a barrage of bullets followed by a thunderous impact.

~ Kennedy

When I woke up this morning, I didn't expect to be strapped into this mech. I was just as surprised as the rest of my brothers and sisters in arms when Sarge ran in. The alarms were blaring and in all the chaos we suited up for briefing. The confusion we thought was all just another drill turned out to be something much worse. I wasn't trained fully as a private, but when I went to take my place to prep the mechs, I was surprised to hear that my name was called for a special briefing as well as a few others I've worked with before. "Kennedy, get your ass to brief now! This is not a drill soldier!"

I had seen many degrees of seriousness on the Sarge before, but this... this seemed different. He seemed to be fighting to keep all his composure, but his eyes seemed almost scared.

"Come on ladies, get your shit and get going! You have zero time to be wasting! Move move move!"

This had to be bad if Sarge was worrying about the order to get anywhere. It seemed like he wasn't given an option himself to be slow either. We were all put on a sprint to get to the briefing room as soon as possible. Looking around the base seemed to be in complete anarchy with helicopters taking off, trucks filled with soldiers leaving the base in droves, even tanks being mobilized. *Were we under attack? Was it the Russians? Did North Korea finally launch? If either of those were the case, I don't know what we were being mobilized for, unless we were being invaded. But who would be dumb enough to even attempt that?*

Entering the small meeting room I sat next to Laurence Bardock, who was checking the buckles and straps on his synaps suit. Squad leader, Vincent Valheart, sat more towards the back of the room, he was taking notes off the boards already, and Patrick Wilcox, another private, was sitting smug as usual in the center of us all, probably just trying to conjure up some smartass quip to get us all to run drills later.

"Hey Bard, what's this all about? I mean I'm not even qualified to pilot one of the Z.F.G.'s in combat yet."

"Man, I don't know greeny. Your guess is as good as any."

"Maybe it's some top secret mission to run a train on your mom new guy, you know, really break her in."

"Fuck you Wilcox, I might be green but..."

"Don't bother private, Wilcox is incapable of any more complex thinking above baser instincts." Vincent chimed in, while writing something down into his notebook.

"Well isn't that just another fancy few words from our little book nerd."

"I believe the term you are looking for is bookworm, not nerd. Haven't you been using those, learn to read books I bought you Wilcox? I mean, I did go all out and get the ones with the big colorful pictures."

I couldn't help but laugh a bit at the mental image.

"What are you laughin at ya little shit? Your ass couldn't even pass the combat sim."

"Maybe he would have had you not duct taped him to the wall," Bardock piped in

"Those are unfounded charges, you can't prove a thing!"

"Enough! Shut your mouths! Eyes forward!" With all the talking we hadn't noticed Sarge walk in and had gone up to the front podium, a well dressed, almost business-like woman, following him in tow.

"Hey Sarge what's all this about?"

"Can it Wilcox, you will be informed in a moment. This is Dr. Andrea Conoly. She is the lead botanist for the Chlor-Reform corporation. Ma'am the floor is yours."

The doctor approached the podium with some reluctance. Shuffling some papers she took a deep breath before softly speaking.

"Hello, my name is Doctor Andrea Conoly. I apologize for the inconvenience, but the matter at hand has become quite the disaster and you as well as other military assets are needed. It appears that at about 4:56am yesterday morning,there was a breach in one of our biological testing facilities outside of Boston. We are still searching for the person or persons responsible. However, we will be keeping all parties involved up to date with that information as we proceed further. The subjects that had escaped containment were infected with a highly reactive mutagenic formula that was originally designed to help with terraforming, as well as deep space exploration on planets with higher CO2 concentrations. After a few failed experiments to properly edit the new code into flora and fauna, it mistakenly created unforeseen... mutations... and became highly contagious."

"I'm sorry lady, but what does that all mean? You said a lot of big bullshit words and..."

"Wilcox shut your hole before I shut it for you!"

"But Sarge, what the hell is she trying to tell us?"

"What she's saying is that they had a pretty big oopsie and something bad has escaped from their fancy building. Is that dumbed down enough for you?" Vincent chimed in, not looking up from his notes.

"Well what kind of fuckery escaped your weird petting zoo?"

Taking another deep breath, it seemed hard for her to even wrap her brain around it. "What escaped was one of our earlier experiments. When the new genetic code was introduced, we saw favorable results. The test subject began to photosynthesize light creating its own sustainable food source using nothing more than the sun and small amounts of water. Its body adapted to different environments quite quickly. So quickly in fact it was as if its body was evolving faster than we could come up with tests to even see its upper limits. That was before we sadly had to attempt to terminate the subject after the first... incident. The subject, while in a test, managed to escape the enclosure and enter one of the scientist's clean suits. From there it mutated within a minute causing my colleague to begin transforming into something horrible. We had several of our team — as well as security — infected within only a few minutes. The genes mutated into a virus, spread by direct introduction via penetration of the skin by vine-like appendages, bites, and we also discovered some spread through the air by pollen that had become aerosolized when the infected reached full maturity.

How did they get away with any of this?

"That's a real sad story, but what the hell does that have to do with us?" Wilcox again spoke out of turn.

"The information I have been allowed to discuss is for your safety. As well as give you all a timeline."

"What's the timeline Ma'am?" I asked timidly.

"From our lab tests we discerned that for the smaller infected, it takes an average of a week to become capable of pollination. However, the larger mutations are unknown. We never dared to allow them to mature that far. Remember our intentions were good, we never meant for this to happen but..."

"The road to hell is paved with good intentions, lady." Bardock spoke up.

"Please understand, we have been trying to come up with some kind of antivirus or something to counteract this from spreading further than it already has."

"How far has it already spread? By your time frame it's been loose for over twenty-four hours now." Vincent spoke up.

Clicking a few keys on her laptop the large screen behind her lit up with an overview map of the state.

"So far we have been able to keep the quarantine zone confined to a few small suburbs surrounding ground zero... unfortunately, our containment teams have been failing to keep the areas properly confined and stragglers have been getting through and infecting on a cross species scale we were not prepared for. That's why I was sent here to beg for military assets to help."

"We understand why you are here, but why us? Our units are only mobilized for urban and confined combat with large scale combatants and multiple soft targets. What are the forces we might be seeing in this situation?"

She looked down again as if searching for an answer.

"At this point I honestly couldn't tell you. From the reports our units have sent in, we are talking about thousands already infected. One of my associates is currently setting up a safe zone in a prison in the Concord, Acton area which should be able to house most of the displaced residents. Your team, as well as others, will be sent in to protect that facility and aid in the extraction of the uninfected. Those who are unfortunately infected will be considered casualties."

"What? Sarge, are you hearing this bullshit?" Bardock shouted.

"Yes , I do hear it, soldier, and I expect you to understand I don't want to give this order anymore than my superiors, but it is no longer in our control. Ma'am if that is all please move along to brief the others. I have a lot to talk to my men about."

With a small nod of understanding she started to walk towards the door only to stop and turn to us again. "For what it's worth, I truly am sorry for all of this."

"Yeah, well maybe next time you won't play god just because you can."

"That's enough Wilcox!"

"Sorry Sarge but...."

"I understand the situation is not ideal for our unit to be deployed on US soil. However, we will be sent out at 18:00 hours. In the time between then and now, you will run diagnostics and prep your mechs for drop. Kennedy, I need to speak with you. The rest of you are dismissed."

As the others filed out, grumbling or questioning what the hell was going on, I made my way to the front. Sarge had reached around the back of the podium and pulled out a file holding it until Wilcox exited with the others.

"Do you feel you are ready for this son?"

"What do you mean sir?"

Staring at the folder for a moment in thought, Sarge handed me the file. "You will not be going to the prison. This file contains the coordinates for the Chlor-Reform facility. It also contains a flashdrive to upload the map layout and the route to take in order to find what boils down to an antivirus."

Shuffling through the papers, I saw a few medical images and containment chambers holding creatures I could never have imagined. I stopped on the last page that simply read "**Advanced tests needed**" with a picture of several vials of an unknown liquid.

"I don't get it sir. If they had this contingency plan, why not activate it when their breach happened?"

"According to the good doctor, they did try. Unfortunately, whoever released the virus also deactivated the safety protocols. By the time anyone realized, it was too late." He paused as he tried to collect his thoughts. "You will be dropped in a small area of Acton not too far from your main objective. We would drop you closer, but the risk of mutants, or as her security guys call them 'the sprouted' on location is unknown. You are to survey the area from a distance and if the location allows, you are to infiltrate the facility and follow the directions from there."

"But sir, I haven't even passed my advanced pilot courses, I'm not..."

"I understand you haven't done any combat drops, but you scored high on your basics and intermediary training. We don't expect heavy enemy combatants to be in the area, only minor, seeing as they appear to be spreading randomly and not organizing. I guess we can at least be thankful for that. As long as you stay on course, resistance should be minimal."

"Permission to speak freely sir?"

"What is it?"

"Why are you sending me to do this? I mean this seems like something that Vincent or Bardock would be better suited for."

"Listen, those three have all worked together on several missions. Seeing as you are still new and haven't quite found your niche yet, I am going to need my most cohesive men working on evacuating the civilians. Besides getting those canisters and venting out, the antivirus might just save the world. Not a bad gig for your first outing if you ask me. Don't dread the situation too much, chances are by the time we are ready to go the boys in green might have this all under control. Read through the file and keep it close. Upload the contents to your suit and familiarize yourself with it." Looking around as if to check for anyone listening, he leaned in and whispered into my ear. "You are on a timeline son, I might not have the authority to stop what is going to happen, but the rumor mill has been throwing around the scorched earth policy. If you are late getting to the rendezvous, that's not too big a problem, but if you can't get that canister and the doctor to where they need to be in the next few days, the higher ups might make a call to literally burn Massachusetts to the ground. If you can't get to the pick up point in the allotted time frame though, I can try and arrange your pickup at another location, but I can't guarantee when."

With that little speech wrapping up, Sarge walked out of the room and I was left standing there not sure how to take on the responsibility forced into my hands. I get that I don't have the experience, but that seems even more reason not to send me into ground zero.

Walking to the hanger, the reasoning Sarge gave just didn't seem to make sense to me. I understand the logic, but still something wasn't sitting right. Entering the expansive building I grabbed the flashdrive from the folder and slipped it into my pocket and began reading the dossier on the building layout and what I may see in the lower lab where the original outbreak is supposed to have originated from. I was still in shock that they somehow managed to collect so much data on these creatures in such a short amount of time, but my concerns were cut short when I felt the papers being ripped from my hands.

"What the fuck is this newbie? Doing some light reading at the end of the world?"

"Damn it Wilcox, give that back I don't have time for your shit!"

Desperately I grabbed for the paperwork, but Wilcox managed to turn and hit me in the stomach putting me to the ground gasping for air.

"Asshole... that isn't... for you to see!" I managed to squeeze out between breaths.

"Well you seem awfully protective of this little folder so it must be something good, and you wouldn't want to keep secrets from the rest of us now would ya?" He said with a glare of malice. "I mean honestly what does Sarge see in you that we haven't already proven to him?"

"I don't know, but I need to follow my orders. Please just give them back, this isn't the time for one of your damn power trips."

"Oh, look at the puppy getting some bark to him." His smile lessened as he tore up the file and tossed it to the floor in front of me. "Doesn't matter I listened in on your little personal meeting and quite frankly it's stupid to send you, of all people, on some fetch quest."

Watching the torn pieces fall to the ground I felt I had already failed my mission and it hadn't even started.

"By the way, don't bother trying to report this. They won't do anything about it given the situation and even if they do, it won't be until all this is over with."

He walked away with his stupid laugh as I collected the pieces as well as what little dignity I could into my hands. He was right anyway. We were technically in an active duty situation and the higher ups weren't going to do anything about some torn papers and bullying.

Gathering myself, I stood up and managed my way to my hanger bay where I found my big booty bitch of a mech. She was the pinnacle of war based technology with some long winded name that none of us bothered to remember, well maybe Vincent did, but the rest of us just called them the zero fucks given or Z.F.G.'s for short. The stock models were standard twelve feet tall at its full height. Chicken walker legs gave the enclosed canopy more stability and mobility in tight quarters. The segmented arms were mounted where you would have your shoulder blades on huge ball joints to allow full access all around you in combat. Picking up the tablet, I read over the weapons loadout I was to be given and I was surprised to see some weapons that were unusual, given they are usually outlawed, but didn't stop me from smiling as I read.

Mine was outfitted with a small wrist mounted gatling gun chambered in 7.62 on my right manipulator arm, which housed an extendable blade for close combat in the claw-like hand. The off hand was to be modified with a flame unit and an auto shotgun was mounted inside the clamp-like hand. The shoulders housed twin mounted grenade launchers which according to the new outfit was to replace one side's usual high explosives with white phosphorus. I had finally been given more than the base model, I felt pretty proud of myself.

Putting the tablet down and looking it over, I couldn't help but notice all the lovely drawings that I'm guessing Wilcox decorated her with. I'll give it to the guy – he sure can draw a realistic dick. Walking around to the other side, I was a little annoyed that he scribbled out my code name and replaced it with 'Growling Thunder Cunt'... with a sigh I shook my head and couldn't help but look up to the ceiling in annoyance as I knew I was going to have to clean this later.

The hours raced by, but I was surprised to see so many hold offs for our deployment. According to Sarge, it was because of the rate at which the virus was spreading, it broke the known quarantine zones in under a day. The reports of dangerous contacts were growing by the minute and the brass couldn't decide on where to send us to be the most effective. We waited so long that it was night now and we were finally given the go ahead to just go through with the original plan seeing as the prison was the last safe spot in the suburbs, and the others were given a side mission to extract a scientist that was overseeing the separation of the infected from the survivors.

Sitting in the cockpit, I felt myself connecting with the machine with each plug that was embedded in the seat attached themselves. It had been so long since the implantation, I had almost forgotten that they were there. With each connection I felt a rush to my nervous system. I had to stay as still as possible since once the final jack was installed at the base of my skull, whatever I moved, the machine moved. Whatever I thought, it would send the signals to make it happen. When the system was first implemented, the stress was too much for one pilot. He went nuts and killed who knows how many people before a tank pinned him to a wall long enough for someone to disconnect him. Luckily we have protocols in place for instances like that to never to happen again.

"You ready?" one of the engineers asked while holding the brain plug.

"As I'll ever be." I said with a small laugh.

I could never get used to the insertion process as my body instantly felt like it jumped from two-hundred pounds to the three ton frame that surrounded my body. My vision switched between my eyes and the fly-like sight of the cameras mounted in all directions at will. I could see the others all testing their respective suits. Bardock was already doing his close combat drills with his demolition setup. His hands were like wrecking balls that had no issue battering down reinforced walls clobbering armored vehicles into scrap.

Vincent was charging some fancy railgun setup that could violate whatever defense it wanted by sending a charged lance of supersonic aluminum at mach fuck-your-concerns type speed. It was a long distance weapon, but up close the thing could punch a hole straight through a warship and destroy whatever was behind it in one go.

Wilcox was staring daggers at me while his mechs' arm unfolded and transformed into a drill, he affectionately called a 'drilldo'. Other than the few specialized weapons all of their loadouts appeared to be similar to mine, consisting of explosives, and flame based weapons.

I couldn't help but think he may have some jealousy built up that I somehow got to save the world mission and he got the escort mission.

"Systems check," one of the many people running around spoke into my radio.

Calming my mind and focusing, I lifted each of my knees to my chest, the corresponding leg would move accordingly. Moving my arms I checked all the joints, my fingers actuated the hands into opened and closed fist like grips. It was as if I had gone from a mortal to a god in a split second. Imagining each weapon activated them and brought up an ammo counter and diagnostics to monitor safety levels.

When all systems were checked, I walked over to the chopper and was lowered into a chamber just below where I was to be attached.

My heart raced as the quick connectors were mag locked into place and the helicopter roared to life and began to rise. It was such an odd feeling watching as the ground shrunk beneath the swaying metallic feet the higher we went. It was the closest I would ever get to actually flying.

"Hey thunder cunt!"

I felt a tinge of aggression burn in my mind before taking a calming breath to respond. "Yes Wilcox?"

"Ha! You have a new call sign. Good luck on your super secret bullshit."

"That's enough! Stay focused," Vincent annoyingly voiced over coms. "We all have our objectives. Kennedy, meet us at the rendezvous point in five hours. If you are not there for any reason, we will send you an alternate extraction point. If enemy contacts are too numerous, call for backup.

"Roger that. Five hours before extraction."

It was a surreal view of the ground below us rushing by. Our heads up displays constantly scanned the environment, marking enemy contacts in red and civilians as blue. What disturbed me though, was that there was almost no blue left in the area. The few contacts we did see were barricaded into homes and buildings surrounded by whatever the enemy was. We hadn't been given too much information concerning the sprouted. However, the generally accepted theory is that the chemical causing the transformations is not picky, and will contaminate and convert anything it touches that is made from biological material.

Seeing the types of creatures now running through the streets, I felt my mind race with possible combat strategies. The suits AI was taking notes based on visual cues and attack strategies of the enemy movements. I still didn't know how the suits worked entirely, but I understood that the only reason we were there to pilot them was because the AI was never programmed to make hard decisions, only do what our brains told it to do.

We were passing over a small town street not far from my drop point, when I saw two blue signatures flare up in front of a large crowd of red. I watched as they appeared to have seen us and one of the blue triangles began to move. From the video it looked to be struggling with something before a flash from a gun barrel took my attention. Then another flash killed a red square in front of them before a third shot upwards striking our helicopter. The only thought going through my head was to help them when before I knew it I found myself in freefall.

Zeroing in on the creature closest to the blue marks I readied my cannon and opened fire. The recoil as the bullets flew was almost non-existent, but the vibration I felt in my arm and the burst of strange colored mist from the now shredded creature, let me know it was definitely firing. I felt the impact as I landed on the remains of the creature crushing not only it, but the car it was once standing on.

I stared down at the two terrified civilians before warning alerts started to pop up all around me. The street had become alive with motion and it was as if instinct took over. My body turned and before I was even on my next target the barrels of my canon were already spinning up. In an instant the red squares began to disappear as the bursts of fire were finally released. I activated the flamethrower and the plume of the flame instantly incinerated whatever it touched.

One of the larger creatures grabbed my right arm and the whole upper body of my mech twisted when the beast pulled. I spun myself to grab my attacker by what I was guessing was its head before lifting and slamming its body into a telephone pole, its body partially splitting in half dropping its organs to the ground. It tried to continue its assault, but a stomp to its back and a few rounds to its body seemed to keep it down.

Looking over my shoulder I saw that the enemy count was rising and they were now coming from the store fronts as well.

"okay, I don't have time or the ammo for all of this." Flipping the switch to the loudspeaker I called out. **"You two, climb onto my back and cover your ears."**

~ Chris

The giant robot had smashed the monster into mush. Its entrails seemed to ooze like it had just been through a blender. I looked to Zoe and we ran for cover as the machine began firing in all directions. The sound was deafening as the cannon on its right arm mowed through the creatures like a weed wacker cutting through grass. In the brightness of the fire it belched out over the road, we could see hundreds of those things coming closer. It was like an unending march of mutation going to war for an unknown purpose.

One of the larger monsters grabbed onto our saviors arm, but was brutally dispatched before it seemed to be able to do any harm.

We were huddled behind a car when a voice boomed from the giant mechanical death machine, telling us to climb on and cover our ears. We didn't question it and I grabbed Zoe's hand so we could scramble up. Grabbing wherever we could get a hold, no sooner had we climbed on, had one of the boxes on the machines shoulders popped open and a series of thumps could be heard followed by metal clanging against objects in the distance before blinding flashes of lights and concussive blasts filled the air. Opening my eyes, everything was now in flames.

A few seconds passed and our metallic friend had begun moving fast. Where we were heading though, we had no clue.

FERAL TERRA

Chapter 4 an old friend

~ Zack

I don't know how long we had been moving, but with the new found strength my little angel had given me, we managed to make it to the mall in no time. Something I would have thought impossible without my new-found abilities. I had managed to not only outrun, but fight the few creatures I needed to in order to survive. Once they were down, Tabby would drain them and pump their life into us.

I avoided as many as I could, I knew she needed to rest and get better between meals. She was such a strong fighter, I knew she would get better soon. I know the last little fight took a lot out of her.

I was surprised at how easily I was able to pull the locked door open. The metal simply sheared off in the locks and the door itself morphed out of shape like clay. It was as if it just swung open by me touching it. I knew I was strong, but not that strong.

Standing in the empty mall, I felt weird. I knew it was after hours and the world was ending, but the liminal feeling of the building itself. There was just something about seeing the once always busy building being dark and shut down that made it all the more creepy.

Walking through the open area, it was strange as anything with electricity running through it appeared to start glowing the more I focused on it. Looking down at my hand, it too appeared to glow in thin lines as if my very nerves were filled with power. The more I stared, the clearer the vision was of all the tiny avenues branching through my body. It was almost as if I was able to see through my skin. "This must be how superheroes with X-ray vision see people. This is an astounding gift."

Even with the acceptance of my new abilities, I understood what my duty was and I couldn't let myself be distracted from it. I made sure everything was clear before finding a spot near a little garden to set up a camp. We had been so busy that I hadn't noticed my baby girl had begun to form a strange membrane over her body.

"It's okay hun, you've been so strong on our little journey, you deserve a rest. Daddy is so proud of you."

I knew I needed to give her time to regain her strength, but I couldn't leave her out in the open. One of those soldiers or someone not knowing she isn't really sick will try and harm my little angel. *They'll just think she's a monster. I know she isn't. She's just... not healed yet. She's not the monster, those people are! I have to keep her safe!*

I felt my body moving as if on its own volition. My hands plunged into the dirt and dug my free arm deep into the soil. I scooped handfuls of the grainy earth and shoved it to the side. Digging as vigorously and as deep as I could, I didn't stop until I hit the concrete below and punched through it in order to not impede her. Pulling my darling from her resting spot in my chest, I howled in pain as if my heart was truly being torn from my chest. Her arm that fed me my strength released its grip and pulled its now knotted root shaped fingers free as they desperately searched for its new home within her hardening shell.

Gathering myself. I held my daughter over the shallow pit knowing that I was burying her for her own good. Blood dripped from the gaping wound in my chest filling the hole with nutrients to keep her fed for now.

Gently, I lowered her down, her rooted hand attaching itself to where I had bled into the hole. Small hairlike tendrils started to sprout out and burrowed deep, quickly latching her into place. I pushed the soil to cover her little body and with a light pat I let her know I was there.

My body felt very weak from all the blood loss, but I still felt the abilities she gifted me flowing through my veins. Laying down, my back against the cold tiles, I felt and heard my stomach growl, I needed to eat. I also needed to bring Tabitha something as well.

Pulling out my phone I saw a surprising number of missed calls and texts from the old bitch. "Oh isn't this convenient."

She was clearly worried as the hundred plus texts were all begging to call her and let her know that Tabitha was okay. Voice mail after voicemail progressively getting more frantic. I didn't even get through a quarter of them before my phone started to vibrate with another call. Not going to lie, the fact she was this desperate was quite entertaining to me. She destroyed me in court after cheating on me. Claiming I abused her and that I was in fact the one who was cheating. A thought entered my mind and before the final ring I decided to answer the phone.

"Hello?"

" Zack! What took you so fucking long to answer, I've been calling and texting you for hours!"

"Good to hear you are alive too dear." I forced the most sarcastic tone I could manage with how much pain I was in.

"Don't give me that crap you asshole. Where is Tabby, is she okay?"

"Yes, she is safe and fine with me."

Before I could continue she interrupted me with a barrage of questions.

"Where are you? Let me talk to her, give her the phone, stop wasting my time and bring her here!"

"Dolly, shut the fuck up! You are in no position to be making those demands. We are at the mall and she is asleep right now. We couldn't even leave if we wanted to. The area surrounding us is crawling with those things. We aren't far from you though, so if you want to come see her, you are free to stop by, but in the meantime we are kind of stuck here."

There was a span of silence. I had never been that assertive with her in our marriage and I'm guessing it threw her off. She was always an "ask for the manager" type so I knew her pride and inability to accept being disrespected would bring her here.

"Fine, I will find a way there, just stay put and you better not let anything happen to her! I know how incompetent you are and..."

"Like I would purposefully put her in danger. How about you have your boy toy bring you. I know how you hate doing anything yourself or taking accountability."

"You listen to me you son of a..." 'beep'

Hanging up the phone I knew she would definitely come now. She didn't know how not to be a bitch. I hope she isn't alone though, we are hungry.

~ Vincent

"**Romeo this is alpha, we are over the LZ. Multiple hostiles are in the area. Permission to proceed?**"

"**Permission granted. Use of force is authorized. Alpha leader, our scan shows that lone wolf is no longer in transit. Please explain.**"

I knew I was going to have to cover for Kennedy, but it seemed like an easy lie.

"**Romeo, lone wolf, had a separate mission. He was tasked to disengage and drop at another location. Details are top secret. Not a need to know. He was informed of the ETA for pick up.**" I did my best to make it sound better than he decided to help some civilians before reaching his real drop zone.

A few seconds of silence was only filled with the light sound of static. They may have been trying to confirm, but all the dispatcher could get was a confirmation of a side mission. I sat waiting until they finally responded "**Roger that alpha, proceed to drop. Collection of the asset is of utmost importance.**"

"Understood."I let out a sigh of relief, had it not been confirmed as needed then it would have been a major shit storm when we returned.

Bardock and Wilcox were green and ready for drop. "**Transport 1, we have been given the go ahead to proceed with the mission. Let's clear the landing zone and...**"

Before I could finish, a barrage of impacts sparked against the hull of the helicopter. Closing my eyes I used the fly lenses to see what damage had been done. There were dozens of sharp needled teeth sticking into the hull of the transport. Quite a few had managed to embed themselves into the armored plating and began to release some kind of caustic fluids, melting into the metal even further and dissolving. Almost as if it was rotting it away.

Soon after another volley of the acidic thorns was heard clattering and I could feel the helicopter beginning to sway.

"**You guys gotta drop now! The rotors are being hit.**" The panicked voice of the pilot came screaming over the radio.

"**Troopers, release!**"

The few seconds of freefall was always the worst. The sensation of being weightless right before impact was my least favorite part. The sudden shock of hitting the ground was instantly filled with gunfire as Bardock was being swarmed by several of the lumbering beasts. Although slow they were like bullet sponges. Even as chunks were blown away, their blood seemed to just seep into the others making them mutate further. Each piece as it hit the ground almost appeared to have a life of its own and began to sprout into some kind of crawling terror. As the creatures closed in on him, he swung his fists to devastating results, but even with how many he was killing, the smaller harder to kill ones began to cover his suit like ants.

Wilcox ran over to help tear the creatures away from Bardock, but the only thing we could do was fight the inevitable. We used our guns to force the monsters back and torched the ground. I primed my railgun and shot a blast towards a hoard of the creatures, the shockwave blowing the monsters to smithereens. That seemed to be the only effective way to control them and keep them down permanently.

In the light of the fire I could make out that some of the creatures were wearing torn military uniforms, and prison jumpsuits. These weren't some faceless enemy invading, these were people, our brothers and sisters of battle.

"Sir! Sir! They've breached my cockpit, they're insi... ahhh!" The sound of Bardock's voice was replaced with a wet tearing sound. I looked over to his unit, only to see him torn through a small hole that had been melted into his shield.

What the hell is that stuff made of that it can melt through ballistic glass?

The monstrosity that had killed him looked like some sort of massive pitcher plant, with stumpy legs covered in vine like tentacles. The weird movements of the muscles mixed with the plant like sinew made the movements of the thing so much more grotesque. I watched in horror as my former squadmate was unceremoniously tossed piece by piece into the caldera of a mouth. As the other smaller spider-like creatures crawled in through the holes to get at the pieces not yet pulled free.

In all the confusion, the mech was in an instant, engulfed in flame. Explosions rocked the ground as Bardock's suits arsenal detonated. White phosphorus fuel and high explosives all erupted into a small cloud of smoke. I felt completely defeated watching as the enemy had killed one of the men under my charge. Add to that, I had one drop premature and possibly shitcanning his mission as well. The goal we had was starting to dwindle. I truly hope we didn't lose a man for nothing.

I felt a rage growing as I fought. We had all but stopped using our guns and switched strictly to the flamethrowers. By the time we had cleared the yard, our fuel tanks were almost empty and our explosive ordnance was almost depleted as well. After all was done, it was as if I was in a trance. The charred remains of the mutants surrounded us. The barrel of my railgun was glowing red from the overheated magnets. I had no idea how much time had elapsed since the shooting started, but it was calming, now standing in the relative silence.

"Sir, are you okay?" The unusually sullen voice of Wilcox came over the radio.

"We have to keep moving, we have already spent too much time here." I didn't know what else to say. It was as if my brain couldn't fathom the situation. This was not what we were trained to deal with. But we had a job to do, and I... I couldn't let the loss of a friend stop us from completing it.

Each step we took was punctuated by the sound of burned bones and wood splintering under our feet. Knowing they were probably the very people we served with and were sent to save, weighed heavily on my conscience. Seeing the door we were told would lead inside it was obvious that the creatures had originated from it. The heavy metal was twisted and melted, more than likely from that thing that killed Bardock.

Tangled plant-life intertwined the entrances' passageway, like some sort of temple hidden deep in the Amazon. Unusual, yet beautiful flowers seemed to spread open in the early morning hours. As we came closer to them, the details began to form. Everything was wrong, bony finger-like stems moved the flower petals that looked like eyelids, moving around the center mass of pustules that were so tightly packed together as if a balloon had been filled with water through a fishnet stocking.

I reached out with my suits' hand and pulled the doors off the hinges, tossing it to the side and readying my cannon. Pulling the mass of fleshy weeds from the doorway, I was surprised to see the floor was littered with parts of those creatures and bodies of those who hadn't been turned yet. All of them were left frozen in positions of pain and struggle. Shallow puddles of strange brown water were on the floor, like there was a fire at some point, but nothing other than what we had torched seemed to be burned or have had any smoke damage.

"Sir, are you seeing this?"

"Stay alert, our suits are too big to go inside, so we need a plan."

"Wanna rock, paper, scissors to see who goes in?"

~ Zoe

We rode on the back of our metal friend in whatever direction he chose. Chris and I haven't said a word for maybe a half hour, in order to avoid bringing more attention to ourselves. We were deep in the woods and the last infected we had seen was back on the street a few miles back. It was very dark here, but whoever Mr. Roboto was, seemed to be able to navigate the environment without light. I looked over at Chris, his shadowed silhouette was barely visible in the moonlight. I couldn't see his face, but I knew he couldn't be too happy that we were heading in the opposite direction of where he wanted to go.

"Hey... hey... Chris?" I whispered over to him, but I don't know if he could hear me. "Chris?"

"You should probably know we are clear, no real need to whisper." the voice from the machine said.

"Seriously, you didn't think to tell us this earlier?"

"Didn't seem like a need to know type of thing. Besides, I can only scan so far ahead. There is no telling what might be in the area."

I didn't know how to respond to that, but we kind of needed to know where we were going and whether or not it's safe.

"How far are we from the nearest apartment complex?" Chris finally spoke.

"I hate to break it to you man, but pretty much all the major population areas are wiped out. This whole town was ground zero. Where I'm heading right now is where everything started."

"And that would be?"

"The Chlor-Reform corporation. It is the epicenter of the outbreak, it's also where there is supposedly a cure."

"Wait, you mean to tell me this was just some company's pet project?"

"As far as I'm aware ma'am."

"The phone call wasn't a prank..." Chris mumbled. "Why are you telling us this? I mean I figure this is probably some sort of cover up mission you are on."

After a few tense seconds of silence **"To be honest sir, given the rate of the spreading infection and how fast things are going to hell. I doubt even with the antivirus, I'm fairly certain we are all screwed. So to me, it doesn't matter. They have already decided that quarantine of the state would be easier to do than it would be for the antivirus to work. Pretty much if I fail in this mission, they plan to cordon off as much as possible and the rumor of burning the whole state to ash has been passed around."**

I didn't know what that meant, but I had a good idea that it meant they were willing to sacrifice the few to save the many. "Do you mean they might nuke the state?"

"No ma'am, the higher ups plan to napalm the whole infected area. It's more controlled and wont cause nuclear fallout. This isn't the movies."

"How much time do we have?" I knew it couldn't be long, given that according to my parents they had already started putting up the walls.

"Currently my mission time says I have just over four hours before it is considered a failure. Unless I can get to the facility, locate the canister containing the antivirus, and get to the pick up point in that time frame. We will have maybe a few days before the barrier is finished. Then within a few hours the first fire bombs and MOAB's are going to be dropped."

I had no clue what any of that stuff was, but I understood that it meant nothing good for us. Maybe if we tried and made it to one of the walls the military would test us and see we were fine and let us out or something, but knowing that in only a few days the whole state would essentially be a bonfire was not really on my list of things to try and comprehend. I knew my parents were close to the border, and I hope they were able to evacuate safely.

Taking out my phone, I wanted to see if they were okay, but I didn't have a signal. I knew I should be worried, but my parents weren't stupid. *I'm sure they are safe. I'm sure I will see them when this big robot guy manages to complete his mission. Yeah... I'm certain of this, but just to be sure.*

Tapping the canopy a few times I felt a need to ask. "So... big robot guy, what are the chances you will succeed at your mission? I mean we both have family we are trying to make sure are still alive."

"Ma'am, I have a name." a slightly annoyed tone was clear even with the distortion of the speaker.

"Well, you could start by telling us or else I'm just going to continue calling you..."

"Kennedy! okay? You can call me Kennedy, and to answer your question, had I not been busy saving you and now having to walk to my dropsite, I would be in a much better position to say yes, the mission will be a total success. However, right now I am in a bit of trouble and need to hope we can get there in the next half hour or so. I don't mean to be rude, but we should probably be quiet for right now. Also, you may want to make a choice. You can stay with me, in which case you are going to need to hold on because I have to increase our speed. Or I can Drop you off at the next area that is clear enough in this direction and close to a quarantine zone." After saying this, he shut off the radio and I could feel his steps hasten. He seemed to be pretty annoyed with us at the moment and I felt bad, but I think we had the right to know what he told us.

okay then,nice chat. I still didn't know what Chris was thinking at this moment, but with how quiet he's been, he couldn't be thinking of anything good. I think it's time I start thinking of how to get out of here, because if this situation is starting to be too much. I might consider Tin-man here's offer. Maybe I would be safer if I stayed with him instead of Chris?

~ Kennedy

"Kennedy, do you mind explaining why the hell you dropped so far from your designated dropsite?" Sarge's voice boomed through the radio. **"Also can you elaborate on why you appear to be carrying extra weight? Do you understand the gravity of importance that hinges on your mission's success?"**

"I don't have an answer for why the helicopter dropped me where it did, sir. The helicopter took a hit from small arms fire and before I knew it I was falling. I managed to save two civili..."

"Are you kidding me?" He said with a more calm tone. "Your suit must have activated the defense protocol and dropped you." A few seconds passed and I was worried something else had happened. "I'm rerouting your course and updating your map. If you drop the extra weight and increase your speed you should make it to the facility within the next hour. We are definitely going to have a discussion when you get back to the barracks. Remember your time limit. Drop the baggage and if you don't bring back that canister there will most certainly be hell to pay. Am I clear?"

"Yes, sir."

"The new route unfortunately will send you through an unknown area. We don't have any intelligence about the threat level due to the trees blocking our view."

"Is there anywhere safe where I can drop off the civilians that is close to a quarantine zone?"

"Give me a moment... It looks like there was one set up in a small strip mall a mile or so in the same direction you are heading. We lost contact with the command there a few hours ago. However, there should be someplace for them to hold up in order for you to continue your primary mission. If you can procure that package, I promise you that we will find them. I understand you feel responsible for their safety, but sometimes in war you have to put the mission over collateral damage."

"Understood sir." I gritted my teeth as the words left my mouth. I knew what he meant, but it was hard to hear. If I were to send these people out on their own now or at the mark on the map, who knows how long they will survive.

Before I could even run the scenario through the computer, I heard someone hitting the canopy. I tried my best to mull over the options and decided to give them the choice. I knew that if I let them go it would be almost certain death, but if they stayed with me, maybe their survival would be better. However that might mean I miss the pick up.

When the lady mentioned that they were trying to find family, I knew they would more than likely want to check the quarantine zone. The guy has been very quiet and not the badass I had seen trying to get my attention shooting shit earlier.

I didn't see a point in keeping anything secret at this point so I was as honest as I felt I should be. They deserve to know that this place was about to become hell in less than a week. Maybe that will give them at least the opportunity to try and either escape the impending doom or find and spend some time with loved ones. Whoever the lady is, didn't seem too enthused by the options though. I think I'll give them some time to decide. According to the map, we are about fifteen minutes away from a clearing I can drop them off at. Either way, I need to step up my speed. My mission counter is marching on and I have a deadline for a safe exit.

~ Chris

The rhythmic stomping of the massive vehicle of death as it carried us through the woods was intense, to say the least. I was still in shock at how easily it destroyed so many of those things in only a few seconds. The power this one person wields is almost godlike. *How could anything stand against it?* Yet, here we are, running away. I understand why. The shear numbers would have eventually overpowered it. I couldn't help but feel insignificant in its presence. I was thankful that whoever was driving it decided to help us, but I still knew in the bottom of my heart that I had to find my family.

I wasn't expecting all the action to happen. I was foolish to think that the helicopter would have just landed with no issue, picked us up, and then we would all be able to fly off into the sunset where I could find my family again. I know they are out there somewhere, but if what he said was true, then my inlaws apartment is probably not safe. They wouldn't have gone there if it wasn't. Where else would they go?

The very thought that everything I was hoping for is again taken from me. I'm riding on the back of this war machine in the opposite direction of where I had been trying so hard to go. Was he even telling the truth? Sure the roads were filled with those things and pretty much everywhere we have gone has been over-run, but there is always a chance, right?

Looking down at my phone, *I still didn't see any missed calls or even a text from any of them. I wanted so badly to call them or to message them in some way, but I didn't want to put them in more danger if they were hiding. I also knew Beth was horrible at turning off her notifications, so her phone would definitely make a sound. I couldn't risk putting her or the boys in more danger because I wanted to be selfish. If I take the option to go to the outpost, or whatever he called the quarantine zone, maybe... just maybe I could find them.*

With every step, it was as if I could feel my hope slipping further away with each thundering step. My choice in the matter also seemed to be dwindling. I had to either hope the quarantine zone was safe, or venture off on my own.

~ Vincent

"Wilcox, watch the door. We don't know what else is here and I may need you to make some noise and cover me and whoever I may find."

"Sir we are only here to extract the scientist I thought."

"I understand that, but would you seriously leave someone in this hell hole?"

A tense few seconds passed as I looked at him before he nodded, knowing I was right. **"I'm not feeling too hot on how this is going to go. So please focus on what we need to do here."**

"No problem sir, be careful."

He walked off, and deployed into a defensive position. As strong as our mechs were, they would only last so long in an assault like we had earlier. I had to make this quick. Disengaging from the interface and opening the cockpit. I hopped out and opened one of the cargo pods in the leg.

Grabbing the emergency rifle, I racked a round into the chamber, making it ready. I made my way clearing corners as I moved through the destroyed prison. Scorch marks and chemical burns decorated the walls in various shades of colored death. *Guess there was fire being used... but why would they have flame units?*

Stepping through the death halls, I did my best to avoid the darker more infested areas. I didn't want to draw unneeded attention from unnecessary gunfire. Even with a silencer, this gun will be loud enough to bring them in.

It was pretty obvious where I needed to go though. The barricaded areas of last stands and half destroyed hazardous hallways only got thicker with bodies the closer I was to the beacon on our target. According to the transmitter he was in the isolation wing. I'm guessing he decided it was the safest place. Judging by the damage though, I really hope this mission wasn't for someone that was already dead.

I was relieved to see that there were less contacts in here than I had thought there would be. The only sounds I could hear were the gentle sloshing of the disgusting water and what I told myself was just sludge.

Nearing where I had to go, it was the safest route I could find. All the others were blocked off by more of those things than I cared to tango with. However, this way had a strange pounding echoing throughout the hall. I couldn't determine from which direction it was coming from, but the sound grew louder with each second. Rounding a corner, I was stopped dead in my tracks. There was one of those things, a humanoid shape to it, leaned to one side as if a heavy weight was pulling on its head.

As soon as I saw it, I stepped back behind cover. I didn't hear any footsteps as I pressed myself against the wall. A few moments passed and the source of the thumping continued as it had been. Peeking around the corner I saw the massive club-like head swinging back as rooted arms stretched down anchoring the body to the ground. It brought its head repeatedly against the now failing security door. Each hit splintering bloody chunks from the creatures head and embedding themselves into the metal, the blood causing it to corrode as if acid was leaching into the steel, rusting it like a ship that's been at sea for too long. Each smack shattering the oxidized chips into the water below.

Looking down, I tapped the screen on my wrist pulling up my map of the area. This was the only way left that was clear for the most part and right behind that door is where the target was. *Fuck... okay Vin, what are we gonna do.*

I watched it for a minute or so, seeing if there was an opening and found that every thirty seconds or so, the thing would stop smashing its face and take a break. In that time of rest, some type of bio-growth would form over the splintered off sections of the things face. Like it was growing some kind of plant based armor mixed with flesh and bone.

Time was running out as the creature began its repetition again. *okay if I'm gonna do anything I have to do it now.* Gripping my carbine I raised it up taking aim. Its head reared back and in the destroyed face an eye rolled around to see me, stopping it dead in its tracks.

I didn't know what else to do, squeezing the trigger, I felt the shots vibrating through my shoulder and the rounds sprayed a thick sap-like blood across the walls as they tore through the beast. It struggled and loud cracks could be heard as its arms and legs broke free from their rooted prisons. The elongated neck swung back and was brought down, smashing one of the limbs into a sharpened spike-like blade of a forearm. Its other arm pulled free of the concrete floor with a massive chunk still attached.

The bullets didn't seem to be doing anything as it began to make its way towards me in a lumbering lurch, dragging one of its legs behind. It wasn't fast, but its reach would take up the whole hall.

"Shit!"

~ Michaels

It happened so fast. When the lights went out I was lucky to find myself in the isolation hall. I knew things were bad, but I would never have imagined that the power was going to go out this soon. In the splashes of light I could see the soldiers firing into the amorphous mass of shadows that I couldn't even tell if they were my colleagues or just the infected. Those military idiots were just firing out of fear, blindly hoping they hit something to live another few seconds.

This god forsaken suit was so encumbering that I fell to the ground as I tried to escape the chaos. The floor was becoming slick with blood and whatever else was spraying the area. I'd be lying if I said I wasn't scared. The screams surrounded me and I couldn't think of anything other than my own survival. In the strobe of automatic fire I saw something. It might give me at least some kind of a chance for survival. Crawling as fast as I could, I made my way towards the sprinkler controls. I had to climb over bodies, coming face to face with those infected or horribly mangled from them. If there was a hell, I'm sure this was a snippet of what it was like.

I felt something grab my ankle and fear shot up from the tight grip. I looked down to see the terrified eyes of the private I had tried to reassure earlier. With each flash I could see the veins in his face already turning purple from the virus. I kicked as hard as I could and felt his grip finally relent after the third or fourth stomp. I saw him rolling in the sludge, clutching at his face. I clawed feverishly at the ground before I finally managed to get my footing under me. I managed to steady myself even with tripping over whoever or whatever got in my way. In my panic, I managed to grasp the valve and began furiously spinning it open. I knew there wasn't much of the chemical still in the lines, but it was something that might weaken the things.

Emergency lights flickered to life as the sprinklers exploded to life, drenching everything with the infused liquid. Those not wearing any protective gear let out cries of pain as their skin began to boil and melt off. Steam escaped their body as it absorbed itself into their pores, mixing with the iron in the blood and causing a severe thermal reaction. It wasn't a high enough dose to kill them all though. I felt the heat of the chemical reacting on my gore covered suit and I had to get out of here before it could finish melting through.

I could see the outline of one of the cell doors in the dimly lit hall. I saw an opening and made a run for it. Grabbing onto the handle I swung it closed as the sound of running footsteps came up behind me. I held the door with all my weight, praying that whatever was on the other side wasn't stronger than me. I felt a few sharp tugs on the door that seemed to be getting weaker with each pull until finally it stopped. I heard a splash as something seemed to have fallen to the flooded floor. Sliding the feeding hatch open, I looked out and that poor soldier was laying there, his body thrashing in the water as the mutations began to manifest. The convulsions stopped after a few minutes, along with all the other noises. The brown dirty looking water began to run clear as the tanks of the plant killer ran dry. The private's body stopped flailing around a few minutes later. His hands falling away from his face, revealing that it was already beginning to change.

The heat in my suit had become intolerable and I hopped onto the concrete slab that was the bed and tore off the dissolving pieces of tyvek. The feeling of the cold water was welcome as it washed over my hot sweaty skin. My shirt clung to my body like a needy ex, but all this fresh water was doing now was diluting the solution. I knew the door wasn't locked, but without my suit on that water was still hazardous until then. It should be safe once the sprinkler reserves are depleted, but I can only hope that it'll be watered down enough that I can get the hell out of here.

I had been waiting there for what felt like hours, but couldn't have been more than a half hour since the water stopped spraying. The screams of the survivors died off long ago, I also hadn't heard any water sloshing around for a while now. Either the creatures have moved on or they are waiting for me to make a mistake. I activated my SOS transmitter in the hopes that someone would come save me, but I knew that was a long shot. If I was going to get out of here, I couldn't rely on the kindness of others during this apocalypse.

Testing the water with my finger, it was slightly irritating, but it was safe enough for me to make my move. I kept my rubber boots on for some protection and slowly made my way to the door. The gentle ripples of water sounded like crashing waves in the silence.

Looking through the sliding door, I couldn't see any movement and with a hesitant hand I pushed on the door softly. It creaked open and I had to take a deep breath hoping it wasn't attracting any unwanted company.

It wasn't even completely open before I saw the privates' body begin to convulse again. He stood up with an unholy sound resonating from his mouth. Not a howl, but a pain filled roar. I slammed the door shut again and tied the handle with the bed-sheet. I wrapped the sheet around the toilet pulling it as hard as I could. No sooner had I done so, when the pounding started. I dared not look out again from fear. I didn't want to die like this.

I don't know how much time had passed before I heard it. All I had listened to for what must have been another hour was the rhythmic beats of the monster trying to smash its way in, but these sounds seemed deliberate. I thought it was nothing more than distant gunfire, when I felt the whole building shake as something set off a series of explosions. I began to feel hope again with the thought that I might be saved, and when it all fell silent again moments later I felt that hope being ripped from me, as if the tease of it was to add insult to injury.

Several minutes passed as my dying hope finally made me begin to think that maybe I should just give up. *Did I really wanna spend the last few days of my life holding a door closed?* Even if I was lucky enough not to die of dehydration, the other option would be them burning the state to ash.

The dents in the door are clearly showing that this door doesn't have much more time anyways. *Maybe I should just open it up and take my chances.*

As the thought crossed my mind, the thumping and shocks to the door stopped and a familiar sound of bullets ricocheting off the door reinvigorated me. My salvation was here and now all I could do was hope that whoever it was, was able to kill that thing.

FERAL TERRA

Chapter 5 call of the voice

~Vincent

I watched in stunned silence as the horrifying creature tore itself free and began to shamble towards me. I fired repeatedly trying to stop it, but the bullets either ripped through it or wouldn't punch through the strange amalgamation of muscle and plant. Every shot was hitting its mark, but not even a stammer could be seen.

Slapping another magazine into place I had to think of something as the looming danger of the creature's aura only got closer. I had to keep an eye out for any friends of his nearby, as I had to tactically retreat. The sloshing of the monster's shuffle began to speed up to a more normal pace to close the distance. In the small spotlights coming from the emergency boxes, I could see new vines wrapping around its calves and thighs, acting almost like tendons to help move the increasingly, more armored upper body.

If I don't think of something soon, the thing is going to be sprinting.
In my peripheral, I saw the glint of chrome and red.
A fire extinguisher!
Finding some cover behind a turned over table, I steadied my barrel and took aim. The creature was now almost at a jogging pace only twenty or so feet away. When it was almost to the big red target I squeezed off a round causing an explosion of white pressurized gas to fog up the area. I watched for another second longer before a massive limb slammed down on the edge of the table, splintering it in half. I barely managed to stumble away as it crashed into the floor splashing water and god knows what, everywhere. I crawled backwards as fast as I could as another giant mace of an appendage came out of the haze, crushing the ground hard enough for me to feel the floor crack and a small shockwave of pressure rushed into me like a strong wind.

I rolled to my left as the thorn-like forearm stabbed at me. I somehow managed to clamber to my feet and dove past the creature just as it swung again, smashing the spikey appendage into the wall and lodging in place. I saw an opening of exposed flesh that had yet to become a solid plate and I didn't have any other choice. I grabbed a grenade from my belt and started firing. Blasting chunks of the things skin and muscle away, I managed to jam the grenade into the open wound as vines started to heal around it. I felt a heavy object hitting me in the stomach and a sudden feeling of weightlessness and pain before crashing through another makeshift barricade. Grabbing whatever I could to shield myself, the beast's back exploded in a flash of gore causing it to fall forward and its club of a head to land in between my legs.

"Fuck... me!" I whispered in between heavy breaths. No ones going to believe this.

"Sir! Sir!Come in! I just heard an explosion. Is everything okay?" Wilcox's voice seemed worried over the radio. Can't say I blame him.

Trying to find the words was harder than I thought it would be, but I managed to get them out. **"All good, there... was a... there was an obstruction and I had to clear it. Over."**

There was a moment of silence before I heard his voice again. **"Thought I lost you too sir. Over"**

"Nope, it's gonna take more than some tree mutant to kill me. Over."

"That's good to know sir. Have you located the nerd? Over."

"Not yet, about to head to his location now. Over."

"10-4, Over and out."

"Yeah... 10-4... Over and out."

Gathering my faculties about me, I knew that what I had just done was incredibly stupid and now it's going to be so much harder to get out of here.

That Doctor better be alive in there, or else I'm about to die for nothing.

Shining my flashlight over to my very dead friend here, I started to feel queasy as I realized that it was only going to be dead for a short time though. Looking over the gaping wound I could see that already, the remains of the torso was beginning to suture itself back together. Ivy-like veins spread out and once they hit a chunk that had been blown free, tiny roots began to crawl in and drag it back to the main trunk.

"okay... it's time to go"

What does it take to kill something like that? I put everything I had into it and it's still not completely dead.

It wasn't long before I could hear the distant echoes of all those incomprehensible creatures making their way to where they heard the dinner bell. "I had no choice!" I kept telling myself that in order to not feel like I compromised everything like a new recruit.

Rounding the last corner, I jogged to a soft stop as the door came into view. A wash of defeat hit me as I saw the door was now wide open and there was a bright yellow hazmat suit face down in the shallow water.

"Oh come on..." I hadn't been fast enough. Walking over to the body, I knew that I needed confirmation that it was him, but the beacon was embedded into the suit, and that was the same reference listed in the logs as belonging to him. If he is dead though, there is a good chance he might be one of those things.

Approaching the body with caution, I began to use the barrel of my gun to flip the bio suit. I was just about to see in through the mask, when a sound caught my attention. Turning quickly, it was just in time as three long sharp needle-like objects flew past me and stapled the tyvek to the floor. I saw an upside down head, the jaw opened beyond what should have been possible, with rows of pointed teeth, like a sunflower ready to seed, aimed in my direction. Instinctively, I raised my weapon only to see that the dangling head seemed to be collecting its breath in order to launch another volley.

Grabbing the doors edge, I swung it shut as a torrent of spikes peppered the rusted metal. Some of which punctured deep enough for me to see the tips dripping something as they protruded through the door.

Sliding the feedway to the side I could see the strange bodied monstrosity was attached to a thick stem, maybe the circumference of a baseball. Three prehensile appendages acted like legs and arms as they dug into whatever it was trying to climb on. I saw a few more scuttling their way up the hallway on all the surfaces. Each one mutated in their own unique way. I closed the hatch again and held on for dear life as another barrage of teeth were shot my way. When another more familiar sound caught my attention.

I heard a series of rapid running footsteps, splashing towards the door in a charge. I held on as hard as I could, closing my eyes for the inevitable. I heard them stampeding, until a sudden belch like whoosh came from outside followed by the door heating up and the earth shattering rumble as the battering ram of a beast crashed into the wall. The few creatures that still had mouths, screamed like distorted banshees before the disgusting popping sounds silenced them. Several more bursts of heat washed over the area just outside the door as I listened to whatever had hit the wall, struggling before it itself seemed to perish.

"It's safe to come out now!" There was a moment of quiet when the voice yelled again. "Well, for right now at least!"

Opening the door, I could see a rather disheveled, tall, blonde guy. He had a flamethrower of all things that he was in the process of taking off. Training my light to his face, I was relieved to see that it was the man we were looking for.

~ Zoe

Fifteen minutes passes much faster than what you would think while stomping through the woods riding Mr. robot here. Chris still hasn't said much, but something is going on in his head and I wish I knew what his plan was. I don't want to be stuck out here by myself and even though he may be a little off, he still seems reliable. I really hope we can find his family, no one deserves dad of the year more.

I was so lost in thought at the time that I almost fell off mechy-mouse when the damn thing abruptly stopped. "Hey!, how about a little warning!" I said, slapping the canopy.

"We're here."

I felt hesitant knowing this is where the one source of safety and us were meant to part ways.

"So... this is it huh?" I couldn't help but let out a subtle sigh, acknowledging to myself that I might not make it another day. I looked over to Chris and we met each other's eyes. Even in the low light of early morning I could see that he also had the look of concern as he took a deep breath and started to climb down. I breathed a breath of relief that I wasn't going to be alone, but the chill that filled my lungs let me know it was a bit of a pyrrhic victory.

"If you guys follow that path for a mile, there should be a quarantine zone. Check in with them and when I get what I need to get, I'll radio in for a transport out of here. Take this radio" a small door opened and a radio was stashed inside. **"And, when you get there, let me know how many are alive so we know how many choppers to send."** He said that with a sense of urgency that didn't fill me with confidence.

Chris stashed the radio on his belt, and we watched as our big robot buddy walked away. *Our only real salvation from this hellhole and its walking away... fuck.. me.* I was thinking this as we listened to the heavy footsteps trample off into the distance like it was some weird western.

"I hate to sound like a stereotype here in a horror situation, but I kinda wanted to stay. Big tonka there, could have definitely kept us safe. I'm just saying." The look Chris gave me was one of someone who was a little annoyed. I can't say I blame him though. I probably should shut up. My anxiety was catching up with me and I couldn't help but try to joke to cope. The feeling that we were now on our own with no guarantee was hitting my chest like a hammer now.

"Hey... Zoe, you okay?"

I guess I had been rambling to myself and Chris seemed to be worried.

"Yeah... yeah, sure I'm good, I'm good good good."

He stared at me for a few seconds as if he could clearly see I was not good at all. "Let's get going then. Maybe that will help us focus." He looked off in the direction we needed to go and started walking.

I was a little on edge, but in situations like this, at the prison I had others I knew I could trust and talk to, but in the few hours I've been with Chris, we hadn't really talked. I knew nothing about this guy, but he didn't seem like a safety risk or anything. Clearly with his limp and beaten body, if he was, I could easily outrun and defend myself. From the looks of things though, I might be with him for a while. Might as well try and fill the silence at least.

"Hey, Chris, can you tell me about your family? I'm a little worried about our situation, I need some help here being distracted from it."

He stopped for a second to look back and he smiled.

"Sure, why not, what would you like to know?" He seemed pretty sincere in his response that I started to feel a little bit better, not a lot, but it was better than nothing.

"What are they like?" It was the only thing to ask.

He took a moment to think of what I assumed was the best response. "To tell the truth... they were my world." The way he said it with a small laugh, made me feel his sincerity in his voice. "Derrick was the first one out, but don't tell Tyler that. He's good at sports, kind of the jock of the family. He always listens, but I know he isn't a fan of following all the rules. Tyler has always had an interest in building cool and strange contraptions out of building blocks and seeing if he can make things move. Beth and I are sure he's gonna grow up to be an engineer of some sort."

"Sounds like you have your hands full."

"Yeah, especially since I've been job hunting the last few weeks. It's been taking everything I have in order to keep them all happy and thinking we are all good, when in reality, our finances were in the downward spiral to Nowhereville." He seemed to trail off as if embarrassed. "You never really know stress until you have others that rely on you for survival, then it's just natural, ya know?

I was a little nervous about answering, but it seemed like he needed me to talk, too. "I... I don't have much family, but I do have my parents. I'm hoping that they managed to get out of the state before they shut down the highways. They aren't in the best of health and are getting up there in age. They were both retired so they didn't do much other than keep each other company. But, I was sure to send them money when I had a little extra so they could enjoy a few meals out every now and then." I trailed off a bit as I felt sad that in reality with their health conditions, they might still be stuck at home. I needed to keep the conversation mostly on him so I didn't get lost in my own thoughts again. "You mentioned your wife, what was she like?"

"She was perfect to me. She was a great mother, could cook way better than I could ever hope to be skilled enough to do. Her very presence lit up the room for me whenever I came home from a particularly hard day, and she was always understanding that some things were best unsaid. I understood she knew I was just putting up a front about how screwed we really were, but she stayed with me and helped me at least enjoy some small part of an otherwise bad day." He looked up into the morning sun and I could see his eyes watering. "She was beautiful. Not just in looks, but as a person," he wiped a tear away as a memory must have come back to him. "I remember seeing it on our first date, we were walking downtown and a homeless man had come up to us and asked for some spare change. She ended up bringing him with us to go get food and she bought him something to keep him warm at night. I saw that same care in her a few hours ago as she was shielding our boys, even when certain death was present. She was still putting herself between it and someone she genuinely cared about. I couldn't live without her and that's why I need to get to this outpost. I need to know the boys and Beth are alright."

~ Chris

I was a little hesitant about getting off of the armed escort, but I understood he was on a mission and only helped us as an inconvenience to him. When we got to our drop off point I was starting to wonder if I should stay with Zoe. she wasn't doing too well and I think what's going on is getting to her.

In order to calm down she wanted to talk and I figured we were in a safe enough spot to do so, given we haven't seen or heard anything dangerous for a while. A mile doesn't seem like much when you are talking about something you care about. I thought I was boring her with my stories about my family and how things haven't been too good for us lately. It was a gentle reprieve from what we have been facing the last few hours.

She seemed to be directing the conversation to just be about me and I think it was to keep her from being in her own head. I told her everything I could and I felt bad when we got to the events leading up to us at the prison. Luckily we made it to the quarantine zone before we got too much further in the conversation. It wasn't going in a good direction and I was already in physical pain, I don't think the emotional added to that would be good. Right now I need to keep my thoughts clear.

We saw the fence as we crested a small hill. They had completely enclosed a large grocery store parking lot with fencing and cars. It was insane to see how post-apocalyptic someplace can look in only a few hours. The problem was that there were broken down sections, bent and twisted like whatever had done the damage didn't even struggle getting through.

"I don't think this is going to be safe Chris. Maybe we should keep going?"

Raising my hand for her to give me a second. We surveyed the area from a distance and saw several trailers marked with both military and medical insignia. It might be a long shot, but if anyone was alive, it would be there or in the store itself. There were a few of those head sprouts growing from corpses that looked pretty fresh dotted around in random spots, but none appeared to be close to the shipping container outpost.

I got up and started to make my way closer, but I felt Zoe grab my arm. "Where are you going? There's those things in there!" She whisper-yelled at me.

"There aren't that many, and we will need something to defend ourselves with. Besides, I'm not leaving here without knowing my family isn't trapped there." I knew if anywhere would have some kind of indication to who is where, it would be on a computer or something. There was still power on, and if there were survivors here, maybe someone could help. This is also where Kennedy told us he would be sending the helicopters when he's done. I looked at her and tried to smile. "Please trust me."

"Chris, listen to yourself. You are beginning to sound crazy."

"Crazy? I just want us to have the best case scenario. If we can get inside one of those trailers, we can barricade ourselves inside and we can hold out. If nothing else we can find food or some kind of weapons possibly. How is any of that crazy?" This seemed like a logical enough answer, but she didn't look too enthused by the idea. Even though she stared at me in silence I didn't want to waste more time crouched here in the woods. I again started to make my way across the parking lot as low to the ground as I could. The soft grass gave way to hard asphalt and in the early morning light it hadn't become blisteringly hot yet. I looked back to Zoe, but she stayed in the bushes watching where I was going.

I practically had to crawl in order to not be seen by any of those things. Once I got to the fence I could see the disgusting things absentmindedly swiveling around like death dealing security cameras, but they seemed to be preoccupied looking at the rising sun. The section of fence I chose to try and climb over was twisted as if something of considerable size had simply reached up the ten feet to the top and yanked it down like it was made of aluminum foil. The whole area in the dawn mist was like looking over a desolate abandoned town that nobody has seen in years. The closer I looked the more I saw as a mold like moss was spreading across the ground where the sprouts seemed to be. It was as if they were infecting the very ground they grew from. I could already see smaller animals like mice wrapped in the living vegetation, either being mutated or digested, I couldn't really tell.

I had better try and steer clear of that stuff, I thought to myself while watching the still living victims struggling to be free from whatever was happening to them. The closer I got to one of the trailers the clearer the sound of the suffering was evident. Desiccated bodies were strewn about the area in various positions of anguish, all of them showing signs of pain in what must have been their final moments. The details became more clear and I started seeing a pattern to the moss. It looked almost as if it had been splashed onto the people, encasing them somehow into some kind of an earthen tomb.

I tried to divert my eyes from the horrific topiaries because looking at them made me worry more for Beth and the boys. I didn't want to think about the possibility that they could be here amongst the living graves. The thought that they might be here and gone, was like driving a nail into my head that I needed to pull out for my own good.

Pushing the thoughts away, I found a path through the infected landscape without bringing any attention to myself. It was as if the creatures were sleeping. Looking back to the treeline, I wanted to wave Zoe in and let her know it was relatively safe, but when I searched for her, I saw no sign she was even still there. *Did she get attacked and I didn't hear her? Should I go back?*

It took some wrestling with myself, but what good would I be? If there was a gun or something in here and I'll be able to actually help, sure, but I was in no physical condition to be street fighting some plant creature.

Turning and pulling the handle on the door, I could hear the tiny roots and vines tearing away from the frame causing me to duck inside as fast as I could in case the noise alerted any of them. Pressing my ear against the closed door, I listened for any sounds that might be something on its way to knock, but to my relief, nothing was coming.

My luck appeared to be going pretty well, too. The power was on and there were a few computers still on. It was a relatively tight fit in here, but there was a door at the end of the hall-like box that was closed.

I ran to one of the computers and began frantically typing into every search bar I found, looking for any information on what was happening out there. However, all of it seemed to have been classified or was being blocked. I was able to find a phone number, but the phone had been shot along with one of the three computer stations.

I must have searched a hundred different combinations of words, only to have none of them work. To say I was disappointed would be an understatement. I eventually gave up seeing that this was going nowhere.

"**Thump.**" I heard something fall coming from beyond the closed door causing me to jump like my heart was trying to hop out of my chest. I went completely still, not wanting to let anything know I was in here. *I knew I should have checked behind there when I got in here.*

Looking around I looked for something to use as a weapon, and the best I could find was something that looked like a long cattle prod. It didn't appear to have any charge left, but I'll take this over nothing. As I approached the door, I heard something clatter to the floor. *Whatever it is sounds clumsy.*

Reaching for the handle, it seemed as if my whole world focused on this one moment. Raising the club, I readied myself. Gently turning the handle, I heard the click as the latch retracted and I took a deep breath.

"One... two... three!" I swung open the door and something fell from the doorway and fell on top of me. I felt my face being covered by something slimy and filled with chunks of something hard. Panicking, I didn't know if I was infected. Not knowing what else to do I brought the bludgeon down several times trying to beat whatever was attacking me before I realized that it wasn't moving.

I was able to roll it off of me and I laid there breathing heavily for a few minutes before wiping my face off and looking at my "attacker". It turned out to be a dead soldier. His missing face indicated he had decided to opt-out, instead of trying to run or escape. I couldn't say I really blamed them, but it didn't take long for me to understand that what was now covering my face was brain matter and chunks of skull.

As soon as that thought came, I rolled to the nearest trash can to puke my guts out. I found a jacket on the chair next to me and vigorously tried to rub the remains off my face. The gory scene was hard to process, but after my cleaning session I threw the jacket over the soldier's body, both out of respect and to keep myself from seeing the horrible aftermath of their choices.

Looking towards the door, the sounds I heard were of the body hitting the door, what I heard after the "thump" though was the gun he used clattering to the ground, followed by the soldiers teeth and parts of their jaw bone.

It wasn't a pleasant scene to look at, but I managed to work up the courage to crawl over to the room and grab the shotgun from where it was laying in the pool of blood. The viscera dripped off of it as I picked it up and I felt myself gag again.

Looking it over, I found that it was still loaded. It wasn't much, but the few shots here could save me down the line. Looking down at the unfortunate soldier, I knew I should search them for whatever I could find.

Reaching down, I did my best to avoid lifting the jacket and keeping the nasty sight to a minimum, but I was able to find that they did still have a handgun as well as a few more shells and an extra magazine for the pistol. I felt wrong doing it, but it made more sense for me to just take their duty belt. There was something inherently wrong that I felt while unhooking it from the body only to wear it myself. It felt like I was desecrating the body, but this wasn't a normal circumstance and I could only hope that whoever finds me will understand.

It's not like I'm stealing it. I mean... they're already dead, and I need it more than...

No matter how I tried to justify the situation in my mind, I felt dirty. Like I was a thief breaking into someone's home and taking whatever I wanted. I shouldn't stay here though, in case the soldiers' friends show up thinking I'm the one who killed their friend. There is no scenario where I look good in a stranger's eyes.

If the world is really going to go to shit like it is now though, I'm going to have to get used to this. I'll have to provide for my family in some way I guess.

Turning to the computer station, I saw that there was a camera set up and I began clicking through the different feeds. I knew I needed to go back and get Zoe, but even at this point I understood that she chose to stay back and I needed a break.

The more I flipped through the footage, the more I felt sad. There were a few cameras that seemed to have been hacked into that showed the inside of the store. Probably as a way to keep an eye on the survivors if they had been staying here. Seeing the mess and the destroyed displays, I felt something strange inside of me begin to grow. I couldn't put my finger on it, but something was off about this whole place. Then it occurred to me. "Where are all the bodies?"

It wasn't long from my little TV session that I stopped and realized that I saw some motion in one of the screens. There was something very large moving through the supermarket. I couldn't make out too much detail, but it was big. The few remaining corpses that had avoided infection were scooped up by strange tentacle-like vines and tossed into some sort of opening that sloshed with fluids. The bodies dissolved slowly I guessed, given that in one of the videos I could see half broken down remains floating in the hellish jacuzzi. I wanted to turn away, but in the next shot I froze.

It was Zoe, she had snuck inside and was collecting food off the shelves. I searched through the feeds, desperately looking for where the beast was in translation to her and in the last camera I could see the whole building. That huge monster was heading her way.

~ Kennedy

With my increased speed from dropping those two off. I was able to make it to the lab ahead of schedule. I had been going over the blueprints looking for the best route when it occurred to me that the shipping docks would be my best bet. According to the map, it was a relatively straight shot to the elevator that I would need to take down to the lower levels. Not only that, but the hallways would be big enough for my mech to fit through, which was a bit of a comfort knowing I might be able to stay protected the whole time.

According to the report the lady gave me, the lab I needed to get to was in the fourth level basement. In the lower levels, the map was dark as if being censored. When I tried accessing it, a simple message of "Not authorized" was prominently displayed across the screen.

Tapping the screen gently, I couldn't help but be intrigued "I wonder what's so secret down there?"

Well, if I was meant to know or needed to know then surely they would have told me right? It's not important anyways, gotta focus on the mission.

Typing in the new course, I took in the weird ambiance of the building itself. It looked to only be twenty stories tall, with the outside looking relatively generic with the windows reflecting the surroundings. The giant Chlor-Reform billboard name at the top did seem a bit tacky, but what could you expect from some multi-billion dollar company though. It did look out of place in the area and should have been in some city or corporate hedge fund district, if that's a thing.

The grounds surrounding the building were littered with the strange infected. However, they didn't appear hostile. It was almost as if they were in some kind of trance and focused on the sun. Their bodies split open like their skin were petals in bloom. The horrifying scene of twisted flesh and muscle clinging to bone as the mutations each had, seemed to be worse than the last as I walked through the nightmare fueled field.

As docile as they seemed to be, I was still on guard. This wasn't a video game or a simulation, I only had so much ammo and due to the rescue earlier, my reserves had already taken quite a hit and I doubt even with this suit, I don't think I could kill all of these things.

Looking at my timer, I saw that my clock was running out and I had to make my next few choices carefully if I wanted to survive and get to the extraction point on time. Luckily the creatures were distanced apart, but I had to try and be as stealthy as possible in a twelve foot tall three ton death machine. With each step I felt as if I should speed up, if for nothing else, to get past the clear and present danger I was in. I could feel the crunch of the creatures beneath my feet and with each one my anxiety spiked as plumes of what looked like pollen would shoot up into the air and would then gently fly in the air to who knows where. Maybe burning the state to ash isn't a bad idea. Who knows what they can cross pollinate with.

Halfway through the field of pain, I became a little more comfortable and began moving at a faster pace. That was until I saw the field begin to darken. Looking up, I saw that the sun was beginning to be blocked out by black and gray clouds. Looking around I noticed the infected began to become more animated and it was only exacerbated once the rain began to fall. It was as if the water acted as a shot of espresso for them and before I knew it, half the things had sprung to life, noticing me quite quickly.

Seeing my path quickly filling with enemy combatants, I readied my weapons and began blasting my way through the swath of diseased. The bullets tore through them easily enough, but the number of them only seemed to grow thicker.

I began to run while barreling past the beasts, smashing them aside and crushing as many as I could in my way. The damage my suit was taking soon began to set off alerts as some of the larger less awake ones began grabbing and wrenching at me as I ran by them. Some even tore chunks of armor off in their attempts to slow me down.

The view ahead of me was becoming a focal point for the sprouted to gather and I had to make a judgment call to make this whole plan work. Launching the last of my grenades I was able to clear my path enough to reach the dock, grabbing the door and slamming it down to the ground. Scanning the area, there were only a few inside the shipping area and I was able to activate my flamethrower, torching them to clear the room.

"Fuck me" I said taking a breath.

Doing a quick damage assessment, I found that I was almost completely out of ammo. I was down to about a quarter in my gatling gun, completely out of explosives and my flamethrower was damaged so I needed to be careful using it, but it was still at a decent level. I also remembered that I still had my cluster shotgun, but that only held a few shots in it and I still had a long journey to the mall to make. The scariest part was that there was some damage to my power bank. Luckily it wasn't too bad, but anymore and the lithium may have ignited in the rain.

Taking in the surroundings, the smoldering remains must have made the room smell horrible. I was glad the air filters hadn't been destroyed. It didn't take long to find the freight elevator located in the back of the warehouse. It looked big enough to hold three or four suits my size, so at least I had some time to breathe.

Walking over through the barely lit room, it was evident that the struggle to get free from whatever had happened here was intense. "I guess everyone made it outside at least. That would explain the welcome party out there."

Opening the canopy I reached down and pushed the elevator call button and took a step back. The clang the feet of this thing made on the concrete rang out with echos in what I assumed was at one point a bustling workplace. There were several unshipped containers all labeled in what might as well have been gibberish. Long scientific sounding words and symbols adorned the sides, but I could see that from the pictures on some of them they had explosive contents or were corrosive.

The explosive warnings I understood, but there were a few that didn't seem to make sense when associated with plant research. *Why would they need some of this?* Some of these crates seemed to have external life support systems attached to them. Others looked like they were more designed to hold something, like they were a prison cell and not a shipping container.

Looking at the floor numbers I had some time as the elevator was coming from one of the higher floors and it was taking its sweet time getting down here. I decided to investigate one of the odd looking crates that had what looked like chemical tanks pumping into it. It wasn't clear what I was looking at, but I could see a sliding viewer hatch on the top. Turning on my floodlights and placing my hand on the handle I felt a sense of dread, as if knowing what I was going to see wasn't something I should.

Sliding the port open, an almost purplish blue light appeared to glow from the window. It was clearly some kind of UV light, but for what? "No..." Peering inside I could see an almost black silhouette of some disgusting experiment staring up into where I assumed the bulbs for the box were located. In the strange hue I couldn't make out too many details, but it looked like it was a rabbit's head with distorted features that seemed to be trying to grow into the metal plating. Its lifeless eyes stared up in absent vision as its body, like those outside, was split open revealing teeth covered peels of skin. The inside looked like it had been flayed open as its body pulsated, appearing almost as if breathing in a dense fog that was being misted into the enclosure.

"Dear god... they didn't just know there was a cure... they created the fucking things on purpose." I tried to radio the commander or anyone once I realized the situation was much worse and not what we had been told, but something appeared to be jamming the signal.

Almost as if sensing me, the horrendous creature's head gently tilted so that one of its dead eyes was looking directly into mine. Its nose twitched and the face slowly began to split open.

Looking away I saw a red button on the side of the crate marked "**In case of danger press here.**" Not wanting to see what was going to come out of the thing, I pressed the button and a small alarm rang before one of the many other canisters attached to the container turned on with a hiss and I heard the creature begin to screech as it pounded, trying to escape its gas chamber.

Not wanting to see what was happening to it, I slid the viewer shield back into place and tried to put the screams of torment out of my mind as I walked away. In my fascination with the infected creature, the elevator had arrived and I didn't even notice.

Pulling the gated doors closed, I could still hear the tortured being as I began my descent.

As my canopy settled back into place with a solid click, all I could think was. *This antivirus better be here and for damn sure better work.*

~ Michaels

I don't know how long I had been sitting in that cell, but the feeling of relief I felt when I heard the gunfire and that club headed idiot stomping away was as if it was the first time in hours I could finally relax from holding that damn bed-sheet. I looked through the view port and saw that there was a soldier in a strange outfit drawing that thing away from the door. I didn't watch for long though as I heard the bullets clatter against the metal as they ripped through the creature.

Ducking down, I had to make a plan. Honestly, in all this time, I had actually started to accept that this was probably going to be my final resting place. If I had known that this was going to happen this fast and I was going to possibly die here in this shithole of a place, I would have escaped long before **Subject-404** was released.

Not wanting to lose this opportunity that's been given to me. I only waited a few moments before opening the door and heading straight for one of the downed guards. Searching through their equipment I found a gun and a radio. I checked to make sure that the coast was clear before I typed in an emergency frequency.

"Red robin, this is Blue jay, do you read me?"

A few tense seconds passed before I heard a response.

"Hello Blue Jay, this is Red Robin, glad to hear you are still alive. What is your situation?"

"Good to hear your voice too. I am still at the tortoiseshell. There was a distraction that allowed me to escape the predicament I was in. You didn't by chance have anything to do with that now did you?"

"You know me so well, I had to call in a few favors and promise a few in order to organize the rescue, but I got the best for you. Not only that, but secondary operations are underway for the more expansive release."

"Oh you dirty little sneak. What's the extraction plan?"

"Your extraction is predicated on the survival of those soldiers, so I would recommend that you remain under cover and help them save you. I can only do so much from where I'm located. Those men will get you to the extraction point, located at the mall about thirty-two kilometers away."

"That's almost twenty miles. How far has the infection spread?"

"I understand your concern, but that's the closest somewhat safe location to send in the cavalry. The virus has spread at an exceptionally fast rate and all the combat data I have been collecting will surely drive the price straight up from projected estimates. As well as our more personal vendetta will be completed."

My lips curled into a smile at the thought. "Excellent, I'll..."

I felt the building shake as an explosion resonated through the halls.

"Red robin, I think I have to repay my savior. I'll radio in with any updates that have relevance."

"Copy that, good luck Blue jay."

"Thanks, I'll need it."

Hiding the radio away, I searched through the corpses and found an arm still holding one of the torches with about half a tank of fuel. "This will do just fine."

I didn't have to wait long before, to my shock, the soldier boy managed to survive. *As grateful as I am for his hand in helping me, I wanted to try and do all this alone. However, given the spread has been faster than I had calculated, I still had use of him and I was happy to see that he was alive. However, the small army of specimens chasing him down was going to be an issue though.*

Watching the events play out, I couldn't help but feel strange and wonder if I had looked that scared when he ran and hid in that very room. I felt a cringe in my spine at how weak he must have looked. Luckily, no one survived to have seen it. I couldn't have that getting back to Robin. She would never let me live it down.

Time was running out for him, but I was fascinated by the speed at which these creatures have evolved. From our experiments in the labs, they were too scared to let the virus progress naturally like this, so I needed to gather this data.

It was intriguing to me that even with the bodies damaged, as long as the brain had something able to connect to it, it would mutate to the point of what it needs to control and give it whatever adaptation it seemed to need for that time to survive or spread.

The head sprouts appear to have evolved in a way to launch its teeth like infectious projectiles. *How were they not shattering upon impact? Have they somehow integrated a way to harden their teeth more than the steel of the door? For a lack of a better term, and horribly out of context, but as a scientist, that is beyond cool. This will make these kinds quite profitable. All we seem to need would be a functional brain and spine, the limbs it will create itself. It must be rooted into the central nervous system.*

Soon the lummox that pounded the beat of my life for the past several hours, came lumbering down the hall. Its body twisted and armored, the door would stand no chance against its fury now. Sure pounding is one thing, but a charging battering ram, no way.

Sensing it was time for me to step in, I charged my weapon and the flickering sparks of light from the sparker suddenly became a jet of blue flame that hissed before flaring to life into a pressurized jet of fire, engulfing everything in its path. The smaller of the creatures fell from the walls and ceiling, dying quickly with their little bodies popping like squishy water balloons. An unfortunate trade off for how easily they would be able to be made. The tanker though, I had to focus the stream on him for much longer and I was relieved it was forced off course and into a wall, cracking it severely from the impact. It did manage to die before my fuel ran out and struggled and thrashed around before going still. I burned it a few more times before calling out to my new friend.

"It's safe to come out now" I dropped my now empty flamethrower into the nasty water with a splash. "Well, at least for right now it is." *No sense in holding onto that any longer.*

I watched as the soldier peeked out at me and looked me over as if he was trying to identify me.

"Doctor... Michaels?" The soldier's voice seemed shaken by the situation he had just been saved from.

"Yes, and who might you be?" I figured play it safe, play it dumb.

"My name is squad leader Vincent Valhart. My team was sent here to rescue you. My apologies, but we don't have time for pleasantries. We are on a time schedule and need to get you to the extraction point. Please follow me."

So much for the whole heroic speech I was expecting, but it is probably for the best that we get moving. I didn't want to be here when the rest of the infected showed up.

There wasn't much speaking as we snaked our way through the corridors of the prison. He would point me in the direction to go and I would go. I wasn't sure how much ammo he had, but it must not have been a lot. With the firefight I heard him having earlier I wouldn't be surprised if he was completely out.

Running most of the way, we could hear the cacophony of the carriers getting closer. Not so much what I was thinking, I would be scared of screams and screeching, but more a mass of varying stomps and scuttles mixed with the occasional sound of something heavy being dragged.

We came to the yard where I was amazed to see a very large exo-suit that was crouched at the doorway. Vincent jumped into it and frantically hit some buttons before the cockpit closed.

"Doctor, duck!" another man's voice boomed out of another machine's loudspeaker.

Diving to the floor I heard something whirring to life before a hailstorm of bullets flew over my head. In between the bursts of fire, I could make out the sounds that he was saying something, but not what he was saying in the deafening roars. Not knowing what else to do I started crawling, staying as low as possible so as to not get hit by a stray ricochet or an incoming enemy.

"Run, now!" There was a break in the assault and the voice boomed again. Gathering my will, I sprinted to the door and ran out, before he leveled the doorway with a giant drill-like arm and collapsed it to the ground.

The robotic form that Vincent had jumped into, turned to me as I stood brushing myself off, trying to retain some portion of my dignity. **"Doctor, I'm going to need you to climb into the harness on the back of my rig. We didn't have a lot of time, so this will have to do."**

I looked up to the hastily attached restraint with a bit of bemusement, but reluctantly agreed.

"We didn't have enough time to connect the transport capsule. My apologies."

"It's fine, I'm very grateful that you were able to save me."

"Sir, we have to get going. HQ says we have a small window of opportunity to get to our rendezvous point for extraction and it's a bit of a hike."

The drill armed suit came stomping over, addressing commander Valhart.

"Understood. You all set back there Doc?"

"Ready when you are." I said as I buckled and tightened the final clasp. "Where are we heading?"

"We are heading to Burlington. We should be there by mid morning as long as everything goes to plan."

"Splendid."

~ Zoe

I laid down, with my back against the little grassy divot, listening to Chris's footsteps eventually fade off. I couldn't bring myself to go through that field of sprouted. *It was clear nobody was alive here anymore, why risk it? For what, a gun? What are the chances someone is still alive here?*

Rolling back over, I saw him looking back to try and see if I was going to follow him, but I wasn't that stupid. However, the feeling that this was probably going to be the last time I ever saw him did make me feel a little sad. Even in our short time together, we did become pretty close. I'm going to miss his family stories. *I didn't want to leave him, but if he was going to make stupid choices like this, do I really want him with me? He could put me into some serious trouble down the line.*

Moving along the shallow embankment, I looked over the edge one last time and saw that he had somehow managed to make it to one of the trailers and was looking for me again, I assumed, before he went inside out of sight.

Am I really doing this? Is he really doing this?

I felt my stomach growl, and I knew that the journey that I was gonna be taking to my parents was going to be a long one. I was going to need food.

Looking back over the hill, I stared at the big supermarket and did everything I could to try and talk myself out of doing something stupid, but it was right here, and I have no clue if I will be able to stop or find any place safe, let alone that might have supplies left.

Well, this is it. I'm sorry Chris, but I think this is where we part ways.

I circled around the parking lot of doom and found a safe way around the perimeter of the building to a side door that had at some point been propped open. Maybe it was one of the last things the unlucky employees did on a break before all this happened. Or it could be the reason this place is a dead zone.

Steadying my breathing, I slowly opened the door and quickly closed it again at the gore filled sight just inside the door. The thing that was pinning the door open was part of one of the employees. Taking a few seconds before opening the door again, I looked down and saw that it was a small leg. Turning away though I came face to face with a hiring sign attached to the door that said **"Any applicants must be at least 14 to apply."** Even though I was hungry, I felt a sickness in my belly for the fact that this might have been a kid, instead of being out having fun, they were instead here working. *I wonder how old you were, maybe it is best the world is going to shit.* The thought bounced around my head as I tried to re-focus and get through the small room that was covered in blood. Except for the leg, the room didn't have any other bodies or remains. There was clearly a massive struggle, and there was way more blood here than from just one kid.

Whatever I was looking for, I had to find it fast. Something about this place isn't sitting right with me. I searched the break-room and found a backpack in one of the lockers. It wasn't much, but it would carry some food. Opening the fridge was kind of a lost cause for anything to eat, but I found an unopened bottle of water and someone else's lab experiment growing in a plastic container.

Stepping around as much of the still slick blood, I got to the door on the other side of the room and looked out into the patchily lit store. Some of the aisles had been pulled down or torn apart. Groceries were thrown all over the place, but looked to have at least a few departments still in good shape.

Sneaking through the downed shelving, I was again disturbed at the lack of remains. It was as if something had simply made them disappear. Not wanting to meet whatever may have done this, I figured I should make this quick. In the flickering lights, I tried to stay in the shadows and hidden as much as possible. It was strange doing this on my own. Unable to watch my own back now, I was starting to wonder if I should go back and try and think of an excuse to talk to Chris and have him come in here with me. "No! I'm not going to put myself in more danger to just lie so I can feel safer. I am a big girl and I can do this on my own." The words of affirmation I told myself seemed hollow even when I said it out loud.

Finding the canned food aisle, I started to hear something approaching from the other side of the store, and it sounded huge. Gathering as many things as I could shove into the backpack, the thuds of whatever it was grew louder, joined by the sounds of metal being bent and twisted out of the way. Stumbling to my feet, I felt something hit me before I was sent flying through the air and skidded across the floor, only stopping when I hit a cooler. A shock of intense pain shot through my body as I felt something break, slowly dulling down until numbness took its place.

I desperately tried to move, but no matter how hard I tried, my body wouldn't respond. I laid there with my face on the cluttered floor, my bag torn open and only one eye able to watch as the shelving of where I had just been crumpled under the weight of whatever had attacked me. A massive tree trunk like leg, the size of a dinner table, hefted an unfathomably large body. Another leg smashed through the racks as if they weren't even there. Again I tried to struggle, my heart racing like a rabbit and my lungs filling with heavy gasps yet I couldn't scream.

More of the creature revealed itself as two more legs hauling a giant pot shaped body of stretched veiny skin. Splashes of some unseen liquid moving inside like trapped waves of a storm. In the shadows created by the light behind it, I swore I saw a human torso fly up into view, only to vanish back into the walking cauldron. Vine covered, malformed arms protruded from open pus dripping sores all over its body, grasping absentmindedly for the next ingredient to add.

Watching the behemoth almost scraping the ceiling from the angle I saw it at. No eyes could be seen, but it moved in my direction as if it knew my presence was near. My panic rose, knowing that it was going to kill me and I couldn't do anything to even try to get away. I tried closing my eyes, but even they refused to listen. One of the enormous feet came down hard and I had to watch as my arm was flattened.

My brain couldn't seem to process what exactly had happened without the pain. I silently screamed on the inside in reaction. One of the creature's vestigial arms felt around, unlit its mangled fingers caressed my face. As soon as it seemed to realize I was there, my eyes watered as I knew what was coming next. Hands in varying degrees of mutation grabbed my lifeless body and the room spun and jerked as it twisted my pinned arm off and raised me up. As my head dropped, I found myself sick as the world faded in and out of existence. *It must be from the blood loss. At least I won't be alive long.*

In the light that managed to get through, I could see the vat full of slime. The soup of corpses in all stages of decomposition were swimming in the liquid as if it were some kind of jacuzzi. As the world tunneled into darkness I felt the splash of the waves hitting my face, followed by my lungs fighting for air as I was dropped into the acidic bath. I did nothing but try to accept the embrace of death only hoping it would be fast.

I felt a sudden shake and the world suddenly rushed by. My body washed free from an open wound gushing from the bottom of the great glutton's underbelly. The room was dark and filled with debris still floating in the air. It looked like a bomb had gone off.

The creature tried to move, but a large section of its body had been blown off, forcing it to the ground. Although I couldn't feel the limbs being pulled, I found myself being slid along the floor as someone pulled me by my feet.

The world was silent as the ceiling whipped by fading in and out of shadow. We stopped and I saw Chris standing over me looking back from where we were and then back to me. The panicked look on his face of not knowing what to do, not even concerning me at this point. I just felt acceptance going through my body with a pleasant chill.

He cried over my body, looking for anything he could in order to stop the bleeding, but he had to have known it was too late. I tried to focus on his lips as he did his best to comfort me. He turned away grabbing the radio from his belt, but a look of defeat hit him from whatever he was listening to on the other end.

He stood up, looking down at me and then to a gun he was carrying. It didn't take a genius to figure out what thought was going through his head. He raised his arm with tears in his eyes, and as I stared down the barrel of the gun, he covered mine.

~ Zack

Tabitha was growing nicely. She's such a big girl now. I couldn't wait to re-unite her with her mother and make her so much stronger.

Going off the text messages that bitch was sending me, I was surprised she really was on her way. I wonder what whorish thing she had to offer and de-grade herself to, in order to convince her boy toy she was fucking now, to come save her precious little daughter. She never trusted me to be a good fa-ther, but Tabitha is doing far better than fine now. I could feel her body surg-ing every time I caressed her growing stem.

The world hasn't gone to complete shit over here yet, so she should easily be able to get here. Well, relatively speaking. I had gone to the roof earlier in or-der to see how everything was going, and I could see that the highway was backed up for miles. There were police and military vehicles at every on-and-off ramp that were holding detour signs on how to get to Boston in alternate routes.

"They must have been trying to evacuate using the pier, or maybe airlifting the survivors from the baseball field. Pathetic excuses of the human race. Couldn't they see that this isn't a curse, but a blessing?" I was disgusted at how these people were acting. It wasn't something that was going to be a pleasant change, but I could feel that those who were going to be changed by my baby girl would be different. She was going to emerge from her shell in a new form and bring us into the light of the future.

I looked down as I felt the vibration of the phone again. A message on the screen saying that the cunt was almost here. Along with some more colorful language about my inadequacies as a man. I had lost my ability to respond a while ago. My hands had become difficult to move as they were going through their changes. My fingers were long, having grown new joints and ligaments to compensate for my new physiology. My whole body had grown, my limbs now like a spider's legs, allowing me to move more freely. The hole in my chest where Tabby had been resting during our trip was now filled with a hardened crystal of sap. I haven't seen my face, but I have felt the changes happening to that and my jaw fell off maybe an hour ago to allow for my new thorn barbed tongue to dangle freely. I understood that those who accepted the gifts would need to be able to handle the changes, and they would in their own ways accept it in the end. We just needed to get them to understand.

Watching the parking lot, I saw my wife's car that I had been paying for, driving in with her new fling behind the wheel. The SUV drove in as the morning sun rose behind them. *I wonder if he's muscle bound like the last one? It'll be more protein for my baby.*

The feeling of my fingers digging into the granite and concrete as I climbed down from my perch was oddly enjoyable. It almost felt like reaching into a gritty putty. Pulling myself up to the lookout over the entry they would have to use, I cracked the door open and waited.

I could hear the woman screeching long before I could see her, and I felt myself salivate at the prospect of maybe eating her myself. She always did say I needed to do that more.

I did my best to stay as still as possible. My body, even with all its new gifts, did come with the drawback of clicking a lot now as I moved. Watching from the shadows, I saw the queen bee herself. She changed her hairstyle to something short, but it looks like she had put on a little more weight. Whoever this dude was, seemed to be some poor schmuck that had no self respect. Sounds like the only guy that would try and tolerate her shit.

Watching them walk in the open and abandoned mall, their auras seemed different from each other. *I wonder if she got knocked up again. Oh what a joy it might be if she's stuck with this idiot because of a kid. Well, I'm sure Tabby will be happy as an older sister. It's just sad that she has to share genes with a horrible monster like her. In all honesty, I was surprised they weren't dead yet because of her incessant yammering.*

Before I lost the dexterity to type, I had told them specifically what door to take so as to keep Tabitha's current state out of sight as much as possible. Wouldn't want to ruin the reunion.

They both carried flashlights and even with my new vision I could see the electricity, not only from the lights, but the nervous systems of the two were vibrant in the dark. Everything seemed as if it was pulsating through a filter of a membrane that had replaced my eyes.

The little sparks as they tried to find whatever was making the click noise was entertaining. I was too fast for them to catch sight of, but the look of concern on their faces as they began desperately shouting for me to come out was so deliciously perfect.

I grabbed the boyfriend first, he was so small and weak, she didn't hear anything except the click as I snatched him up. His muffled scream as I raked his face across my chest ended when I threw him to the ground from the ceiling. Sixty feet left him with a few seconds of free fall and the splat of his body breaking on impact was enough to send Sarah into a screaming fit before she ran deeper into the mall.

Picking up the now very squishy body of her fuck-boy, I gave chase knowing she was going exactly where I wanted her to go. I ran ahead of her and stowed the body of the man away near the main atrium and set off again to find Sarah. It didn't take long though. She was never a bright bulb and was so predictable. She ran into her favorite store and it worked out best for me because it took up two floors. I could get in easier without her seeing me.

Crawling through the upstairs entry, I went to the overlook and just as I thought she would, she hid in the makeup department. The pulse surrounding her was so intense that I could almost taste it from where I was observing her form. As quietly as I could, I climbed down the escalator and found a few items and tossed them through the theft detectors at the door, setting off the alarm.

She shrieked at the high pitched siren and took off running again. This was more fun than I thought it would be. I easily herded her by throwing things or letting her catch glimpses of me until she was exactly where I wanted her.

It was almost like watching a movie as she ran into the atrium and stopped in her tracks. If I still had lips I would be smiling at the face she was making. Dropping down behind her, she spun to look at me. Before she could run again, I grabbed her around the waist and lifted her up. Standing at my full height I held her tight and raised an oddly jointed finger pointing at the beautiful blossom that was the beginning of our daughter's new life, and then turning her to face me. This whole experience filled me with so many beautiful memories, but it was time to add the final one. I decided I didn't want to contaminate my baby's perfect form with the addition of this sluts blood. However, I didn't want her to go to waste either.

Using my pinky and thumb I wrapped them around her arms, crucifying her in my palm. Letting my tongue reveal its full length, I dragged it across her body, tearing her clothes and cutting into her skin as it went. Her screams of terror were like music to whatever my ears were now. I jammed my tongue down her throat and flogged it around like I was using a snake to clear a drain. Twisting and turning it all around. The rage I felt wondering how many dicks she sucked while we were together fueled me to go deeper with every plunge, before ripping it out along with whatever had gotten stuck to the barbs. *Did you feel that hunny? Was that deep and hard enough for ya?*

Holding the now lifeless body, I took joy in watching as the sparks traveling through her body faded away, I didn't want to even allow her to change into one of us. She didn't deserve the gift.

I spent the next hour or so devouring her corps when I heard a chirp of static and a voice. Looking for the source I found that it was coming from the boyfriends body. Turning it over I saw a small walkie talkie halfway out of his pocket.

"I repeat, this is Private Kennedy with the mechanized division. I have an open urgent message to any military personnel. The package has been recovered, but my suit is damaged. This is a priority request. Need assistance getting a package to extraction at the mall in Burlington at all costs."

A few seconds had passed when another voice responded.

"I'm on my way, stay at your location and activate your beacon."

"Understood."

The radio went silent after that and I felt joy knowing that we were going to soon have more guests. Hopefully by then, Tabitha will be ready. If not, more fun for me.

FERAL TERRA

Chapter 6 A call for help

~ Kennedy

The gears of the elevator sounded like they needed to be greased. *The fact that this whole thing was something purposefully made, was killing me, knowing now that this was an accident that could have easily been avoided... I gotta stay focused. There are obviously going to be some surprises down here, I just hope one of them doesn't jump out and get me.*

The elevator slid and bounced to a stop at my floor and the whole place was dark. The emergency system down here must have been damaged and the lights were all out. "Great... that's just funderful."

Flipping on my night vision, a high pitched frequency squeaked on and the whole room became bright with a green hue. The fly eye cameras were kind of intense and it wasn't my favorite choice, but it was better than stumbling around in the dark inside of a giant maraca grasping for whatever might be canister shaped. Speaking of which.

Typing up the file, a picture of the vessel popped up and I wasn't shocked that it looked about as generic as the building upstairs. It was about the size of a thermos, with a few buttons and what looked to be places for tubes and whatnot to be attached. A big valve was on the top and if my knowledge of movie based evil corporations was of any good, it was probably red. I couldn't tell at the moment because of the green color washing over everything, but I'll see if I'm right when I get outside.

Marching through the hall, the doors seemed to be reinforced. They had what looked like bulkhead style spinning handles, like you would see on a submarine. Massive bolts were twisted into place by thick steel handles. Each doorway had a small glass viewer, that if I wasn't in my suit would be at about head height. Everything looked like it had to be manually closed by hand. *They must have done that for safety in case the power went out. At least they were thinking of some kind of failsafe.*

I followed my marked path, trying my hardest to not stop and look through the glass. I didn't have time. Besides, if what I saw upstairs was anything to go off of, whatever is in these ones, must make that rabbit look like child's play. The thought didn't give me any reassurance, but at least they were... "Shit..." With the limited range in the dark, just out of view, I could see that something was very wrong. A few of the doors were wide open. One of which had been ripped right off the wall. Parts of the shattered hinges decorated the floor. A smear of what must have been the unlucky SOB standing in front of it when it blew open, was stretched across the floor. Where the door had stopped and slid down the wall was where the rest of the person was smeared. I had to turn away from the sight. The body wasn't even in a solid state anymore, and I really didn't want to puke in my cockpit.

I counted three open cells and started a scan for anything that might be alive down here. The computer picked up the tracks leading away from their respective contaminants and seemed to have gone everywhere. The scans also picked up that there were a number of dead bodies or places where bodies had been, going down the same path I was meant to be following. Intermittent spots where the creatures must have stopped to attack their next victims, glowed with where they had been jumping or moving in circles, possibly fighting.

Where there was blood, there also appeared to be some kind of spongy looking moss mixed with mushrooms. The tendril-like roots seemed to branch out as if in search of something more to feed on. It was like walking through the woods and seeing a clover patch or little moss mounds, only these ones seemed to be actively moving, slowly, but still moving.

Stomping past some of the dead scientists, I saw that some were torn to shreds, but not before having been mutated. It was as if whatever killed them, didn't want there to be any of those head sprouts growing up. The remains had been pulverized and only allowed for the most basic of growth I assumed.

Watching the map, I could see that there was a turn coming up that would lead to some kind of storage room, where my goal was located. Coming around the corner, there was a set of sliding metal doors that had been broken and bent with a hole ripped through it large enough to fit a truck.

Stepping up to the mangled mess. I tried to bend the hole large enough to fit my mech through, but even with all the added strength, it didn't have the power needed. The metal, even though it moaned and lifted, it just refused to budge. *What could have been strong enough to do this to it?*

Reluctantly, I took a few steps back and depressurized the cockpit and opened the front hatch and grabbed my carbine. As I was about to hop out, the rotted stench of the room assaulted my sinuses and I dry heaved while covering my mouth. It was like I was breathing in a dumpsite for roadkill mixed with compost, with a gentle hint of cut grass mixed with ass. "Jesus Christ..." grabbing my respirator and throwing it on as fast as I could. It helped with keeping the smell at bay, but there was still some seeping in through the filter. Hopefully the plastic barrier would keep it from trying to get in through my eyes, too.

Turning on my headlamp and the flashlight mounted on my small rifle, I disengaged from my unit and stepped onto that strange sponge-like floor. Each step squished and felt like I was walking on raw wet chicken and water balloons. The odd substance would slide and stretch into fluid filled pustules. Each one filled with seeds that almost seemed to swim in the thick mucus.

Taking a moment to adjust my footing, I did my best to ignore the very gross situation I found myself in and climbed through the tangled mess. Looking at the small computer screen on my wrist, I saw that my path was going to take me to the right. Looking up, I was surprised to see a faint white glow coming from that direction and I took off. Moving tactically through the room of towers and huge test tubes filled with who knows what kinds of horrors. I found the candle in the dark.

Looking at my computer again, it verified that what I was looking for was inside this container. I pulled a link cable from my pocket, I hooked into the tower and started entering in the passwords that the file said to input and before I knew it, several locks and little bars unhooked and slid away with a small puff of cool clouds revealing the canister, surrounded by frost. A digital thermometer displayed across a screen read that it was being kept at negative two hundred degrees.

The file stated that as long as the vials were kept from reaching above freezing, it would not turn into its gas form and dissipate. In order for it to be viable to save the world, it had to be at minimum, in liquid form – which would start to happen around the negative sixty degree mark.

Tapping a few more commands, the vial rein-cased itself in the metal tube and I was able to remove it from its cradle. Strapping the complicated looking case to my belt, I turned to head back to my suit when I heard heavy footsteps approaching followed by a fluid filled roar.

Guess I stumbled into whatever had gotten free.

~ Chris

I didn't have much time to think. Grabbing the shotgun and with one last look over the trailer's internals, I rushed out the door where the sunlight blinded me for a second. Rubbing my eyes, they adjusted to the brightness and the thoughts started racing as to what I had to do.

The sprouted still seemed to be mesmerized with the sun and I wasn't going to question the small grace from whatever god may still be looking down on me and took off sprinting towards the big grocery store. The sliding doors were shattered, I nearly fell as I slid through the piles of glass that littered the ground.

Stumbling inside of the darkened store, I didn't need to listen, but saw the massive four legged beast crashing through the displays and knew that I was running out of time. I tried to find a clear route to where it was going, but everything was blocked.

Climbing over the debris and slipping on what I was telling myself was just spilled food. I was getting closer, but at a hindered pace. It was a fight for survival just trying to navigate the labyrinthian maze that was only getting more difficult with each passing second.

With the weapons I had, I stood no chance against this thing, I held out hope that I might be able to save Zoe. *Maybe I could cause a distraction, draw it away?*

Ducking down I managed to dodge a flying piece of sheet metal as it cut through the boxes of whatever was behind me.

Turning down another aisle, I found myself in some kind of random assortment of football and beer displays. It must have been for some kind of summer tailgate party supplies, but what I did see of use, was a box with a portable grill on the front.

Grabbing the box, I ripped open the top and shook out the cheap metal grill and found what I was looking for. A small compressed gas canister filled with propane. *Maybe I can make up for my lousy shooting earlier.* Tucking it into my armpit, I ran as hard as I could and was horrified to see I was too late. The creature had Zoe in its multitude of branch-like arms. Her lifeless body dangled over the edge of what looked like a gigantic pitcher plant's mouth. Time seemed to slow down as I watched her battered body being dropped into the creature. My stomach dropped and I stopped thinking.

Hurling the small cylinder of gas, I raised the shotgun and fired two shots. I didn't even think of the recoil and when the kickback to my shoulder hit, it sent me to the ground. The explosion from the tiny container sent shrapnel tearing through the leather leaves and splitting open the belly of the infected monstrosity, draining its digestive fluids all over the floor. It reared back in pain and several bodies in all stages of digestion spilled out in the deluge of liquids.

The massive wound forced the odd shaped creature to stumble to the side as it lost its balance. Seeing my opportunity, I ran in to find if one of the bodies I saw ooze out was Zoe, and I was relieved to see that she was, but something was wrong, she wasn't moving.

Rushing to her side, her eyes were open, but she didn't seem to be there. Her gaze looked off into the distance and the life that used to be there was dulled and vacant. Her body was twisted in an odd position and her legs were almost touching her head. I looked down at her and she was mangled and injured almost to the point where I couldn't tell if she was alive or dead.

"Zoe! Can you hear me?" I could still see her chest rising and resting, but still no response.

" ... Fuck, okay, Im sorry, but I need to drag you away from here!"

Scooping up her feet, as soon as I lifted and began to move them a series of cracks made me shudder and I felt how limp they were. Worry washed through me, she wasn't answering me because she couldn't. Biting my lip, trying to hold back my look of concern and trying to block out the sounds her body was making.

Reaching back, I pulled the door open and I found we were in some kind of break room. Going back to the door I barricaded it with a table and came back to try and get some kind of reaction to know that she was okay, but the acid-like slime was already beginning to eat through her skin. Her flesh began to bubble on her face and some parts of her clothes had begun to break down. Exposed muscle didn't even twitch as the sizzling fluid ate through indiscriminately of what it touched.

Time was still a warped perception to me, and the situation I was just dealt with was too much for what I could handle at the moment. I was so fuzzy in thought that I jumped as the radio squealed to life.

"This is Private Kennedy with the mechanized division. I have an open urgent message to any military personnel. The package has been recovered, but my suit is damaged. This is a priority request. Need assistance getting the package to extraction at the mall in Burlington at all costs."

The message repeated two more times and I was put into a dilemma from hell. I couldn't leave her here like this, but I couldn't carry her with me. Kennedy needs help and I'm the closest person to him that can possibly help. If I go to help him, I'll be able to save my family, but what do I do with her? I don't know how much time had passed as the scenario kept playing in my head. Minutes, seconds? Who really knew? All I knew was that I was now standing here with a gun to the head of someone who has been there and helped me through this endeavor and I don't know if I can pull the trigger.

I kept apologizing, not even knowing if she could hear me. Tears rolled from my eyes as I tried to just make it quick for her. The look in her eyes had nothing to give me a modicum of an idea if she understood what I was about to do, yet I felt an immense guilt weighing down on me as they seemed to stare directly into my soul.

I looked at the gun one last time and I placed my hand over her eyes. I squeezed the trigger and all I heard was a "click". I was out of ammo.

I fell back from the immense pressure that hit me like a ton of bricks. I was hyperventilating at what just happened, and now I couldn't even bring myself to end her suffering. I still had the pistol, but I don't think I could handle putting myself through the stress again.

"Hang on, I'm going to get you to safety, then I have to go help Kennedy. okay?"

I knew I wouldn't get a response, but the affirmation I was trying to tell myself so I didn't feel like a piece of shit, didn't seem to be working.

Noticing the tingling on my hands, I realized that I had some of the digestive slime on them. I went to the sink and began scrubbing with soap and eventually the stinging stopped. I looked through the lockers and found a jacket and a blanket.

Removing her drenched clothes, I did my best to wash off the goo, but with every scrub more skin was pulled off or left loose as if it wasn't attached anymore.

Wrapping her body in the jacket. I lifted her and carried her back to the trailer. I pulled the dead body of the soldier out and laid Zoe down on the floor as gently as possible. I couldn't find anything to dress her in, but she would at least be safe here until the medical evacuation team could come and save her. All I had to do was get to Kennedy and she would survive.

I did my best to make her as comfortable as possible, or as much as my conscience would allow me to feel comfortable before I left. Standing in the doorway, I looked down at her broken and hollow body with shame.

"I'm sorry I'm such a coward... I'll be back to help you... I'll help everyone."

Closing the door, I ran back to the woods. Finding where we had been dropped off, I began following the trail of deep footprints. My only hope is that I'll get there in time.

~ Vincent

"This is Private Kennedy with the mechanized division. I have an open urgent message to any military personnel. The package has been recovered, but my suit is damaged. This is a priority request. Need assistance getting the package to extraction at the mall in Burlington at all costs."

"Sir, rookie's in trouble." Wilcox radioed in and I heard something I hadn't heard in his voice before, there was concern.

"I'm aware, but we have our orders." Even with the hiccups that we had at the prison, we were still moving according to schedule. Our speed though has been hindered by the addition of the scientist, but we should be on time for extraction. We couldn't deviate because of a setback. I understood the importance of rook's mission, but ours took priority. Even if the canister didn't make it, we needed Michaels so they could make it again. The only reason the canister was a secondary was if the scientist was dead.

"Sir, we can't just leave him there... Sir!"

" I hear you private, but we have to consider the mission. We need to get this guy to the extraction point and if we turn around now and go back for Kennedy we will miss our window."

"That's bullshit and you know it Vince! You can't honestly..."

"Remember your rank, soldier! I understand your concern, but we are talking about possibly billions of lives around the world if this guy doesn't get flown out of here. We can not risk those odds for one soldier. As much as it pains me to say that, we have to think of the consequences of our actions." I felt horrible saying it, but it was the truth of the matter.

There was a long pause and I saw Wilcox stop moving. I already knew if I turned around he was only going to argue more. Pulling up the time clock, we only had a few hours left before our ride wasn't coming.

Opening a private message chat, I couldn't verbally tell him to go, but if he were to go on his own and he managed to survive, the worst the higher ups would do is chew him a new asshole.

"**Listen, I can't tell you to go get our boy. All our conversations are recorded in these things. You have three hours to go get him and get to that mall. I will do what I can to stall, but be prepared for a sit down when we get back from going AWOL.**" I typed out the message and there was a tense pause and the indicator of a message being typed was on screen before it disappeared and in true Wilcox fashion I heard a booming voice from his loudspeaker.

"**Sorry sir, but you can keep going and abandon your man, but fuck you sideways, I'm not leaving him behind.**" With that being said, he raised his manipulator as if to give me the finger and started sprinting.

"**This is a court-marshal action soldier, get your ass back here!**"

"**Suck it sir!**" That was the last thing he said before he cut communications. It took everything I had not to laugh at how easily he was willing to accept a dishonorable discharge. *Even though he acted like a manchild a lot of the time, he was a solid soldier and a good man at heart. I'm really not going to like yelling at him for the show later.*

I heard a couple taps coming from my guest followed by him shouting. "I think your friend is abandoning us!"

Trying to think of an excuse, I figured there was no sense in lying. "**He decided that going to help someone over following the mission took precedence. We are going to the extraction point and will be leaving with or without him.**"

There were a few seconds and he shouted again. "Not much of a soldier if he can't follow orders, now is he?"

I was annoyed at the comment, but had to keep up the ruse in order to also save my ass from a verbal assault later. "**Yeah, but that is something that if he survives, I'll deal with later.**"

"Fair enough, I'm trusting you to get me out of here alive."

"**I know, hold on tight, I'm going to start going faster and it may get a bit bumpy back there.**"

I wasn't going to let him get away with insulting one of my men, so I'm going to make this next ten miles very uncomfortable for him.

~ Kennedy

The massive bear shaped beast began circling me. Its body was easily twice the size of a grizzly and it was covered in tendrils that seemed to move independently from the monster. Its long face was made up of three jaw hinged sections that rubbed against each other like tongues rolling over one another in anticipation of its next meal. As I leveled my weapon, the black pupils adjusted to the light and revealed blue bloodshot veins pulsating through the green and yellow predatory eyes. Something about this one seemed different than what I had seen so far. There was intelligence behind those eyes and not only that, but burning rage, and I think it thinks I'm the one who did this to him.

The tentacle-like growths began to ooze some kind of substance in anticipation and something told me I didn't want to get it on me. Its green tinted fur along with those weird growths flattened and I felt that it was time to move. Keeping the light in its eyes, I started taking small steps so as not to startle it and instigate an attack, but it followed me with its stare and I had no way of getting to my mech without going right past it.

Using what little I could see, I started moving towards what looked like a set of towers. My hope being that once I get out of sight of it, I could start running. Even with the Beowulf ammo I was packing in this thing, I don't think it would put that thing down.

Looking to the pedestal I had taken the vial from, I got an idea. Removing my flashlight from my gun, I slowly backed up to the stand and as I passed by it I did my best to smoothly slide it into the empty cavity still pointing at the creature that was standing still, but focused on the bright light.

Stepping behind the display I turned off my headlamp and peered around it. The beast was fixated on the light and I took the opportunity to start moving in the shadows of the room. I made it to another container and I heard several loud thuds followed by something shaking and then the light vanished from the room.

I shot a look towards the display and found that it had swallowed the flashlight thinking it was me. The monstrous thing pounced and in an instant was ripping the heavy vault from its stand and crushed the whole thing like it was made of aluminum foil.

Taking the hint, it was time to leave. I began sneaking as fast as I could while the failed experiment was rampaging. It was distracted so I was able to get back to the main entry, but as I began to clamor over the destroyed door, my footing slipped and I smacked my head, turning on my headlamp. In that instant all the aggressive howling and growls stopped and an eerie silence filled the room.

Looking back to the now destroyed and clawed open pedestal, the horrifying beast was staring directly at me.

"Shit!"

It charged as soon as I turned and managed to frantically get into my pilot seat. Taking a few steps back, I started to turn to run, but before I got more than a few steps the whole suit was lifted and thrown like I was no more than a child's doll being discarded across the room. The ground shook as the thing closed the gap and again tossed me into a computer station in a shower of sparks.

Rolling onto my back, I raised my flamethrower, but just as the flame began to spray, the creature grabbed the barrel and crushed it causing it to backfire and a huge flash filled my vision as the tanks ruptured and exploded.

The stick went dead and warning signs blared where my suit was now damaged beyond repair. The only things I had left to fight with was my combat knife and hopefully my scatter-gun. A huge crack had formed across the glass of the canopy and I could barely see through the spidered spread. The beast was staggering and appeared to be injured, but was determined to kill me.

The limping creature charged towards me and I flipped the switch dropping the large blade into place and I swung at it. I felt it contact and cut deep, but the monster was on top of me. I tried to retract the blade, but my arm was pinned.

The creature's tendrils excreted that strange fluid again and as it dripped down onto the armor plating,it began to fizz. The metal began to rust and melt and I had to think fast. In a panic, I spotted the big red oh shit handle and a thought popped into my mind. I gripped the lever and pulled it as hard as I could. A split second later, the heavy glass canopy jettisoned with enough force to shove the creature off of me and stunned it long enough for me to get up. The legs of my machine were in rough shape, but I was able to run with a limp. I could hear the thunderous footsteps as the beast was chasing me down and I got desperate. Spinning at the last second, I used the inertia and centrifugal force to whip my dead arm around and smashed the creature in the face, tearing off one of the mandibles on contact, sending it flying.

I was almost to the elevator, and again the beast hit me from behind. I stumbled, but was able to keep my footing. I tried spinning again but the creature grabbed the arm and out of desperation I pulled my carbine and began unloading the whole clip into the creature's head, eviscerating it and forcing the beast back.

"Jesus H Fuck! Just fucking die!"

Changing the clip, I started running again and made it to the elevator. Turning around, I faced the creature and saw that it was now standing and it was clawing at its chest. The absolutely massive monster even with its missing head, stood easily twice the size of my mech. I stared in horror as it burst open, revealing a mouth that bellowed out a deep distorted growl that shook me to the bone.

"Fuck this, fuck this, fuck this!" I kept shouting as I repeatedly hit the up button and the doors slowly closed as the beast charged again. The door locked into place and as the elevator began to rise, I heard the gates being ripped free and a horrid guttural noise that wasn't even something I could attach to an animal anymore, echoed up the shaft. I managed a few breaths as I knew that situation was over.

As the doors opened on my floor, I felt the elevator shake and a clawed paw tore up through the floor. I stomped down on it and the room shifted, dropping slightly. "I can't do this here!" Falling slightly, I had to climb out using my one good arm and I engaged my knife. I saw the cables holding the elevator and the emergency brakes keeping it on the floor. Grabbing the brake pad closest to me, I was able to rip it off the rail, dropping the box more. I could still hear the thing fighting its way through the floor and I began hacking at the cables. The frayed steel snapping as the weight it could handle lessened. I don't know if it was out of insanity or not, but I began stomping on the top of the elevator until it finally gave way and the screeching as the elevator drowned out whatever the sound was that came from the beast, until I heard the crash of it impacting the bottom.

I didn't have time to catch my breath as I knew my time was now very limited, and there was no way for me to get to the extraction point in time. I had to get a message out to come get the football. Hopefully the sprouted ones outside went back to looking at the sun.

Hitting the open button I was relieved to see that they had gone back to their trance like states. My suit was in no condition for the trip. Falling to a knee I used my one good arm as a shield and sent out an emergency broadcast.

After sending out the call for help, I stood up and began trying to make it to the treeline, but fell over and found myself face to face with one of the heads of teeth. An instant later I felt nothing but pain as it launched its barbed spines were lodged deep into my body and I felt them injecting. I reached for my radio to warn whoever may come this way, but it was too late. My muscles went numb and they wouldn't work anymore. I kept trying until the world went black.

~ Wilcox

I didn't have much time. *Doing the math, as long as I go get that idiot with minimal issues I should get there right on time. If not a little late, but I'm sure if anyone can hold off on pulling out its Vincent. Dude is a massive ass kisser.*

With the crap show that this whole mission has become, I'm surprised we only lost Bardock. Never really liked him, but the way he went out was no way for anyone to go. I had to mute my intercom because of the screams. I knew it was too late to give him a mercy killing, but the creatures were piled on top of his suit and I needed to do something. I made his death not be in vain, and I bombarded the group like it was my in-laws' house. *I guess I still haven't processed that.*

All this for a nerd and his science experiment gone wrong. Hell, had that cute doctor lady not told me to take a look at rookies paperwork, I wouldn't have had any clue where he was heading. She told me that his mission outweighed ours and that the research trumped the man. That and she offered me a shit ton of money to be sure that canister made it back safely. So, who am I to say no to early retirement and a hot chick?

The fact they sent a rookie to do such an important mission did piss me off, but the kid was just following orders. Sure I razzed him a lot and was a dick, but it was to help build his character. The smartass wasn't going to last long with thin skin here. From the sound of his voice though, he was definitely in some rough shape.

My hope is that he at least managed to get someplace safe so I can just grab the can and move on. In this situation, I'm sorry man, but if you can't keep up I gotta leave you behind. Sorry your first mission is your last. Sucks to be you.

Putting my suit on auto pilot, I started contemplating what story I was going to have to come up with to explain why I left the new guy to fend for himself and the best I kept coming back to was that I could claim he was infected. Who would question it? I mean I could easily just take the canister, kill Kennedy and then move on. Even with the satellites watching from above, I doubt they have a good enough lens to see if I was telling the truth or not, as long as I was quick of course.

Mulling over the ideas, the time passed and I started thinking of what I would do once I got my money. Sure there was travel, but I know I'm going to blast through a bunch of hookers and parties with the first half of it, but the other half I'm gonna have to be smart with. Maybe I'll start a business? Put it in some high yield bank savings or maybe stocks?

I was so lost in thought that I almost hadn't noticed the figure walking ahead of me. It was some scrawny white dude who looked like he had been through the ringer. He saw me and started waving his arms trying to get my attention, but I didn't have time to stop and chit chat.

Passing by, it was funny how small an average sized person was in comparison to my suit. I wonder if he saw me laughing. *Hope he understands that I'm a busy man.*

Thinking it was odd we were heading the same direction, I figured it was just a coincidence and he was probably just turned around out here. Given the way the world was right now, I probably should have stopped to tell him to go the other way to get to an evac center, but that's just wasted time.

Seeing that the path ahead was clear, I increased my pacing and the man just became a small dot in my rear-view camera. I was only a mile or so away from where that dumbasses tracker was indicating he should be, so I started to mentally prepare myself for the shoot first take canister second scenario I kept replaying in my head.

~ Chris

I had started off strong at a hobbled run, but that confidence soon left once I realized how far I was going and just how hurt I really was. I had chosen more a... brisk pace and had no clue what time it was. My phone had apparently been crushed in the attempt to save Zoe. The screen had been smashed and it didn't even turn on when I held the power button. When I noticed it, my hope that I would get a call from Beth or the boys died. I really had to make this work and help Kennedy now, this was probably my last chance to see them again.

Maybe an hour had passed since I started following these tracks and I heard the familiar sound of robotic footsteps approaching. I got excited that maybe Kennedy had managed to get his suit going, but looking into the distance of where I was going I couldn't see anything. *I knew the walker was loud, but how far could the sound really travel out here?*

With every step I heard, it became clear that wherever the sound was coming from it was getting close. Looking around I saw the giant machine stomping its way down the path and I realized that it couldn't have been him.

Waiting until the machine was close, I think the pilot could see me, but I waved anyway to try and get his attention. "Hey! Over here!" I shouted and did everything short of throwing something at it, not wanting to piss off the driver.

There was no reason they didn't see me. However, they just walked by me like I wasn't even there. Ignoring me as it trudged along down the path, my shoulders dropped trying to figure out why they wouldn't even so much as acknowledge me. The only thing I could think of was they were also heading in the same direction as me. *Maybe they ignored me because they are trying to help Kennedy? Maybe I just wasn't important enough for them to bother with saving? I don't blame them, I wouldn't waste my time saving me either... I didn't deserve it.*

~ Zack

Tabitha has grown up so much since her last feeding. Her vine covered stem was thick and her bulb was massive. The sunlight that lit up the mall through the skylights was so beautiful and filled me with warmth. I felt rejuvenated and a sense of being high had taken over in a relaxing way. I found myself being compelled towards higher ground. My movements were sluggish and moving my limbs felt labor intensive. Like trying to punch in a dream, only all over my body. Whenever I rested from trying to move, a rush of comfort would hit me like a bucket of water being splashed on my skin.

I wonder if Tabby is feeling the same right now. This euphoric feeling was something that if she was sharing it, would be the best father-daughter bonding experience. My little princess is growing up so fast.

Since Sarah's... departure from this world, we have had a few guests sneak in. They were fun to play with, but my daughter needed to feed more. The first few weren't too worrisome, a few college age kids. They had tried hiding in the furniture store. They must not have ever had to search and see if someplace is truly safe, because they came right in and acted like it was their living room.

I almost felt bad interrupting their... activities, but I couldn't very well allow them to expose my little girl to that kind of behavior now could I? She was much too young for her fragile little mind to understand. I had to make an example of them.

I wasn't sure if I should have distributed their blood as nourishment. As soon as they were joined, Tabitha's body changed. Little polyps formed over her stem, finger-like branches grew sticky with sap and moved as if in search of something. I have smelled something in the air that was oddly alluring and sweet ever since. It also seemed to break the hold the sun had making me more sluggish. I felt a reinvigoration take hold in its place and I found myself being drawn near to her. I didn't feel that I was worthy yet though. It was going to be her birthday soon. Maybe I should go find her a gift or offering? Prove to her I was a worthy protector.

I had to leave her side and explore the town surrounding our little safe haven. I didn't travel far, only a few small stores that surrounded us. I couldn't get the smell out of my mind and an unbridled rage seemed to be growing within me the longer I stayed away from her. The disturbing feelings welling up within were unrelenting in their draw, and I forced myself out of the building and in search of something to vent my aggression on.

With every person or rival I came across, I felt the need to challenge them to some degree. My form had begun to become more defined and muscular. The more I killed and fed, the more my body would engorge and become heavier. My skin became callused and hardened. The few unworthy I came across wielding guns, couldn't even leave a mark on me. Their bullets would bounce off and for the few that did manage to find a weak spot in my carapace, I made sure to make them regret it.

My skin has broken open and I could feel something under the leaf-like peels wriggling like maggots in an old steak. My sluggish body began to return and my drive was only made worse by the sun and its addictive drug-like effect it was having on me. It only added to my rage when I went into any of the darkened storefronts. The feeling as the rush quickly left my body made me increasingly more aggressive.

My thoughts had become less and less coherent and all I could think about was how much I loved my daughter and how she will be so happy to see how strong I truly am for her. How worthy I have become for her love and I came to the understanding of what this feeling I had was telling me to do. I had to return to her, I had to join with her once more, and show her how much I love her.

By the time I returned back to the hive, I could barely fit through the double doors. No longer fearing for what may have visited in my absence, I strode through the glass as if it was nothing more than a shower curtain. The log-like spikes covering my body shattered the doors and gouged out chunks of the overhang with an ear-splitting screech as they dragged along the metal within the concrete.

My feelings of what I must do were mixed, but I understood that no one else would or could ever be worthy to be in my position and in my mind this needed to be done to ensure her survival. As I got closer to the atrium, I noticed a large bright light, like the one from all the unworthy, only it was three or four times bigger. *Is there another? No! I am the only one to be with her!* There was a smaller glow coming from beside it, and I knew that that one was human, the other I had no clue. But the fact they were staring at Tabitha the way they were, spiked my anger and I lost my senses and charged. I didn't want to give whatever that huge glowing object was a chance to hurt my love. In my head I was screaming for them to leave, but all that came out was a roar of hatred.

The big machine that turned to face my attack, raised its arms and I felt several heavy impacts against my chest, but it meant nothing. My family was in danger and this weapon was about to meet its match.

~ Michaels

Dear lord, was this rescue the most uncomfortable thing ever. My balls were almost in my chest due to this damn harness riding up with every jolt from the idiot inside the suit taking probably the most indirect path he could to get to this damn mall.

I'd be lying if I said I wasn't a little unnerved by how empty the town was, but with what was coming this way I wasn't surprised. There must have been a chaotic exodus away from here, there were abandoned and destroyed vehicles scattered around that looked like even before the monsters showed up, the panic alone had already done plenty of damage. People were always the weakest of willed creatures when faced with their imminent demise. If they only knew what the future held for them, they wouldn't even have bothered leaving their homes.

It was surreal smelling the fresh cut grass from those interrupted mid yard work, it brought back memories of the times in the labs. So many of the experiments started off with that scent. We had spent years mapping the genome of predatory plants and fungus that could control living beings. It was fascinating work.

The prospect for the consumer market was limitless in what we were going to do. Insecticides would be a thing of the past, no longer would we worry about the cancers and mutations they caused. The poisoning of the ground waters would be limited to near zero. For the industrial market, the boosted transformation by genetically modifying the local fauna to have larger root systems and leaves to bring in more of the toxic air and purify it. This could reverse the effects of global warming. We could have used it to help bring life to deserts by increasing the humidity and creating plant strains to survive on little to no water, but still produce the needed moisture. It was such a noble cause and I was proud of the work I was a part of. There were even talks with different space organizations that we could use our research to help terraform another planet, and not just the usual suspects like Mars or moons like Titan, but places that we couldn't even consider before. We could use panspermia to send the basics of biological life to whole other galaxies.

My associates and I, especially my newest lab assistant, Ms. Conoly, was one of the few who shared my vision, and over time we found ourselves bonding over our shared love of the potential of how our research was going to change the world. Needless to say, our interests eventually spilled out into our private lives and we started dating. Over the following years I had waited to propose to her. I had everything planned out, but the cards of fate decided to flip and brought that to a halt.

I had been with the company at the time for close to a decade. We had brought them so many new products derived from our experiments that I was rest assured in my mind that when I went for the promotion to be a leader in our company, that I would get it. Once the meeting I had to attend that day was done, I would know that our financial future would be set and we could finally get married.

I remember staring at the ring. It wasn't much, a small diamond and an ornate gold band that looked like the branches of trees wrapping around her finger to hold the stone. I had been saving up for a while, but I felt it was perfect. Although simple, its beauty was like our love. Brought together through mutual wants and soon to bring something spectacular into the world. *Oh how wrong I was.*

That meeting wasn't for a promotion or even a raise. It was for me to discuss the military applications of what we had built. What we had created was meant to bring us into the next stage of human evolution, take us from the primitives of fossil fuels to true renewable self sustaining energy by making bio-organic life that could power itself with nothing more than the sun. No wires or metal needed. Capacitors and batteries would have been nothing more than things of the past, this wasn't meant for war.

Yes we had had a few situations of isolated tests showing that the mutagen could sometimes spontaneously change to infect insects. On one occasion it had caused a test animal to bond with the spores, but it was never anything purposefully done. When the plants bloomed and the infected spore-like pollen entered its body, the rabbit reacted normally at first. Nothing even seemed to show that a cross contamination had occurred. It wasn't until a week later that the effects started to show.

Its cornea had changed to an emerald green and gold swirl that illuminated under ultraviolet light. It had become lethargic during the day as well. We had decided to put it under observation as subject zero. We expected the bugs to be subject to some change as they were going to be what was used as the transfer medium in the wild, but this was something we didn't think was going to be possible. We had specifically designed it to not be able to do this, but I guess life will always find a way to adapt.

We had monitored it for several days as its body morphed and changed into something that was nothing more than a pained existence. It had become too much for one of our weaker willed assistants who activated the sanitization protocol. They burned it, as well as the other animals it had come into contact with to ash, and we vowed to never speak of the isolated incident. We then made sure to try and eradicate the defective mutant genes that caused the spillover. It was an unfortunate side effect, but we did fix it.

Well, as I was realizing that someone in that lab hadn't kept their mouth shut. The military bio-weapons division had caught word of it. They had offered my director a very large chunk of military funding and his moral compass decided to take a break. To say I was angered by this would be an understatement, but I had no other offers or prospects, and if I left here, anywhere I went to would be a step down in my career. We couldn't afford to downgrade to the degree we would have to for me to be a badass and quit right there. Instead, I made the only choice I could. I shook their hand, and agreed to see what I could do.

I took the rest of the day off under the guise that I wanted to celebrate, but in reality I spent the few hours I had mentally preparing myself to have to face my future wife with the news that we were going to be making weapons for those we were hoping to end the need for. That night pulling into the driveway, I shut off the car and sat there for a few minutes silently cursing myself out for how things were going to be now. That's when it hit me. *Maybe we still could make a world that no longer had the need for armies. If there weren't any left to fight, then we as a society could progress and our work could go back to what it was meant for.*

Running inside I grabbed Andrea by the arm and led her to the living room to sit on the couch. I tried to explain my reasons to her, but she at first was beyond disgusted with what I had to tell her. However, after I explained my plan she seemed to come around to the idea that we can use this to our advantage and get even for the bastardization of our work. If they wanted a weapon, we would give them a weapon that would make them wish they had left well enough alone.

We never deleted the results from that failed experiment in case we needed to ever reflect on what happens when you don't take all precautions with your choices. We poured into our work all of our resentment for being used for something as stupid as a soldier's plaything of war. We added more aggressive plant-life gene strains that would give them an ability to feed and hunt in order to sustain themselves. If the army wanted a weapon it didn't need to feed, the pigs could feed themselves. For when they died, we looked into species that would poison and strangle those who ate from anything grown or breathed in its fumes. We took some of the code needed from the manchineel tree and white snakeroot. For some of the smaller iterations we used other more potent poisons that we would change the creature to search for water sources and intentionally make themselves die in order to poison whole towns, and to be sure it was permanent, we spliced in a viral strain of oddly enough the common cold. It would always be present once released and no one would be immune.

As much as it pained and sickened us, we understood that this was something that needed to be done. We, of course, showed them we also had a cure for the presentation, but that was only for an "isolated incident" and they would never be the wiser.

We executed our plan by orchestrating a breach. I felt terrible making Edwards open that door. I assured him that **Experiment-404** was going to be sedated. The combat data we got was amazing. Turns out when you inject a bear with a cocktail of the virus and a liter of synthetic adrenaline, it becomes quite powerful. **404** was already a massive grizzly, but once that mixture hit its bloodstream, it was game over. It already stood at fourteen feet and weighed over a thousand pounds, and that was before the experiment was started. When I was done with it, Pooh bear was twenty-six feet tall, and built like a tank. Whatever we had done seemed to have reawaken dormant genes in its DNA. Its limbs grew to carry the newly bulked weight. Its claws became machetes, able to slice through farm animals with ease and with all that had been done to it, its predatory instincts were on par with almost sentient beings. To be completely honest, that was the only experiment that truly terrified me, and that's why I chose it to be the catalyst for my new world. A monster is only considered a monster because we don't understand its nature or why it does what it does. I think I owed it to this miracle of evolution to stretch its legs and establish itself in the pecking order of the natural world.

I watched through the cameras as the doors were each opened. It was a routine sample test for those involved, the other teams for **Experiments-403** and **402** were as safe as they thought they were, but that aggression boost for **404** was my first real taste of a pyrrhic victory. I lost several of my team, but what happened needed to in order to get the point across.

When the general or whoever it was stopped by that day, he said he wanted to see the combat data, he didn't say how he wanted to see it, and what better military to test it on than one of the strongest in the world? If I had known that this, our current predicament, was going to be the result in less than twenty-four hours, I would have been sure to have been long gone before I got called into babysit the dead and dying like it actually mattered. I'm just glad Andrea wasn't in the building when the shit hit the fan. The only reason I was still there was because someone had to be there to sabotage the lockdown procedures.

Once **404** broke quarantine, all hell broke loose. The beast slaughtered its way through the containment lab level like a hurricane through Florida. Those that managed to escape but were wounded, were the carriers for the initial few cases of infection. The close proximity they had with the others only made things spread faster. The security teams tried to contain the mayhem, but a few button presses later, **403** and **402** were jolted awake with their own doses of wake up juice and they had no issue breaking through the doors and rushing up the stairs. Both had their specific skill sets for hunting, **403** was an infected wolfdog, and **402** was a large cat breed, I believe it was a jaguar at some point, but I honestly couldn't remember. They had both been alpha level tests, but **404** was considered violently unstable, and was prone to last second mutations that would always inevitably lead to close calls. Its escape attempts would have surely led to a successful one eventually. That's just basic statistics. In this case, it just happened to have a helping hand this time. When we did our best to evacuate, it ended with my colleagues being airlifted to a safe zone, but the transport I was on was sent to that shithole and now I find myself here. Piggy backed on this guy, who I am very grateful for, but this area is just empty. Sure I've seen maybe one or two sets of eyes here and there staring out at the robotic monkey here, but this area is relatively untouched.

Marching through the parking lot, we could see that this place must have cleared out quickly. There were abandoned cars with open doors, some were still running with the radio emergency broadcast repeating in the vehicle graveyard. The virus hadn't appeared to have spread here to too high of a degree yet. There were a few bodies here and there in the beginning stages of transition, but no real immediate threat. My concern was that I wasn't seeing what had killed these people.

Unhooking my harness as we stood outside the massive building, I hopped down from my metallic chariot and had to seriously adjust myself. We took in the strange liminal feel of the empty mall standing there. The vacant feeling of nothing living surrounded us and a tinge of concern started to rear its ugly head. The only sounds we could hear were distant shots as the infected ones were coming. We just seem to be counting ourselves lucky at this point that there were minimal contacts along our journey.

Looking up at Mr. Valhart in his little bubble cockpit, I wondered how long we were going to be standing there. "So... we just going to stand here looking at the building, or are we going to head inside?"

His response was him lifting a gigantic robotic hand up with one of the fingers up, like he was a dad telling a kid to hold on while on the phone. Throwing my hands up, in a "what the fuck" kind of shrug, I saw him mouthing something and it occurred to me he probably was actually on the radio with someone.

Watching how it was going he seemed to be annoyed, but whoever he was talking to seemed to be not letting him get a word in edgewise. When the conversation appeared to be over, he threw something and he didn't seem happy. Not too long after that, he frantically searched for whatever he had thrown and whatever he was hearing now seemed to be making him happy to hear, before finally looking back down to me.

Flipping a switch he finally spoke to me. **"Transport has been delayed for at least a half hour. Let's go inside and we can try to find someplace to bunker down."** Pushing another button a small panel slid to the side on one of the legs. A small backpack was nestled in it with a pistol stowed in a holster attached to a belt. **"Put these on. We don't know what's in there and you need to be able to hide if need be and you can't do that while strapped to my back."**

Inside the bag were some of the bare essentials. Food, a water bottle, knife and a gasmask. As well as some basic medical and survival stuff.

Stepping inside, we were welcomed by the feeling of loneliness. The void of people in the place and it only being lit naturally, brought a feeling of unease. My gut was telling me something wasn't right here, but other than the expected lack of people, I couldn't put my finger on what it was.

We walked the ghostly quiet mall, the sounds of our footsteps the only thing echoing in the silence. The grinding of gears seemed louder from my companion and when I looked back to him, he seemed to be scanning the area. Looking around there were gouges in the marble and granite surfaces, like someone had been shooting in oddly consistent groupings of bullets in paths along the walls and ceiling.

Walking up to a pillar, I started to recognize the pattern. Reaching my hand up to the punctures it dawned on me. These weren't bullet holes. There was something in here with us.

The big mech had stopped just around the corner from where we had come in and I ran to catch up. "Hey Vin... cent... whoa..."

We came to the main atrium and I was speechless at what I saw. Something I had only seen in the lab, but on a much smaller scale. We had made them in order to concentrate certain genes and then mix them with other varieties of the plants. This one appeared to be of the female strain which means a male must be close by, but the male would in comparison have to be huge to us. We had used simple bugs and small rodents, but this... this would require a huge matured male in order to pollinate and then some extra. What we were seeing was a bloomer. If the male manages to make this thing go to seed, our plans for revenge would be beyond what we could have ever dreamed.

~ Wilcox

Coming over the hill, I was a little taken aback by the haze that appeared to be emanating from the field of the sprouted dead. The only thing standing out was the destroyed mech that was knelt down in the middle.

"Well, I have a few grenades left, if I bombed him from here it could destroy my money bag though. Damn... guess I gotta go say hello."

Checking my respiration systems the filters were all still working optimally and I had plenty of ammo. Approaching the downed machine. **"Hey rookie, I've come to retrieve the canister and save your hopeless ass. So how about you meet me halfway and at least stand up!"**

I was almost to it when I saw my first sign of life. I was maybe ten yards away when the body sparked and twitched. **"Kennedy! Wake your ass up man, we don't have time for you to be..."** I was almost right on top of him when the suit spun and drove a fist directly into my chest, cracking my visor and sending me staggering back.

You just made my job easier. Raising my cannon the barrels spun up to speed and I unleashed a barrage of bullets into the armored carapace, but he rose like they had no effect on him. As his body turned, I saw the vines and twisted roots feeding into the limbs. The mass of knots and branches filling the cockpit spread apart as it stood to its full height. The screaming humanesque face splitting open wider than it should have been able to spread. The power coming from the mutant was impressive and in the rage filled roar that was being released, I saw a glimpse of my prize deeply sunk into the fleshy wood that encased the long lost pilot.

"I hope you understand this isn't personal." Firing another burst, the bullets tore into the bulky frame with little effect. The limbs enclosed the head and it charged. It swung its robotic arms wildly, the one being completely remade as it was brought down in a hook shaped blade, like a scythe being brought down in an executioner swing. I brought my drill arm up to block it and the point drove itself through the steel like a hot knife through butter and locked itself in place as it began to branch out into any open crack it could. I tried to activate my only close quarters weapon, but the growths had already shorted it out and were trying to make it one with veggie man here.

I activated the shotgun mounted in my right hand and began shooting into the invasive arm until it was weak enough to snap off in a mixture of blood and sap, spraying and smearing on my windshield. I felt a series of blows smashing into my chest and I blindly fired in the general direction. Hoping to hear something that would give me an edge.

The best I could see was a vague shadow that was washed out in the smudged light. As my ammo counter went down I couldn't even see if any of those shots did anything. I was missing half of my suit's left arm, but I still had the upper portion I tried to use to block from the haymakers that this thing was pummeling me with. The robotic nub was ripped off into a sharpened spike that had little other use. A crack formed across my screen as another devastating hit sent me to the ground. I spun to my stomach when I saw a shadow that had leapt into the air and was about to land on me. Another series of impacts and the muddied ground darkened my visor with each hit driving me deeper and deeper into the muck. The cracks became bigger as the pressure increased and I had to think of something.

I could see my grenade pack was still above the dirt and I made a desperate shot on the side I thought the possessed cyborg was on. Launching an explosive, I was blown over onto my back again and my sensors went off with warning signs that there was severe structural damage. As if that wasn't bad enough, there was another series of secondary bangs destroying half my canopy and taking the last of my bombs away. I felt the flames singe and scorch my face. The smell of burning hair filled the air around me and I knew I was not in good shape. But I could buy a new face as long as I survived and got that damn container.

Looking through the fresh hole, I could see that Kennedy was on the ground, its leg missing along with one of its feet. It was still trying to struggle to attack me. I brought myself to my feet and made my way over, keeping as much of its body in my line of sight as possible. Each step made me feel almost sad at what had become of my squadmate. It's one thing to kill someone for a selfish reason, but this felt different.

Kicking the flailing body onto its back, I plunged my robotic hand deep into where the canister was and pulled it free as the growths tried to spread to my clawed manipulator. I used my leg as leverage and shoved the creature's body back. My weapons were depleted or destroyed and quite frankly, I just didn't like the guy enough to stomp him out.

Raising the metal thermos into view, I saw something else that was shiny and dangling in my grip. I brought it closer and I saw that it was his dog tags. It was funny, I had worked with this kid for so long, but never learned his first name. Snatching it from the robotic hand, I wiped the strange blood from it and started to laugh. "Your real name was Hortense! Oh god, I wish I had known that while you were alive. The jokes I could have made. Well, lost cause I guess. By the way, thank you for doing the hard part. But, now I have to find a way to get back to Vince and the nerd. Nice seeing you again, though."

Turning away I began walking towards the big building hoping to find a still functioning car to hotwire or something. Doing a coms check, I radioed Vincent to tell him the good and the bad news.

"Alpha this is rogue, do you copy, over?" I repeated the call a few times before I finally got a response.

"Rogue this is alpha, good to hear you are still alive. What is lone wolf's condition?"

"Lone wolf..." I sighed for dramatic effect. **"Lone wolf didn't make it. The sprouted got him."**

There were a few tense seconds of static before he responded. **"Rogue, were you able to secure the package?"**

"Package is secured, looking for alternate transportation. My rig has a few dents and scratches and I can't show up for departure like that now can I?"

"Understood, we are at the extraction point. You have maybe a half hour to get here."

"Affirmative, I will be there."

Looking around I could see a few vehicles that looked to still be of use. "Well, hello there."

Making my way over to the shipping dock, I saw that the only one without something blocking it was a tanker truck of some sort. It wasn't the fastest of choices, but I'm sure it would plow through whatever gets in my way. As I was about to pop open my cockpit and make a run for it, I heard someone shouting from behind me.

I turned to see the man from the path running down the hill pointing at where Kennedy had been. I could see that the creature's body was grotesquely warped as the infection mutated him beyond any form of recognition. If there was any part of Kennedy in that thing before, it wasn't there anymore.

"Now what am I gonna do?"

FERAL TERRA

Chapter 7 the end is near

~ Chris

He saw we were heading the same direction. The guy didn't have to be a prick and just leave me alone. I was a little pissed at the unknown pilot who left me on the trail. *Oh yeah Chris, this is a great idea. Let's save the world by going where the big robot man had his ass kicked with nothing more than a god damned pistol.* Degrading myself in thought was all I could think to do to pass the time. Walking down the trail was slowly killing me inside at the thought of what Zoe must have thought of me, worse than that, what would Beth think of my actions? *Yeah hunny, I helped save the world by abandoning a woman that was so horrifically hurt, I couldn't bring myself to be man enough to put her out of her misery. Sure, that would end well, ya fucking weakling.*
My self deprecation was interrupted by the sound of something clanging in the distance and automatic fire. "The hell is that?"
Jogging along the trail as best as I could, I found myself looking over an open area of land, towards the center and surrounded by random sprouted, were the two robots going at it, and it looked like my friend from the path was getting his ass kicked.
He was prone, belly down, and the other who I had to assume used to be Kennedy, was pounding on the other like a gorilla. The damage was unreal, how easily it was being smashed. All I could do was watch before a sudden blast sent both of the suits flying apart from each other. Pieces of both of them rained down across their battlefield. Before another explosion rocked the body of the soldier's mech and sent more of the suit into the air.
I was shocked and felt like I couldn't breathe. The warrior wasn't moving and what was left of the cyborg looking monster was flopping around like a vicious primordial fish. My hope was dying and I felt myself wanting to give up. There was no way I could kill that thing.
I was contemplating what the hell I was going to do, when I saw the horribly damaged suit begin to move again. Not only did it move, but it was able to stand up. For the first time in all the craziness, I was genuinely happy. The lumbering wounded machine made its way over to the downed creature, Its body still flailing and trying to pull itself towards its approaching execution-

er. Lifting its heavy foot, he kicked the monster over and stood pinning it down before reaching down and ripping something from the root covered cockpit and shoved the creature aside.

He must not see it as a threat anymore or something, but it still looked like it was trying to kill him. I started climbing down seeing the lone soldier walking towards the tower in the background. I tried to stay low and kept an eye on the cyborg. It was still moving, but it didn't take long before I realized that its limbs were getting longer and regrowing.

"Shit, Hey! You, look out!" I screamed, waving my arms and doing everything I could to try and get the soldiers' attention. By the time he turned around the infected Kennedy had reformed enough of its lost pieces to begin galloping on all fours like an animal. The whole head of it was encased in thick wooded armor. The sections opened and closed like a gigantic mouth. The metal splintered through the thin layers of vegetation covering its back. It looked like something was sparking underneath the chitinous leaves.

What could be powering that thing?

I was running as fast as I could towards what looked like a truck depot. The sprouted beast of a man was now in a full out sprint, its limbs now fully formed again. Its goliathian strides closing the distance between itself and the now realizing soldier.

Everything seemed to slow down as the creature closed its fist like head and the robot's arm swung to give it one good hit. As the fist collided with the creature's battering ram like skull, the fingers and arm crumpled in and blew it apart. The impact sent the rest of the body flying into a sparking ass over head tumble, only stopping when he hit a concrete pylon.

The monster skidded to a stop, digging its tree like fingers deep into the cement. It spun to face the decimated remains of the suit. The mushroom shaped head of the ram opened up revealing a screaming and flayed, bloody skull. Its eyes, piercing and focused on the motionless pile of metal before closing itself up and charging again. I had to turn away as the suit erupted and was completely obliterated.

I stood paralyzed in fear as the colossus turned its attention to me. The mouth of it ground over itself brushing the few chunks of metal that had managed to penetrate and get stuck, shaking it off. The horrifying visage of the center of the hellish flower opening its distorted green and red muscled face made me want to shit myself.

I did the only thing I could think of and pulled out my gun and started firing. The bullets sinking into the brawn of the skin, they did nothing to slow its assault. When the slide locked back, I turned and ran as hard and fast as I could. I could feel the earth quake as it got closer. Its muffled cry, rumbled in my ears between the beats of its feet hitting the ground. I didn't need to turn around to see how close it was until another sound came out of nowhere. It was a truck horn followed by a screech and a cloud of dirt engulfed me as I fell to the ground.

"Hey! Get on the fucking hose and spray that thing!"

I was so surprised that the man was still alive that I froze for a second. "Lets go pretty boy! It's getting back up!"

Looking up to the top of the truck and over to the humbled brute, It was straining itself as it tried to stand back up, but broken tendon like vines were snapping under the weight of the impatient creature. I rushed to stand and climbed up on top of the truck's tank. Pulling the valve lever, a stream of high pressure water shot out, a rainbow forming in the mist and sun. The sparks increased on the back of the timber monstrosity before there was a bright flash of white flame that burst free, setting the whole thing on fire. The flames burned like a jet engine and an instant later the whole thing vanished followed by a loud bang. A shockwave pushed me back onto my ass in a bright flash of light.

"Whoa man... I always wondered what would happen. Not gonna lie, that was fucken awesome." The disheveled looking soldier laughed at the situation. "So, I think that makes us even."

"Even?"

"If you hadn't been screamin and hollerin', that first hit would have killed me."

I laid there for a moment on top of the truck catching my breath.

"So what's your plan? Gonna stay up there or get in? Make your choice quick though, I'm on a time restraint and I believe all the ruckus is waking up our garden friends here."

Rolling over to the ladder, I looked over the field and all the infected had been slowly moving in closer to join the fight. I climbed down and hauled myself into the cab of the vehicle quickly. The chipped tooth smile of the oddly dressed marine and the half brush burned off, bloody bald spot on the right side of his head welcomed me. "Jesus, are you okay?"

"I got what I needed, I'll be good as new when I get back to base. By the way, I'm not Jesus, name's Wilcox."

Before anything else could be said, Wilcox shifted the truck into gear and floored it, making me fall into the seat. *This guy is insane.*

~ Vincent

I was hoping for this mission to have just been a simple in and out and here I am fighting some kind of blooming onion from the depths of some psycho's imagination. The doctor ran someplace and my ammo is doing nothing to this thing. It moved unnaturally fast for something so big and now it seems to be stalking me from somewhere. For someplace that's this well lit and with how big that thing was. *Where could it have gone?*

I tried shooting it, but that did nothing, burning it only seemed to piss it off more. We've been doing this cat and mouse game for fifteen minutes now.

"Alpha, this is Romeo, do you read?" My radio popped on and the dispatcher's voice made me jump.

"Romeo, this is Alpha. Currently in a predicament, LZ is hot."

"How many contacts?" The voice on the other end seemed like they weren't surprised.

"One stationary and the other is on the move. Whereabouts unknown."

"Roger that, clear the landing zone, extraction is inbound."

No shit, what the hell do you think I'm trying to do! I would have said that, but that could get me in a little bit of trouble and the last thing I wanna do is make our taxi service mad at us. **"Can I get some kind of support? Are there any friendly's nearby?"** The radio was quiet for a few seconds again. **"You have your orders."**

What the hell is that supposed to mean? I'm almost empty and that thing has already destroyed my railgun. Bullets aint doin shit to it. We were drastically unprepared for this mission and from what I'm seeing, some pertinent, need to know information.

I really wish that they would send at least a care package. It's not like I'm asking for a flying fortress or anything. Of course with the way this thing has been acting, it almost seems sentient. Like it's trying to pull me away from whatever this flower thing is. Maybe I can get it out of hiding if I mess with whatever it's protecting.

Cycling through what inventory I had left, I only had a few signal flares and about a handful worth of scatter rounds. Looking around the open area, I tried to find anything I could, to make a plan that might actually work, but everything around me was just clothes and electronics. I knew it was watching me from somewhere, but I might have to consider leaving my suit again and heading up the escalator to the food court. If nothing else there was oil and salt.

Oil and salt... was this really what I was trying to think of. Oh yea salt the earth, maybe it'll die of thirst. It's a giant tentacle sticking out of the ground! However, oil is flammable. Well, it's as good a plan as any and it beats standing around with my dick in my hand.

Opening my suit, I instantly felt naked and like I was being watched even closer now. I didn't even have my emergency gun because that prick ran off with it.

Each step I took away from my little peanut shell of protection made me feel dumber for having left it. Looking over the railing I could see a cell phone sign and a couple jewelry stores. Nothing out of the ordinary. I moved as quietly as possible, stopping occasionally, because I could hear the sound of the creature moving somewhere off in the distance.

Okay, it's nowhere near me. If I'm lucky I can search one or two of these restaurants and make something to blow or burn that thing up. Then get back to the suit and we can be on our merry way.

Sneaking up and over the display of some Japanese cafeteria hibachi wanna be place, I dropped down and started looking for anything of use. I wasn't surprised to find several large containers of fryer oil. Food had been left on the flattop and had long since burned to the point of becoming part of the grill. Even the fryers themselves were still on and would occasionally pop from condensation dripping into it from some unseen source.

Going into the back, I relaxed a bit now that I was out of the open area and was able to search a little faster. Looking under the sink I smiled as I saw a container of drain cleaner, and near the prep station was some aluminum foil. "Awesome, now I just need to find some containers and I can make something." Then it occurred to me. "The fryer oil containers!" Grabbing two of the heavy jugs, I took them over to the railing and dumped them out over the side. No clue if they would catch fire, but I needed to try.

Going back into the kitchen, I started pouring the clog remover into the big container and tried to think of a way to make it a little more deadly. I needed something that wasn't going to cause a strange reaction though. *Duh, the jewelry store!* Tearing off a piece of the foil sounded like thunder in the quiet and I felt like an idiot having forgotten that it was loud as shit. Ripping the foil into tiny pieces as fast as I could, I put them in a bag and moved as fast as I felt safe going.

As I stepped inside I heard a very loud crash and a roar of pain echoed throughout the mall. Instantly, I hid inside the store and held the slippery vessel to my chest. "It must have been trying to find me and slipped on the oil. A small smile from the mental image of that terrifying creature slipping around like some cartoon character, spread across my face. I had to have been losing my mind to think laughing at a time like this was a good idea.

Suddenly, another howl filled the halls and I stopped laughing as another sound resonated. I didn't see it, but I heard my mech as it was torn apart. Chunks of metal clanked and bounced off of whatever they hit. The sounds of the window store fronts being shattered. All my hope drained from me as the reality of my plan to kill this thing wasn't in the best of shape. "Fuck!"

Putting down the container I started looking for keys to open the display. It didn't take long before I found them on the other side of the store, still in the lock. The whole time I had the cover of the monster curb stomping my suit like an unwanted prom baby to not worry about noise.

I opened the display and filled my pockets with as much gold and platinum that I could. Turning to get back to the home made bomb though, I saw the root like fingers grabbing the railing as it lifted itself up to the second floor. Its weight caused the heavily waxed floor to crack. I went prone to the floor and I waited to hear the footsteps. Taking a chance, I looked over the top of the display and all I could see was the beasts writhing flesh vines moving like worms as if adjusting to whatever move the rest of the body was making. It was trippy, watching something that all my life I've only seen stationary like a tree, move the way it did. It was surreal to see bark moving over muscle like skin.

I only had a few handfuls of diamonds and metal, a sentence I never thought I would say, but I needed more to make this thing better than a glorified fire cracker. The floor shook as the thing started to move in search of where I could be. The sounds of crumbling concrete falling to the floor did not fill me with confidence as now I had to worry about the structural integrity. *If I was lucky, maybe it would fall through the floor and I could make a run for it, or with luck being as it was today, I would fall through and be crushed to death.* Opening another display, I continued to fill my pockets and prayed that the sound of jewels shaking in them didn't get its attention. Stealing another look, I saw that the walking terrarium was on the other side of the escalators and I had a small distance between us. Its back was split open in several places and tendrils of fungus were whipping in all directions. With each jerking motion a cloud of what looked like dust would gently fall to the floor.

Taking a few deep breaths, I felt a cough wanting to rear its ugly head and I did my best to stifle it. I waddled with all the extra weight throwing me off balance in my crouched position. I was almost to the I.E.D. when I coughed, causing me to trip and the sound of all the shiny bits of metal danced across the floor in a sprawling wave as they burst from my pockets. *Seriously Vince?* Scrambling to my feet I already knew the thing was on its way to fuck my world up. The running stomps followed by a sudden silence and the heavy thud as it leapt from the other side of the walkway. I didn't have much time as it was now right where I needed to go. A large deep creviced bark covered arm reached in smashing through the displays, its body too big to get into the store. I ran to the other exit, but it didn't matter as it had already started to move in order to give chase. I was trapped and it didn't seem keen on letting me get a head start. I tried to find a way out, but it all seemed useless.

"Hey you big son of a Bitch!" The voice was familiar as a series of gunshots sprayed across the back of the creature. "Come give Willie a suckle, ya overgrown weed."

The creature's arm crashed through the wall as it spun to see Wilcox standing with his rifle in the air waving it around like a madman. He looked like he had been through a woodchipper, but was still doing all he could to distract my pursuer. Seeing my chance I ran for my chemical experiment. Snatching it as I sprinted past. I made my way back to the restaurant. I had a plan... ish.

~ Zack

I wouldn't let these filthy degenerate bastards defile my dear daughter's life. They were here to hurt her! The machine's guns made no difference as the bullets would just pass through me. My princess's gifts took away those useless organs, the weaknesses of man mattered little to me now. The parts of me that are taken will only grow back stronger.

The closer I got, the more I felt my rage rise. They were too close to my baby. I couldn't allow them to hurt her!

I saw the pitiful tiny man run off, his light bright with fear. I would deal with him later. It wouldn't be an issue to hunt him down. I towered over this armored piece of food. It was going to be like tearing open a tuna can.

He tried burning me and that ended when I grabbed the nozzle, crushing it and bending it out of the way. The ash it created would only feed my body more. This manifestation of evolutionary godhood was meant for one thing and one thing only. Once this little spat was done, I will become one with my darling to bring forth our children. They will protect us and we will spread our love all over the world. The seeds I will sow with her will be the beginning of a perfect next step. The planet will know her as their queen.

The blows as he did his best to defend himself with, were laughable. He did manage to shove me back. I simply charged in again. He brought up his weapon and I saw a massive glow of energy building and I drove my fist towards it as it transferred into a projectile. The piece of metal traveled so fast I almost didn't feel it as it ripped through my fist and blew out the back of my arm. It did little to slow my fists' momentum and I could feel my body healing together as I impacted the barrel, bending it in like it was nothing more than a piece of wire.

Wherever my hands would grow into, I grabbed a hold of the mechanical monster and lifted it into the air. I felt joy as I heard the metal stress and moan, the look of concern of the tiny pilot as he flipped arbitrary switches. He had nothi...

I felt a sudden impact staggering me back and saw the flames at his feet as he flew away, smashing into my darling's beautiful stem. He marred her skin and scraped away a swath of her delicate finger like hairs. The impact rattled her all the way up, forcing her gentle petals to sway, almost hitting the arch of the ceiling.

All my anger changed to worry at the anguish I brought upon her. I did something unforgivable. I let out a primal howl at my stupidity and moved away in fear. I had to draw him away from here. Her life was in danger if I kept the unclean one here. I couldn't allow him to touch her again.

I did my best to act injured and began moving as far away as I could. The minor injury he did manage to inflict was already healing. The weeds of my veins intertwined to suture the gash closed and the sap encapsulated the wound. I made sure to stay in his view until I knew he saw where I had gone. I waited for what felt like an eternity before I looked back to see if he was following, but he was just standing there. I was confused, the big shield on his face was looking up to the second floor. *What is he looking at?* Following its gaze, I still didn't see anything that could make him freeze in place like that. *Maybe it can't move?* Thinking of all the possibilities, I found myself moving closer trying to see if I could simply drag him away. It wasn't a question of if I could overpower him, but of how.

He didn't even seem to see me coming. *Was I blessed with the ability to be a chameleon in the light? Who knows, but I was crouched and ready to pounce.* My body crackled with anticipation, just as I went to leap at my prey, my body twisted as I felt my grip on the floor leave and the gravity of the world gave me a lesson as my body crashed to the ground.

I tried to stand, but my body was not able to stay standing until I forced my gnarled fingers into the floor and drove my trunken feet down like jack-hammers, cracking them for traction. Still the man stood motionless and I couldn't take the fact that he didn't find me a big enough threat to even face me.

I roared in anger and attacked the motionless titan, releasing my fury like a hurricane. A tsunami of hits denting in the metal and pulling off parts like a child would a butterfly. Each hit was more devastating than the last. Finally, I stood over my downed opponent. I wanted to see my enemy and devour him to prove myself to establish my dominance. Stepping on the remaining leg I ripped the glass canopy off and threw it away. I looked back to the seat ready to pull my trophy out and I saw nothing but an empty torn apart cushion.

The suit's power blinded me from his light. *Where was he? I will kill him!* Grabbing the railing, I tried to pull myself up, but whatever was on the floor kept me from lifting myself as fast as I wanted. Slowly I pulled my body up and the floor dropped as I climbed over the rail, destroying it in the process. I moved to the other side looking for anything that could be his light. I listened for any sound, any smell, any chance, and I was going to shatter every bone in his body and drink him like a juicebox.

I stomped trying to scare him out of hiding like the rat he was. Making my way around the escalators, I was only getting more aggravated. *There was no way I was going to allow this little...*

I heard the sound of metal ringing off the floor and whipped my head around. I saw the glow of the little shit and I allowed my instincts to take over. I launched myself forty feet and smashed the floor even more and immediately clawed at where I saw him. I would catch glimpses of him moving and match where he went. He was cornered and had nowhere to go. He was just out of reach before I felt a series of small impacts dot my back. I heard someone shouting at me, but I couldn't understand them.

I turned away to see who else I would be hunting down. After seeing his burning flame of a light I knew I must have him, but later. I felt the little vibrations as the original target of my aggression had managed to sneak by. I chased him around the corner, seeing him hop over one of the countertops, I followed him there and as soon as I forced my head into the opening, a burning sensation splashed against my face, forcing me to stumble back. I tried to wipe it away, but the blistered splinters popped like boils on a sunny day. One of my eyes was sealed shut as the molasses-like fluids dripped down from the searing wounds.

In my blurred vision, I made out the amorphous blob of that little bastard running off and I wasn't letting him get away again. I charged in the general direction I saw him heading, and he was standing where I had clamored up. His light had traveled to his feet for some reason, but I had no care or worry as to why. I stomped over bringing my fist down and crushing the tiny nuisance beneath its girth. Grinding my palm I relished in the feeling of... it wasn't bone... and I felt nothing squishy. My vision was still obscured and I dragged my arm across my face to scrape off the hardening burls giving me a clearer view. What rolled out from the destroyed mass was a white plastic head. *What?*

The light I was now standing over grew and a loud bang deafened me. I didn't know if I was flying through the air or falling. It lasted no more than a second before I felt the impact. Followed by the heavy chunks of flooring crashing down on me.

~ Wilcox

I tried to keep a small friendly conversation with this guy. I knew that it was a stupid idea to pick him up, but he did have a hand in saving my life. Not only that, but he also managed to kill... that thing back there. I didn't feel right calling it rookie, whatever that creature was... it wasn't my squadmate anymore. Not gonna lie to myself though, I felt kind of bad for how it had gone down. Sure I was going to kill him anyways, but he didn't deserve that.

The actions of that fight replayed in my mind. I couldn't help but laugh at the fact I had survived because I wasn't properly buckled in. When that thing hit me, I had flown free from my seat. Skidding against the concrete, I was lucky to only get a bad case of road rash. But it was nothing given the money I was about to get. I'll trade a couple grand for a few million anyday.

"So is that it?" the dude said, gesturing to the canister.

"Is that, what?" he shouldn't have known anything about what this thing was.

"Is that the cure? Kennedy had mentioned it before dropping us off... It's why I was walking down that path. I heard his call for help and I had to do something if I was going to see my family again." His voice trailed off when he mentioned he was on a mission of his own. I can respect that. However, the fact he knew about this was a liability. He may need to be left behind, but I can still use him as a distraction if need be.

I didn't want him to get the wrong idea about this ride, so I decided to humor him. "Yes, actually it is. Why do you ask?"

He had a small smile and sat back like a weight had been lifted from his shoulders. "Thank you to whoever is out there." He said, staring up into the sky. "So there is a chance we can end all of this?"

"Of course, and all we gotta do is get this here tin can to the proper people who are meeting us at the evac site and the science nerds will get the ball rollin. That means I'm safe, you're safe, and your family will be safe as well." I patted him on the shoulder and he looked like this was the first piece of good news he had had in a while.

"Hopefully it's in time for Zoe as well."

"Whose Zoe?"

He seemed deep in thought for a moment before his tone changed and he sounded sad. "She was who I had been traveling with since the outbreak at the prison. I had to leave her behind at the outpost Kennedy sent us to. It had been attacked and she went looking for food I guess in the store, but she was attacked and I... I was too late. I couldn't bring myself to do what I should have done. But, with this, maybe there is a chance her life could be spared." All the happiness in his body melted away. *Was he about to cry? I don't know if I can deal with this dude crying the whole way.*

"Hey, hey, hey man, no need to get sad and cry. You did the right thing. You could have done the simple thing and killed her, but you saw the chance to save her and you are taking it. Don't dwell on what choices might seem horrible at the time, because sometimes you gotta be a monster and selfish to protect those you care about. So, man the fuck up buttercup, because we are gonna save your family and this Zoe chick." Just as I had hoped, the look in his eyes seemed to brighten up at the pep talk. "I gotta ask though... is Zoe hot?" I said with a wink. He didn't seem too keen on saying yes or no, but I had a feeling she was. His smile gave it away.

I managed to find a quick way down the highway that wasn't backed up with abandoned cars and I was happy to see we were going to be there in time. Weaving in between a semi and some compact piece of shit, we could actually see our destination at the next exit and it was unsettling to say the least. Someplace that twenty-four hours ago was probably bustling with life. It looked normal, but with the lack of artificial lights and all the signage from the stores not being lit up made even the giant building seem dead. A feeling of hollowness emanated from it in a weird vibe that I understood was telling me to not go, but we had to. Then I noticed another thing that explained why I was feeling weird about this whole situation. *Why weren't Vincent and the doc on the roof?*

Shifting down to a lower gear, we approached the intimidating building at a crawl. I know we weren't late. *He would have let me know in some way. He would have made them stay or left a god damn note. Something!*

Walking up to the entrance, the main door was shredded. Whatever was in there was huge, but this could have been done with the Z.F.G.. *Maybe they were just inside, ya know out of sight out of...* my train of thought was cut off by the sound of something very loud roaring inside the mall.

"Mind... that sounded big."

"Are we going in there?"

I didn't even bother responding to that idiot's dumbass question. Shoving the canister into his hands, I ran up a flight of stairs to get a better vantage point. It didn't take long to see what was causing all the racket, and it was ugly as sin. It was a straight shot in order to flank it, and I could only assume that it was preoccupied with one of the people I'm here to see. Thus making this a very inconvenient situation.

My training kicked in and I found myself a place to get a good angle. Even with all the chaos, I was in stunned awe at the size of the plant growing in the center of the room. *No! Don't get distracted, I needed to pull that strange bagpipe looking prick off of whoever he was trying to get at.*

In the flurry of swipes it was throwing into the jewelry store, I was able to make out that "who" was in danger, was Vince. Leveling my weapon, I shouted whatever came to my mind and opened fire. The massive thing turned to face me and I saw Vincent slide out at the opening in the beast's distraction, but just as soon as it saw me it turned back to see him escaping and went in pursuit. I didn't have much time so I ran to where I saw them heading and heard the thing scream in pain and Vincent came running around the corner again carrying something.

"It's a bomb!"

"A what?"

"A fucking bomb!" he dropped the container and I could already tell from the bulging sides it was going to blow at any moment. Looking around I saw a mannequin and put it next to the shady looking explosive and ran.

Catching up to Vincent. "Where did you go, freaking window shopping?" He yelled at me.

"Needed that thing to stay there long enough for..." Boom!

A loud bang followed by the sounds of crumbling rubble and another scream, bounced through the amphitheater that was the building, ringing our ears.

"What the hell was that?"

Vincent looked back at me with a smile. "Improv!"

~ Michaels

Watching that thing charge at us scared the shit out of me. I had to run, what good would I have done in fighting it. I ran into a department store and was hidden in the clothing racks. That specimen is beyond perfect. It was exactly what I would have expected from an infected male dominant. I must retrieve a sample.

I heard the fight stop after a loud crashing sound, that I could only assume was my bodyguard getting his ass kicked. Going into one of the checkout stations I looked through for anything that could be used to house said sample, and keep it alive until I was able to escape. In my search I found a variety of plastic bags, but I didn't know how big I would need. I also found some hand sanitizer and tape in an abandoned purse.

Pulling a small knife from the backpack on my shoulder. I did my best to clean off any contaminants that were on my hands as well as the tiny blade, by using the hand sanitizer. It wasn't the best, but it was better than nothing. Sneaking my way over to the doorway, I couldn't see the monster, but I heard the cockpit hissing as it opened and the soldier hopped out. I wanted to get his attention and maybe see if he could cover me as I collected a clipping, but he took off up the unpowered escalators and out of sight.

Damn! If I'm quick I should be able to get over there and get something I can analyze. I can't let this opportunity slide past me.

Keeping as low to the ground as I could, I moved from one piece of cover to another, without any issue. That behemoth of a creature had run off somewhere on the other side of the building. It looked to be wounded, but also seemed to be trying to lure Vincent away from the large female. *Did he see us as a rival?* Looking over, the machine was horribly damaged, but had what looked like a purplish green fiber, and chunks of plant-life starting to grow wherever the fleshy substance had bled onto. A thin film of moss had begun to grow, dark red tendrils of roots were spreading along the surface, sliding into every crack. Small oddly shaped flowers that looked like the massive one in the middle of the room, sprouted out and appeared to be reaching out with tiny moving stamen, as if actively seeking out pollen. Their little bulbs opening in spiraled falange like petals. Small balls of moisture were excreted from them. I picked up a random piece of debris and upon poking one with the tip, the substance stretched away like a cheesy pizza slice before hardening into a thin needle like spike and breaking off in a glitter of tiny sharp looking particles wafting in the almost nonexistent breeze.

"Fascinating, this is far beyond what I had expected. It's creating its own life, but this looks to be a female plant... do these smaller ones also have more than one gender?" I felt a certain type of giddy at the idea that this virus was already advancing to a level that we hadn't predicted it would get to unless unchecked for years. *It did it in just over a day. This is definitely a breeding pair and this is their mating ground! I will never have this opportunity again. I must gather what I can.*

The excitement of all the possibilities we could use this for was too much to think about at the moment and I needed to refocus. Zig zagging my way towards the big mama plant, I found the gouge that must have been created by the fight before. "This must be why it ran away... it was trying to draw him over there so they didn't hurt you anymore."

This was astounding that not only were they creating new forms of plant life, but would the offspring be animal or plant based? Whatever the case, I must get a part of the male sample as well.

Bringing out my makeshift collection bag, I removed some of the smaller offshoots and with a quick look around, I saw the male approaching and I dropped down behind the growth. Hurriedly, I taped up the plastic envelope and put it in the backpack. I was panicking with each heavy step getting closer and I closed my eyes as tight as I could, to not see if this monster was going to kill me. A few steps later and I heard all hell break loose behind me. I knew if I looked I would be dead. I stared straight ahead when I felt I could no longer keep them away from the beast. A few moments of silence and then I heard the most violent beating happening before chunks of scrap metal and electronics flew in all directions. A few seconds had my curiosity get the better of me and I looked over the ledge to see the monster fling the glass encasement across the room in anger and begin climbing up to the second level. Its body morphing before my very eyes, as long, what I was assuming were stamens protruding from its back grew and a powder began to shake free in its wake. "That's the pollen."

I waited until I saw it finally hoist its heavy frame over the ledge and I made my move. Pulling a piece of tape from the roll, I swiped it across the floor where I saw the dust drop. It wouldn't take much. Looking over the no longer sticky side of tape I saw the dark almost mold colored pollen and I found myself satisfied with what I had and I started making my way to one of the back hallway doors. *No need to risk anymore.*

I didn't have to go far before finding a staircase. Following it up I started climbing the ladder to the roof when I felt the whole place shake and a muffled rumble vibrated the walls. Opening the latch I shoved the small door and the bright sun hit my eyes. There had to be a way out of here. I saw out of the corner of my eye another ladder and I started walking towards it. I still had the gun. I just needed to make it out of here.

Just as I was halfway to the gate, I saw movement and I brought the weapon to bear. I had never really shot a real gun before, sure there were the torches and chem throwers I used, but I don't know what kind of reaction to expect from this thing. I didn't even know if I could kill whatever was coming.

"Hey! You there, can you open this gate? I cant open it from this side." A strange but oddly familiar looking man was trying to open the locked gate, but appeared to be having issues.

I let out a nervous laugh and dropped the gun down to my side. I walked over to the guy, he was breathing like he had just run a mile. "You okay man?"

He looked at me with a weak smile and between deep breaths." Yeah... just a... just a little out of shape."

Using the butt of the gun I was able to break the lock and open up the mesh chain link door. I helped the slightly chubby guy onto the roof and I saw something shiny dangling from his belt. I felt a rock of dread fall into my gut, It was the canister. "Where did you get that?"

He suddenly stopped moving, taking a step back trying to hide the metal tube from me. He looked me over and his eyes stopped on my shirt. It was embroidered with the company logo. "Don't worry, I'm not going to hurt you. I work for the people who made that." His tense body relaxed a bit and his shoulders dropped as he must have thought he was safe with it.

"Yeah we were able to secure the cure for this whole thing." He held up the cylinder and even with my mask on I was scared of if that thing broke open anywhere near me. That wasn't the cure, that was the pure strain. That was Virus - 451208, that was the final product. I felt a sudden hit of joy though. This could be the final nail to really teach those military assholes that some things just shouldn't be made into weapons.

Before I could process what was going on, the whole building shook again. We both turned to look towards where the shaking started as the glass erupt- ed and the gigantic bulb forced its way up. The petals peeled back and opened up, revealing that each one was coated in teeth like seeds and tentacle-like stigma. A guttural sound like a whale mixed with a fog horn quaked through the air with such force I could see the sound waves. I could feel the concussion in my chest and we both stumbled back a few steps.

"Dear god... it's beautiful."

Looking back at my little bio drug mule, I got an idea.

"What's your name?"

He looked at me weirdly before answering, like I was insane or something.

"My name is Chris, why?"

"Chris, the only way to stop that thing is to get the vial inside of that canister into that thing."

A bewildered look as if the assumption of my questionable sanity was answered, stared back at me. "The what in the what now?"

Chapter 8 The final solution

~ Zack

I couldn't be brought down like this, I wouldn't let myself be embarrassed in this way in front of my love. Flexing my body, I felt the rubble shift and could hear the smaller pieces fall to the floor. *I need to get to her... I must... (grauh) finish this.*

I thought about everything. All the pain, the lies, the bullshit with her sick monster of a mother and her manipulative ways. How the world is going to shit, has brought us so much closer in our time of need. *I wouldn't, I couldn't allow myself to let her down.*

Dragging myself free from the concrete, I felt stuck. Looking down there were several pieces of rebar deeply embedded through multiple parts of my body, anchoring me to the floor. I tried removing them, but in my weakened state I couldn't, and my blood had already begun to assimilate the chunks. I wasn't going to be stuck here like a statue, only ever allowed to look at my dear Tabitha, but never hold her. "No!"

I felt my body fill with a new found vigor as I pulled my leg free. The rebar hurt as it tore through my muscles until I felt a jolt of pain as the limb came off. I stopped for a second, but the warmth I felt knowing I was getting closer to her, helped me fight through the pain. I howled as I broke my healing ribs in order to lift myself up and off a jagged piece of concrete that had been fusing to them. The open wound letting me see my heart racing at the small triumph of escape. My right arm had been crushed and had already begun to heal in its new twisted angle. I tried gritting my teeth through the torment, but even my mouth seemed to have been destroyed in the fall. My whole existence was anguish as I crawled across the sharp debris. Like sandpaper, it ground away at my stomach, leaving a bloody trail behind me.

Don't worry baby, daddy is coming.

I used whatever part of my body I could in order to keep pulling forward. By the time I reached the base of her throne, I knew it was time. My princess and I were to become one.

Heaving my body, I brought myself up and dug my roots into her stem. I felt an instant sensation of pleasure as our bodies became one. I stared in amazement as all the small finger-like extremities stiffened and began to flower and unfurl. Her body quivered and shook with the experience until finally the beautiful bulb that was her head moved like an elegant dancing snake.

It swerved around and waved before splitting open releasing a thick fluid that bore life wherever it landed. The serpent-like head turned to me, and I felt her gaze fill me with life. A long purple pistil squeezed its way through a hole in the tip of the tightly packed petals, several tiny spines with luminescent ball-like tips emerged from the appendage. The spheres about the size of an eye, seemed attracted to me, and I knew my princess could finally see me again.

With one more surge of energy I felt a euphoric wave as the spines on my back released all that they had. In the black cloud, I could see the dots of light swimming through it and collecting all that it could. As my vision faded and blurred, I hoped she understood how proud of her I was. With joy in my heart, I felt myself finally become one with her.

I will always love you.

~ Wilcox

I can't believe how badly this plan has gone down the toilet. Even with Vince's chemistry experiment bomb, that thing is still alive. *What the hell did we have to do to get out of here?*

As soon as we heard the roars again, we shoved our way through some side door and started hustling to the roof. I knew it was a long shot, but there had to be a way down from there and I could grab the canister back from what's his face, and find a way to get out of this state before it becomes the next burning man effigy.

We were maybe fifty feet down a back hallway before I heard something coming from behind us. I turned to see what the commotion was and as soon as I saw the writhing mass barreling towards us I knew I had to drop the dead weight.

I took off running like a bat out of hell. Soon followed by Vincent running alongside me before he passed me completely. He took a sharp turn out of sight and I didn't see it fast enough and I couldn't stop now to go back. There had to be another stairwell or a door further down the hall. Coming around the corner I saw several doors. One marked an exit, but the door was blocked by a bunch of shipping crates. I tried running to each door as the rumble grew closer, but they were all locked and required some kind of pass card or something to get through.

Panicking, I ran to the crates and started to climb over them. I made it to the door, but before I could open it, I felt the pressure of the big wooden boxes slamming into my back, forcing out a quick squeal of pain before I was launched through the door.

I found myself bouncing and sliding to a stop as the giant root system seemed to stop at the doorway. Looking up to the sky I saw something fly off from the top of the roof and I instinctively rolled out of the way to dodge it as it fell.

It hit the ground only a few feet away from me and when I looked to see what it was, I started to laugh. It was the canister, and I was going to be rich.

~ Vincent

We stopped running when we realized that we were no longer being followed. Wilcox definitely had a good idea with the mannequin. I didn't know how long it would be for the chemical reaction to happen, but those precious extra seconds were what we needed. It was at least hurt enough that we could get to the roof and radio for our extraction.

We could hear wailing as we opened the door labeled **"Employees Only"** and only hoped that we could get out of here before it was ready to fight again. We felt the building violently rattle followed by an indescribable noise bellowing through the narrow hallway.

"Oh, no no no no no! What the fuck now!" Wilcox stopped and turned back to look at me before we heard the sounds of doors being bashed in and his eyes widened while screaming "Run!"

Looking over my shoulder, a mass of tumbling vines and roots were heading right for us. I turned and sprinted as fast as I could, passing Wilcox and turning up to the nearest stairway. I took as many steps as I could in each stride before stopping at a landing. I turned back to see where Wilcox was, but in the noise of the thunderous stampede, I heard a short but distinct scream before it was snuffed out and the building trembled again.

I put my head down for a moment of silence. I knew I had just lost one of the best men I had ever served with. Sadly though, I couldn't give him the proper respect and I had to get to the roof.

There was a small card reader next to the door, but yanking the fire alarm that was next to it, deactivated the lock. The door swung open and the first thing I saw was a crazed man running towards something. I looked to see where and the giant sprout from inside had burst up through the skylight. Whip like limbs were tearing chunks of the roof down, and its blossomed head was brimming with an unfathomable amount of teeth and tendrils.

What the hell is going on? Who was that and what did I miss?

I turned back to where the man had come from and I was shocked to see that Dr. Michaels was climbing down an emergency ladder. We locked eyes and he yelled for me to run while swinging his arm in his direction. I didn't have time to save the civilian. I had a mission to complete.

~ Chris

It happened so fast I couldn't really react. Wilcox shoved the metal container into my chest and he took off. I waited around for a few minutes unsure of what to do before I started hearing gunfire and what must have been explosives going off. I panicked and started running, I ran about half the length of the parking lot and hid inside the bed of a truck.

Looking up at the sky, it was clear and a beautiful blue. I hadn't ever really stopped to look up since becoming an adult. *I guess it's just one of those things you stop doing and never notice.* As a kid I took it all for granted. Spent all those years outside, never thinking that I would miss this, something as simple as hoping to see a plane flying overhead. The gentle breeze as a cloud float-ed by like a puff of cotton candy drifting in the wind. Birds fluttering about as they would chase bugs… all of that, and one day I just stopped looking up. I think I remember it now though, it was the day I met Beth. I was seventeen and I was with my friends on our way to a party in the middle of the woods. We had been told that one of the seniors was throwing it and that if we could get there, it would be fun for everyone. Problem was that we were all stupid kids back then and Bobby, the friend who told us, gave us the wrong direc-tions. So, instead of a party with stolen booze, the cheerleading squad, and my crush, we were wandering in some farmers field surrounded by cows and an abundance of literal bullshit.

Sure the first few minutes were all tiddly ha ha's, but after two hours of mind-lessly walking in the dark. We had become lost when we had, in our infinite fricken wisdom, chose to head into the woods. The fact we were also sharing a bottle of horrible tasting whisky, also did not aid us in our predicament. What did help us though, was drunkenly stumbling across the main road. In our idiotic state we had looped around and found the road we had parked the car on, but had no clue how far or in what direction we had to go to get back to it.

Picking a direction, we started to walk, and that we did for what must have been another few miles. We were all annoyed and we were damn sure going to make certain Bobby wasn't going to live this down.

We saw a pair of lights heading our way and we were all too tired to worry about stranger danger. It was a small town, everyone knew everyone else. However, who would have thought that the headlights we saw bouncing down the old road that night would change my life forever.

When the farm truck jostled to a stop alongside us. We all kind of looked at each other puzzled, like we weren't sure if we were really seeing a truck or if we were just really drunk and all hallucinating.

"You dumbasses need a ride?" I was a little shocked to hear a woman's voice. When the dome light turned on, my jaw must have dropped a little. It was Beth, the girl I had been crushing hard on since we were in ninth grade. She was one of the few occasions in nature of being a ginger in all the right ways. Her hair bottle died a deeper red than it was naturally, but her almost white skin made her freckles stick out, but in a way that looked like a natural blush.

She had such a great smile and was genuinely a good person. Always willing to help, and also happened to be one of the few girls in school that actually talked to me and not in a way that makes me feel like I'm being used.

"Hey!" She said, snapping her fingers. "It's late and y'all seem to be a little lost. Are you okay?"

No one else seemed able to answer given they were completely wasted and I knew I couldn't let this opportunity pass me by. It must have been the liquid courage when I stammered out what I was hoping to say of yes, but what did come out was "dear god, you are the most beautiful woman I've ever seen." To this day she tells people that she knew we were wasted and needed a ride, but even with my wobbly vision, I swear I saw her crack a smile before telling us to get in. I had hopped into the front and the other guys had climbed and or fallen into the back of the truck. I wasn't sure which because I was as focused as I had ever been. Almost to the point I'm sure I looked like a serial killer.

"You okay, Chris?" She said with a weird look on her face.

Trying to act cool, I tried to stop looking at her like a creeper and did my best to straighten up my clothes so as to at least appear like I was cooler than I really was. "Oh yeah, I'm good, I'm good... yep... good diggity."

"Alrighty then, where are you guys parked?"

We all looked at each other and shrugged "We thought it was this way."

"Well, hate to break it to ya, but there ain't nothing that way for a good ten miles."

Clearing my throat a bit and not wanting to sound like directionally challenged morons. "We meant that way." We all pointed in the opposite direction and she let out a small laugh and a sigh before putting the old truck in gear and we started to move.

She drove us to Bobby's car, which was about five miles the way we had just come from. We had a fifty, fifty chance of picking the correct direction, but that misfortune was the best night of my life. When she was about to drop us off, she took a look at me and the boys and told us to give her the keys. None of us were in any condition to drive and she wasn't really interested to find out in the morning we wrapped ourselves around a tree.

Bobby and whoever we were with that night got a little pissy, but reluctantly gave up their keys before staggering to the car and promptly passing out as soon as they hit the seats. Now what happened next I'm a little hazy on and Beth swears to me nothing happened that night. But according to her, I was feeling dizzy and a little sick. She, not wanting me to hurl inside of the truck, offered for me to lie in the bed for a bit. I remember looking at the stars and as my body felt like it was spinning I felt something warm cuddle up to me before I passed out.

When I woke up I had trouble moving and I saw the dumb founded looks on my friends faces. "What?" Then I looked down and nuzzled into my chest was Beth. That warm feeling I had felt was her curling up next to me and covering us with a jacket. I didn't want to wake her, so I told the guys I'd catch up. After they left I just laid there for a while staring up at the morning's blue sky.

I didn't want the feeling of her being by my side to ever end. When she woke up, we shared an uncomfortable laugh and she seemed a bit embarrassed, but her beautiful brown eyes met mine and somehow in my hungover state, I felt confident enough to give her a kiss. She gave me a second small peck before getting red in the face and offering me an awkward boner of a ride home. A few weeks later we started dating, but ever since that kiss I hadn't looked up to the sky, I was focused on her and doing anything I had to in order to keep her happy.

Lying here now, I knew I had to be here in order to get the cure to who needed it. I had a responsibility and if I ran away now, I'd be letting my family down.. I'd... I'd be letting Zoe suffer and Kennedy would have died for nothing. This was no longer me looking for them, this was me trying to save them, to save everyone.

Sitting up, I searched for where they might land a helicopter or whatever they were sending and figured the roof was the best option. There were too many vehicles in the parking lot and there was no way with the back ups on the highway that they would get an armored transport through there at any sensible time. So the roof it was, and I could see the way up down one of the alley's.

I need to do this. I need to be the man that Beth and the boys deserve. Rolling out of the truck bed, I found myself filled with a new sense of purpose and ran as best I could with a limp towards the ladder. As I began climbing up I hadn't realized how high off the ground I really was until I looked down and felt a bit woozy from vertigo. Pulling myself close to the rungs I felt all that bravado quickly leave and I had to focus on something to get my mind-set back. I started to reminisce about the day the boys came into the world and that seemed to help get my bearings back.

Beth and I had been sitting in the house making jokes and seeing if I could bounce gummy bears off her belly and into her mouth. I remember getting a respectable ten to hit on target. However, the eleventh when it bounced, it hit her in the face and she had a strange look, followed by my ass feeling very wet.

"I think my water just broke."

"What, now?"

"Well it's either that or I just pissed myself."

"To be fair, both are..."

"If you ever plan to get laid again, you better shut up right now."

Not too long after that she started feeling a lot of pressure and pain. I stood up and rushed to her side, but it was like a bad comedy as I tried to help her up. We had known she was having twins, but her stomach was so big it would make her top heavy whenever she tried to stand and we would have to be sure I could catch her. I managed to stifle my laughter at her attempt to run with her waddling as I knew she was still fully capable of slapping me.

The groans of pain as she started to feel her labor pains hit were coming in waves of sirened moans. I must have made the usual thirty minute drive to the hospital in ten minutes. It was like I was in some action movie car chase scene, but I was the only one that knew. Dodging and weaving through traffic like a madman, I'm sure if Beth was paying attention she would be yelling at me for being so irresponsible. I didn't care, I was going to make sure she made it to the hospital and that she would make it there as fast and safe as reasonably possible.

Looking back now in that moment I was the biggest threat to them. If she had yelled, it would have been totally justified. I'm ashamed for having been so juvenile in my excuses for being a hazard to them, but I was about to be a dad and I just wanted what was best for them. I also was stressed, wanting to be sure they were all safe. Logic really does go out the window when you want to protect the ones you love.

When I screeched into the emergency offloading area, the security guard rushed out to tell me I couldn't park there, before I shouted that they could tow it, but first I needed to get my wife inside. As soon as the words left my mouth there was a small army of nurses that swarmed us and brought Beth inside. The guard offered to park my car and not even thinking I tossed him the keys before running inside.

It was a flurry of excitement as one of the nurses shouted to the others that they didn't have time and that my wife was going into the final stages of labor, something about diameters and I think I heard the word crown thrown in there. All I knew was that one of them shoved me into a room telling me to scrub up before I was escorted to the delivery room.

It is incredibly emasculating seeing your wife in so much pain and knowing you can't do anything to take it away. I went to her side as the doctors did what they had to do. I held her hand and I felt her grip tighten like a vice with each hit of the contractions. Each push must have been an act of herculean effort, as I felt her squeeze harder every time. I felt something break in my hand, but I had to be strong because whatever I was feeling I'm sure she felt a hundred fold.

We were in there for at least two hours before the final push for baby number one to come out. Derrick was a big one. He weighed in at about seven and a half pounds. Tyler on the other hand got stuck on her pelvic bone. No matter how hard she pushed, he just refused to pop out. They ended up having to do an emergency c-section. It was so hard to be strong for her during that operation, but she did it and our beautiful boys were born.

Looking at my hand as I grasped the final wrung before the door, I had to fight the tears back, remembering all that we had been through. I didn't want our argument to be the last thing I remember of her. I was going to find them when this was all over and we were going to be together and I will never let them go. No matter what.

As I went to push the door though, it only racked back and forth. It was locked. "Seriously?" I tried over and over to shake the thing open, but it was not budging. I started to lose hope and contemplated climbing back down, until I saw a man climbing out of a hatch. He looked around like he was lost. When he looked towards me though, I didn't think he could see me. So I pulled myself back up with a boost of confidence and I started yelling like crazy to get his attention. He noticed me and ran over. He broke the lock and helped me onto the roof.

He had told me his name and he looked familiar, the yellow pants he had on looked like the ones the hazmat soldiers at the prison were wearing. I saw the embroidered patch on his shirt and I felt a wave of relief having found someone who I could trust to find the right people to get the cure to. When I showed it to him though, he seemed almost scared for a second.

Before he could say anything else, the building's roof exploded open and a massive tentacle like flower erupted from the center of it. Its bulb opened into a nightmare of destruction.

I was so entranced by the thing that when Dr. Michaels said that we would need to feed the cure into that thing. I hesitated and thought I had a stroke. "Did you just say we need to get this container into that thing?"

"Not the canister itself, but what's inside. Here, give it to me!" He grabbed the container and after a few button pushes and twisting it open, a small test tube came out of it and when he removed it, the weird looking thermos closed itself back up. We felt another rumble and he threw the useless metal tube over the edge and shoved the vial into my hands.

I didn't know what he wanted me to do. I was scared beyond anything I had experienced up until now, and I was terrified that if I didn't do anything, the world would end. He could tell I was hesitant and he grabbed my shoulders. "Listen, I know this is a lot to ask, but all you have to do is throw that little thing in your hand into that monster's mouth and you can save the world. That big ass monster over there is something that when it sends out its seeds, if they have the cure in them, it will spread. It will reverse all of this. Do you have a family or friends that have been affected by this? They can all be saved or kept safe, all you have to do is get that tube into that thing's mouth!"

What he was saying was insanity, what was I supposed to do? As crazy as it sounded though it made sense. I mean this... whatever this virus was that was infecting everything, seemed to spread through contact and maybe whatever comes out of that thing will spread the cure... right?

"Come on man, the fate of the world and all you love is literally in the palm of your hand." He placed his hands on my shoulders and looked me in the eyes. "Please trust me, I made this cure. If you don't do this... here and now. Even with the contingency plans in place... I fear it won't be enough."

The look and tone in his voice were sincere and I felt the words inspire something in me. I was tired of running. I couldn't be a coward like I had been with Zoe. I had to dig deep and bring out the man I was meant to be and do what I had to in order to save my family even if it meant... I didn't want to think about it, but I had to risk it all.

I didn't understand this feeling coming over me and I looked the man in his eyes again. "Are you sure this will work?"

"Yes, of course it will." There wasn't even a moment of hesitation. I felt so much emotion welling up inside and I turned and ignoring the pain, I ran as hard as I could towards the squirming mass of ever changing plant-life. Its body was now rising up and down and it was trying to escape its confinement. Its mouth of petals filled with thousands of teeth and seeds. Its slobber splashed to the ground bringing more life wherever it hit. I had no choice but to run through the puddles of growth, I could feel the roots digging into my flesh through my jeans with every step it caused me searing pain, it was too late to stop now. I had to keep fighting forward. I belted out and shouted as loud as I could, doing everything to get its attention. I felt myself slowing as the mutant plants grew across my legs. Each step they would grip into the concrete and I had to tear my feet free, just for another excruciating step to be taken.

Digging deep I mustered an immense amount of willpower I never knew I had and found myself at the edge of the destroyed skylight. The creature's trunk-like roots pulled free and allowed it to move more unhindered. I could feel my own little anchors turning me into a statue, the only choice I had left was to make my decision. Kneeling down, I crouched to give my body more momentum to break free from the bonds and leapt with all my might towards the rising snapping mouth. I felt no regret in my heart and whispered to myself "I love you," a final goodbye to my wife and sons. Smashing the vial against my chest I accepted my fate with honor.

~ Wilcox

I snatched up the metal vessel and started to run as fast as I could. I didn't have a clue of where I was heading, but I knew I had to get there as soon as possible because it was a much better place than where I was now. It was clear that whatever transport we were waiting for wasn't going to be landing anywhere near here anymore. There might be a safe zone up the way a bit. Didn't matter at this point, I just needed to find a military vehicle and borrow the radio. *That shouldn't be too difficult now should it?*

I could hear the destruction of the building behind me. I could see that there were two people on the roof, but I couldn't tell if it was Vincent, the doc, or that freaking goober that dropped my moneybag off the roof. "Oh shit! The canister, is it broken?" in a frenzy of concern, I looked over the container. I took some solace as the only damage done was that there were a few dents from where it had hit the ground.

"Oh thank god, if only I knew how to open it though, but I guess as long as whatever it is in there is sealed in this thing, they can extract it. I am only being paid to bring this thing to that cute little doctor. I never promised in what condition it would be in. After all the headaches this stupid thing has brought me, the fucken bitch should be glad I don't shove it down her throat after the payment clears.

Lost in my thoughts, I was climbing over a guardrail and looked back to the roof. Whatever that big plant thing is, was thrashing around like a dildo on a power drill. Its enormity grew beyond the building itself and the walls were already bulging, if not collapsing from the rising pressure from within.

I could see the two figures running away from the crumbling debris. I could see the yellow from here and knew that at least one was the doctor. The sounds the creature made were otherworldly and stole my attention from trying to figure out who the other person was. The view of the thing rising really put into perspective how important this little tube was. *Maybe I can double the offer?*

In the distance from where we had driven in, I could see the hoard of infected trickling in. The bigger beasts were easier to make out in the army of distorted nature, but the shambling and twisted forms of those that still looked humanesque disturbed me more. All the differing forms made me wonder if they were all still in there? Were those that were infected still conscious of what was going on? Did they have any control, or were they simply driven to spread, or worse, were they just along for the ride unable to stop themselves? I remember growing up and watching old movies filled with zombies and monsters. It's what I was raised on. Mom was an alcoholic, drug addict, and she didn't care what happened to me as long as she could get her next drink or fix, and good ol' dad was too busy trying to be a big man while in reality he wasn't worth anything of substance. Neither would have even remembered my birthday unless grandma stopped sending me money on it.

The memories of the classic films always gave me an escape from the reality I had as a kid. In a way I kind of always wished for something like in the movies would happen. I would fantasize about a world where the cannibalistic monsters had removed everyone else and I would just, "survive off the land," and all that childish crap. How I would defeat them all with a rock tied to a stick. It was my little hour and a half reprieve from the real world of those two always fighting. It was a small span of time where I didn't have to repair something, like when my mom whipped a liquor bottle at my dad for being a perv, missing and lodging it deep into the wall. Or when my dad would beat on my mom during the arguments, sure I'd try to stop them, and mom was no saint usually being the one to throw the first punch or insult, but it would just end with one of them shoving me away. Well, until the last time.

It was a school night and I was up in my room watching a movie before bed. It was some cheesy alien take over apocalypse deal. I used the sound to drown out the noise until I heard a loud thud and the old farm house shook. It was getting close to bedtime and I had a test in the morning. I was hoping to get some decent sleep beforehand because my grades had been slipping. I hadn't had a good night's sleep in so long that I was passing out in class.

Going downstairs, I saw my dad leaving and my mom was panting at how mad she was at him. It was like watching animals fight whenever I couldn't get away. She looked at me and I already knew what she was going to tell me. "Go get your fucking father, he's threatening to kill himself like a coward again!"

I didn't even bother arguing at that point anymore, because it was a lost cause and I didn't want her wrath aimed at me. I just reluctantly put my shoes on and went out in the night to look. It wasn't a long search this time. He was just hiding by the front porch, but because there was almost no light in the rural area of town we lived in, he figured he was hidden enough.

"Come on dad, this is ridiculous. Just come ins..."

"Shut up and take my side!"

"Take your side on what? I don't even know what you guys are arguing about."

"It doesn't matter what the fight is about. You take my side or I'm telling her about your little hidden stash."

"My stash of what?"

"Don't "what" me, your porn stash ya little shit, and you know how much she hates that. You see what she is like with me, what do you think she will be like with you?"

I didn't know what to say, yes they had both used me as a therapist after their fights before, trying to explain their sides, but this was something different. The little sessions were obviously to manipulate me, but this was just blatant blackmail. He was right though, and I was only left with three options. I could take his side and be his little bitch, he could tell her and I could risk her hitting me with the vacuum, or I could tell her and hope for mercy.

I stepped back slowly with the realization of what was really going on now and I needed a second. A second that I didn't get, because as soon as I stepped inside and closed the door, my mother was there and ready for round two. Instantly a barrage of questions about where dad was, did I find him, where is he hiding? Living with them while they were arguing was like being interrogated, but now I had the added bonus of whether or not my dad had the balls to say he found my stash and I, in my glorious wisdom, chose that moment to just come clean and brace for the hit, hoping that it would be hard enough to put me to sleep. When I was younger she would just scream in my face for days at a time for something as stupid as me failing tests, but with this... I wouldn't have put it past her. Especially right now.

I tensed, waiting for the hit, but it never came. Instead what I saw as I opened my eyes was my mother standing there, fuming with rage before calming down enough to speak. "What?"

I didn't know how to answer, I mean how was I? I figured I'm already in the pan, I might as well hop into the fire. "Dad..."

"Dad what?"

"Dad told me that I had to take his side or else he was going to tell you he found my porn."

The look on her face was scary. Usually it's very easy to tell what kind of reaction she was gonna have, but this looked like I had short circuited her aggression with her disbelief. I was just concerned about what this was going to lead to.

"Go get it!" she said through gritted teeth.

"What?" I was confused.

"Get upstairs and bring it down here."

She was pissed, but for some reason, it didn't seem to be directed towards me though. I went upstairs and went through my tapes and could only find two of the VHS's. I was panicking, but who knows what was going through that woman's head right now, and I already came clean so maybe she will believe it's just the two.

I didn't want to keep her waiting, so I grabbed the tapes and went downstairs. Passing through the stairway door, I found my mom in her smoking room. She was smoking a bowl, which she held in her hand as she was holding her head up like she was exhausted.

I brought the tapes to her and she looked at me, not with disgust, but like she was disappointed in me.

"I want you to understand something. I understand that sex is a normal thing that most couples do. I understand that there is "normal porn" and weird stuff, but what your father is into is scary. It's not normal, it's disgusting and beyond what is okay." She handed me the tapes back and now I was really confused. "Its normal for a boy your age to have this stuff, but what isn't normal is that your dad chooses to masturbate instead of fucking his wife."

Seeing that clearly what I was holding was going to hurt her, I chose to destroy the tapes. I didn't know if this was some elaborate manipulation of hers, but it would look better and also save me three days of her screaming in my face.

It wasn't too long before my dad finally came back inside. I'm sure he was done with the mosquitoes biting him. He saw that I was talking to mom and I don't think he heard or saw what had been going on. Mom instantly ripped into him though and when he tried to get me to take his side I said no. He tried to pull his trump card and told her about my stash, but she threw it back at him by asking how he knew about it in the first place.

After a back and forth of bad excuse after bad excuse. When he found himself completely out of options, he jumped on my mother and started choking and hitting her. I freaked out and tried to pull him off of her, but he grabbed my shoulder and shoved me across the room. I cut my shoulder on something and I ran upstairs. Searching for something I grabbed my little target crossbow and for the first time I was able to draw the string back in one go. Loading the arrow I did the best I could to mentally prepare for what I was about to do.

Coming down the stairs I felt the tears in my eyes, but the determination in my soul told me I had to do this. I had to put an end to this fight. I walked past them and I stood about six feet away. I turned and shouted "That's enough! Stop!" I held the crossbow up and aimed it right at my dads face when he turned to look at me. My mother went into pleading mode and begged me not to shoot. I could feel the tension built up in the trigger as my dads face changed from his smartass condescending tone to one of understanding he was about to die.

I had played enough video games and watched enough movies to know that if I was to survive an apocalypse, I would need to know what it was like to kill a person. I must have stood there for only a few seconds, but it felt like an eternity before my mom clamored into the line of fire. I had hesitated, but I knew I was going to pull the trigger.

Not a day goes by that I didn't wish I had just shot him. Maybe that's why I feel so okay in this new world. There were so many fond thoughts of the past. Who would have thought that my childhood dream of living in an apocalypse would come true and the reason why I survived was because all those walking dandelion fucks look like more disfigured versions of good ol' dad. Haven't talked to them in years, maybe when my business is done here I'll go finish up what I should have ba...

My thoughts were interrupted by a high pitched whistle and I was driven to the ground. I tried to move, but looking down I saw some kind of giant seed embedded deep into my waist. My hip was blown out and was pinned. Whatever had hit me was buried deep in my abdomen and punctured the asphalt beneath. It was strange, I didn't feel any pain. I tried to move again, but whatever was in me wouldn't budge. I was going into shock, that was obvious to me. My body felt weak and shaky, I looked down and saw what looked like a big ass sunflower seed attached to a tooth's root system. Four, very long chitinous bone spikes protruded from my side. I tried grabbing ahold of them to release myself, but they were so sharp they sliced through my hands as they slid across my palms. I felt something moving inside my stomach and the sounds of cracks forming. A pop resonated in my ears and I was sent spinning away landing against a car. My brain couldn't process what was happening, but when I looked down I saw I had been blown in half. Each little bone like fragment burrowing into my wounds as my organs spilled out of me. I looked off into the distance, the titanic plant mothers bulbous head was open and launching its seeds in all directions. It was like watching mines being launched off of a giant whip. Each flick, sending hundreds of bone-like shrapnel in all directions.

"Man... child me would have been fucked." As the world grew dark, I could feel the little pieces of mother digging deeper and spreading within. "Guess... there are worse things... than being in an apocalypse..." *I could feel them growing and bringing me closer to mother.*

~ Vincent

"Doctor Michaels, we need to go! Get down that..." The building rocked violently and I was forced to look back to the demon that was this creature. The man I saw running, struggled to the ledge and a few seconds later he dropped down into the opening. *Was he insane?*

Turning back to the doctor, I saw him already climbing down the ladder. Rushing to join him as the beast seemed to be reacting to something and was tearing the roof down. *If I didn't hurry I'd be torn down with it.* Looking out over the organized junkyard of vehicles, I saw an abandoned news van. *That's our ticket out of here.*

I hopped over the edge of the metal gate and slid down to meet Michaels at the bottom. "This way, we have to get to that van and send out a message!" I grabbed his arm and pulled him in the direction we needed to go.

Dodging through the cars, the sound of the monstrosity behind us seemed to follow as it destroyed its prison. There was no point in looking back now, I already knew what was coming and I wasn't going to waste my time. I saw that Michaels looked back. "Get to cover!" he shouted before jumping under the nearest car. Following suit, I heard hundreds of whistles screeching through the air. The banshee-like wind was possessed with whatever being blown through it and as it began to impact the ground, it was like an artillery bombardment peppered the area. The sounds of the hoods of cars being smashed in and windows shattering filled the air. The mortar-like bombardment echoed as chunks of what looked like bones came soon after.

Taking a rushed look around, I understood what we had just avoided. All the teeth shaped seeds were being launched in all directions. When they detonated they sent their shards in all directions. Each one grew vine-like legs and scuttled away as if they were spiders in search of prey. Michaels had already pulled himself out from beneath his bent in half shield of a car and was almost to the van. I saw him grab the handle and try to open it, but it wasn't budging.

Scooping up a rock, I ran behind him and smashed the window in. Unlocking the door I jumped into the driver's seat. Flipping the visors and checking the glove box, I found the key in the cup holder and shoved it into the ignition. Michaels crawled in just as I hit the gas, slamming the door closed on his legs. He let out a shout of pain and I grabbed him by his belt to lift him the rest of the way in.

He held on for dear life as I bobbed and weaved through the abandoned vehicle graveyard. I couldn't stop driving and I had no clue the range was on those seed bombs either. Looking at the Doc rubbing his leg, he was not in a good mood. "Do you know how to use one of those radios?" I asked him.

He looked like he was about to hit me with the glare he shot me. "You almost broke my damn leg and you wanna know if I can press a goddamn button? Yes I can use a fricken radio!"

"Good, then get back there and send a message to this frequency." I pulled my emergency contacts sheet from my shoulder pocket and handed it to him. "Whoever answers, tell them to connect you with sergeant Phillips. It is a priority situation and we will need air strike authorization to destroy the target at the mall."

With all the swerving, he was able to make it to the back and I heard him flipping switches and pushing buttons. "Oh that's what that does?"

I heard a click and something bright lit up. "What was that?"

"It was the camera feed, I don't know how to turn it off. Oh, I found the radio button though."

"Congrats you want a fucken cookie, send the message!"

" You could be a little nicer ya know."

"Michaels, not now! That thing is too dangerous to let live for any amount of time."

I heard him type in the frequency and start asking for someone to connect him to the sarge. After the longest thirty seconds, they must have understood the urgency and I heard him relay my message. I heard the voice on the other side say we need visuals on the target and I blurted out. "Turn on the news!"

"Sweet mother of god, the hell is that?"

"That's the target sir! We need immediate burn of the area! We are clear of the blast zone."

A few seconds passed as another volley of those seeds smacked the ground like meteors. The subsequent explosions rocked and dented the walls of the van, like we were in a beer can at a frat house. "Air support inbound, escort your friend there to the nearest open area for emergency pick up. The chopper is on route and we have you tracked on screen. Do you copy?"

"Copy sir!" jerking the wheel I hit a corner and almost tipped the van over.

I saw a parking lot and the helicopter was about to fly overhead. Luckily they saw us as we pulled in or else we would have had to wait for them to circle around. They dropped ropes and harnesses and we rushed for them. We hooked in and gave the sign to pull us up. They instead had to fly up and out as the jets flew over them.

We could see in the distance how large the Lovecraftian monstrosity had grown to. Its body movements almost in slow motion from the sheer size of it. It launched more of its deadly seeds, shredding one of the jets, but the others got close enough to drop their payloads in return. The plumes of smoke and fire rolled up into the sky as the creature struggled and finally broke free from the confines of the shopping center. Napalm wasn't enough, but it was no longer my issue. More bombs and missiles were launched at the lumbering beast, but it did nothing to slow it down. Where it was going, I didn't know, it simply walked as it scattered, like some war engine version of Johnny Appleseed. Branch-like limbs shot out pillars of spikes, destroying the jets as they strafed it with machine gun fire. There was no longer anything I could do. I took a breath of some minor relief, but I had no clue the horror that thing will bring in the future if it isn't brought down.

~ Michaels

Watching the magnificent creature move was a sight to see. I wish I knew where it was going, with all that power it could go anywhere. The flames danced across its back like ballerinas in the production of their lives on a moving stage of death and destruction. Spreading its brood across the land in a path of survival, it swatted its would-be attackers like flies, in its search for meaning. I had to laugh on the inside as the military's weapons seemed to have little to no effect on my beautiful creation.

Clutching my bag to my chest, I knew that eventually the ordnance they used would escalate until it would eventually kill it, but I took some reprieve knowing I had my samples to keep its life going. Sure it would never be as strong as what I brought about with that idiot's help, but it was enough for me to know my research was safe. Now it's just a matter of watching this little experiment as far as it will go. I felt like a kid watching food in a plastic container as it became a little planet of life. The first few blooms of mold, the small bugs we didn't know were in the vegetables and meats eating and thriving off the rot and decomposition. All in the hopes to see something interesting. At first this was all revenge for molesting my life's work, but the more I look at this petri dish of death, the more I am beginning to think that I truly missed my calling in this line of work.

The flight was uncomfortable, sure they were able to bring us into the chopper eventually, but the uncertain looks the soldiers gave us made me feel as if we weren't welcome. Looking over to Vincent, it seemed like he was getting the same vibe of the situation as well. They didn't seem like what the army would send in, they didn't even have insignia for what branch they were a part of.

The way they were watching over us was not the way I was used to traveling with a military escort. *These people reminded me more of the rumors I had heard from the... oh shit!*

These weren't soldiers, these were the containment crew. I leaned over as if to whisper a thank you to Vincent for all his help, but when I got close enough. "These aren't your brothers in arms." He looked back at me and nodded with a smile. I hoped in an attempt to hide that he understood the situation. He also gestured with a low hand signal to not do anything stupid. I hope he had a plan.

We sat there with the turbulence dropping us every once in a while until we could see that we were being taken over a massive wall made of concrete and shipping containers. I watched as the realization of the situation set in. *Was all of this planned before I even put my idea into motion?*

Clearly they didn't want us dead, they could have just left us in that hell if they wanted that. *Then what was it they wanted? No, that couldn't be it, how would they have known it was gone? Was I considered the next best thing?* I couldn't help but have concerns as if this was planned, who and why though kept making it bounce around my head like a hyperactive toddler.

As if sensing my train of thought, Vincent placed his hand on my shoulder, trying to comfort me. This wasn't right, something truly was not sitting well with this situation and I didn't know how it was going to end.

As the helicopter began its descent. I felt a knot in my stomach. *Had I really only made it this far to be sent to prison? No... no I wouldn't allow that.*

When we touched down, the door opened and one of the unnamed men helped me down. We were taken to separate rooms, and I was told to change out of the clothes I was wearing. Looking through the bag they had given me, I found what looked like hospital scrubs and a mask. Putting them on, I checked my bag and found that the clippings I had managed to salvage were in good condition. In fact the finger-like appendage was already moving again. It was in search of something. I would need to find it someplace to be housed in the meantime, but it couldn't be here.

Going to the door, I cracked it open enough to see if there was anyone around. There was a guard outside the door, but he seemed preoccupied with a conversation on his radio. Something about how he should be jealous of how his buddy was escorting some hot scientist chick.

"Yeah man, she's just my type, too. Short black hair, nice little wiggle to her. Hell I bet she moans like a banshee in the sack."

"Whatever man, I wouldn't try nothing if I was you. She may be a baddie, but focus. What you think is gonna happen if you try and make a move and she turns out to be some MMA champ and kicks your ass from here to next Tuesday?" My guard said with a laugh. I knew instantly that scientist was my fiance.

"I'm tellin ya, ya boy here is in love." The voice on the radio responded.

"Well then, stupid cupid, y'all got a new call sign, but if you succeed on your suicide mission, send pics, don't be stingy." I didn't appreciate how they were talking about my soon to be wife.

"Definitely, oh gotta go. Taking her to see the other survivor and then we headed to you. Maybe I can frisk her for safety concerns."

"Ya know what, you deserve the beating she about to give you. Over and out." They ended their conversation and I at least knew she was still here. The best part, she was heading this way.

~ Chris

The prism of color blinded me, the feeling of being surrounded but alone filled me. I could feel the presence of thousands of others. Screams of torment and fear filled every second of this unbearable nightmare. Everywhere I looked seemed to zoom in and show me some random location as if I was looking through the eyes of another.

Whenever my vision became one of the countless eyes. I could hear their thoughts. The person inside of the creatures. Some were panicked, scared, and terrified because they couldn't control their bodies anymore. Others laughed either from their mental state cracking under the reality or were legitimately enjoying watching what their bodies did.

I saw through the eyes of an infected child, jumping and swinging around a house. Killing her family and infecting their corpses. Another man pleaded for the violence to stop as his body destroyed a barricade and attacked a tank. Ripping armor and whatever else was in its way before pulling a soldier through the hand size hole it eventually made.

Some of the visions were dark, when I zoomed into them, all I could see were memories. The hosts appeared to be dead, but their roots had found soil and were still connected. I rewound the memory of one and saw the last moments before it changed. He was someplace that looked familiar. The walls were high and made of brick, the barbed wire that coiled around the tops. The soldiers scattered around, he was at the prison.

I watched as he was in line and saw that the nurses were doing their light tests. I was about to zoom out when something caught my attention. There was a glimpse of red hair, a slender arm and a little boy. I watched a little longer and another little boy was ushered along with the woman. Following where they were getting taken to in line. I saw the nurses shine her and the children's eyes and they were taken to the left and down a hall. The next few people were taken to the right. As the body I was in looked around in a panic, the woman turned her head and in that moment I knew It was Beth and the boys.

I felt excitement, this is what I had been searching for all this time, but *where were they going? Where were they being taken to?*

I could only watch and try to see more until a bright light flashed into my eyes. I looked away in reaction and lost the connection. Frantically, I began searching through every dead sentry I could find that was in the general area before I stopped when Derrick's face was in view. I felt so much warmth, but could see he was clearly injured. I tried to reach out and touch him, but I couldn't feel a thing. It was like punching in a dream. All I wanted to do was to feel his face, but I couldn't even reach out. Then I saw Tyler and it became clear whose eyes I was seeing through. But if I was seeing through hers, then that meant... *oh please, don't let this be true.*

It happened so fast, the infection had already started to show visible signs on the boys. Their skin becoming crackled like bark, their bodies morphing into something horrible. I wanted to cry and shout, but I was helpless to even comfort them. Beth was strong and never let go of them, no matter how bad they were getting, she held them tight. As she changed with them they began to meld together and when they did, it was as if we were all together again.

I did my best to accept the news that they were at least together when they changed. When a face appeared in a little window on the door to the cell they were apparently in. My sadness was replaced with rage as the man I saw was the same man from the roof. The one who convinced me I was doing the right thing by sacrificing myself. He looked down and to his right before saying something I couldn't hear. a metal tube extended and took up a small slot on the door, His body jerked like he was gesturing and giving a command to someone else, all of a sudden the vision began to violently move, the psionic screams of my family rippled through me as what looked like chemicals rained down on them from the small opening. I felt the pain that they felt in that moment and I had to fight to keep watching. I may not have been with them in their final moments, but I wasn't going to leave them. I felt as their lives drained away, dying in a way that was absolute torment. Beth tried her best to shield them... but it wasn't enough.

I zoned out when the wails of pain finally stopped. I made sure to remember which cell was theirs as the sight pulled away. There were no words for the emotional trauma I was feeling. The mental and emotional scar that was now embedded into my soul, I knew would never heal.

"You miss them don't you?" A small distorted child-like voice seemed to resonate through me. "My daddy cared about me like you care about them. He even brought mommy, but he wouldn't let her near me. He said she was a bad lady and didn't deserve to be with us anymore."

"Huh... who... what are you?"

"My name is Tabitha, what's yours?"

"Chr... Chris, and yes I miss them dearly and I don't know how to even begin to feel knowing they have been gone all this time."

"I'm happy to meet you, Mister Chris. I've been scared and all alone for so long now. My daddy was taking care of me, but he's gone now. He protected me, he made sure I grew up big and strong."

"Wait... are you... I mean we... How old are you?" The sound and cadence of the voice couldn't have been an adult.

"I was eight, I think. It's been so lonely and all I hear are the people yelling and crying, but you mister, I can talk to you. So that makes me happy. I'm not alone anymore. All the others just ignore me and I can never get their attention. You seem like a very nice man."

"What makes you say that? I'm a coward and a fool."

"Not from what I see. You seem like you are always trying to do the right thing. I'm watching you now through the others. You are a good person and I'm sure my daddy would feel I would be safe with you."

"Watching me through the others?" *Was she able to view them all at once?*

~ Tabitha

"What happened to you?" The new person's voice asked me.

I remember holding onto daddy as he took me away from the scary jail. I remember all the yelling as he kept my eyes away from seeing all the bad things people were doing and the scary monsters. I could feel them near us and how they wanted to hurt us, but also over time how they didn't mean to be hurtful. They just couldn't stop themselves.

He protected the best he could, but I was very sick. I remembered what happened to grandma and how she was very angry and attacked us. I know now that she didn't mean to hurt me, she was just sick, too. I wanted daddy to be strong because he was sad and I held him so tight that it was like we were together.

Then the big scary animal attacked and I felt a connection to it. It was angry at us, it wanted to hurt daddy, but if it did then I would have been hurt too. I reached out and it didn't stop, but I made it. I didn't want to hurt it. When my hand went out to block it from hurting us, I felt a strange sensation as I connected to it. Daddy was feeling weak and I wanted him to feel stronger. I made it give him strength. I felt his body feel better and he was able to keep his promise. I felt sad as the monster's life seemed to go away, but we were safe.

He must have felt better because he was moving faster and was jumping really high. He kept on telling me he was going to keep his promise to me, but when we got there, he must have thought I was asleep. I got scared because he laid me down on the dirt and started to cover me up. It was dark and scary. It was so long before I started to hear the others. I saw just as you saw, through the eyes of him as well as them. It was scary what I saw him doing and everyone else doing, but he was doing it to feed me. To care for me. He wanted me to be their queen.

So I tried really really hard and I started to grow. The bigger I was, the happier he seemed to be. When the big robot came and hurt me, he protected me again. Even though it hurt, I knew he didn't mean to. It was like I could listen to his brain, but he couldn't hear me saying it was okay.

When the army men tried to hurt daddy, I tried to make them stop, but daddy was hurt after they tried to blow him up. They made him feel pain and for what he did for me, I wanted to protect him. He came to me and hugged me one last time. He gave me his life and for a short moment, I felt he could finally hear me tell him how much I loved him.

I felt so sad at him going away that I needed to escape. I was upset that I couldn't do anything, but with what his life gave me I felt I could break free. I tried to find some way to move my body and with all my sadness and anger I was finally able to make myself move. I don't know what I was doing or thinking, I just knew I needed to get free before one of the bad men hurt me.

Then I saw a new light, it looked like my daddy's and it was flickering like a star. When I tried to look at it, I felt the same love and determination I felt with dad and I thought it was him, but all I saw was a long fall and a big scary monster at the bottom of the hole. I didn't know the monster was me until you had fallen into the monster's mouth. That's when I felt you joined with me. I instantly felt your memories and saw everything about you, and your family. I wished for you to find them and tried to turn your sight to them.

I knew they were here with us, but I don't know how I knew. I wasn't sure if you could hear me, but I understood you were safe. I can take you to see them. I can take you anywhere.

I felt his essence wanting to speak, it was saddened, but I felt his response like a warm hug. "Please take me to them."

I was filled with excitement and we were able to escape that bad place. I felt something hit my body, but it wasn't going to stop me from helping this daddy with finding his family. I could see the airplanes flying around me and I swatted at them like they were bugs. I was so big now and I know my daddy would be proud of me.

~ Vincent

They separated us at the gate and I was being taken for debriefing. They sat me down in a small interrogation room which was a little odd. I don't know why they sent private contractors to collect us, but if they had wanted us dead, I'm sure they would have already dropped our bodies in the infected zone.

A few minutes had passed when I heard the door open and the female scientist from the mission briefing stepped inside. She was more prim and proper looking than before, if that was possible and she held a clipboard under her arm. She sat down across from me and I instantly felt discomfort. It was as if I was in trouble for something, seeing as her once sad and apologetic demeanor from before was replaced with someone that appeared cold and robotic.

She looked into my eyes and I felt hypnotized by hers. The green and yellow tint with the black hair was for some reason giving me dominatrix vibes. "Hello Vincent. I was informed that you and Doctor Michaels were the only ones to survive the mission."

"That is correct ma'am." I didn't know what was going on, but this didn't feel like a normal debrief. *Where was Sarge? Where were the other brass that I usually had to discuss the mission details with?* I figured my best course of action would be to just answer her questions and maybe I'd be able to walk out of here alive.

"I'm going to make this very simple for you," she said before placing the clip-board on the table and sliding it over to me. "If you sign this it will save you a world of hassle down the road."

I stared at the small contract worth of papers and then back to her. "What is this?"

"This is an NDA that states that in the course of your mission there were mishaps along the way and two of your men went AWOL. It states that both of them died, unfortunately due to their choices. However, it also states that you as well as Private Kennedy were able to stay on your respective missions as well, even though he was dropped too far from the mission landing zone. Although the good private was killed in action, and when you came to where the locator beacon was activated, your mission also ended upon finding Dr. Michaels. The good doctor wasn't able to be saved during the rescue proceedings. Try as you did, he was infected and you were forced to kill him. By signing this you will be obligated under top secret clearances to stick to this story and this story alone. In the event you breach this contract you will be arrested under the law in accordance with whatever we deem necessary and in turn be imprisoned for the rest of your life for treason. However, if you abide by the contract, you will be reinstated and given a medal of bravery as well as a promotion to your next rank. I have arranged for an acceptable sum of money to be allocated to your account and we can all go on living our best lives."

It was eerie hearing the calmness in her voice. It was as if this was a daily occurrence for her to say to someone, but my curiosity was nagging at me. "May I ask a question?"

She nodded and put her hand out as if to say proceed.

"What's going to happen to the Doctor? He is still alive... isn't he?"

"Do not worry about him, the reason it is worded in this fashion is because his research would be considered against a few international laws. There is a plan in action that is meant to move him out of the area and hide his identity. If he is reported killed in action, then it makes that plan a lot smoother." She sat back in her chair relaxing a little bit. "Mr. Valheart, I'm not trying to be an enemy here. I am simply trying to make life easy for both of us. The Chlor-Reform corporation is a very well known and powerful company, if word got out that we caused this incident and the loss of hundreds of thousands of lives, it wouldn't be the best image and would result in a global economic tragedy. We can't have that now can we? So please, sign the paper so we can get cleaned up and get you a nice meal." She put on a smile that seemed almost reptilian. No sincerity at all, but I understood my current predicament was a position of going with the flow of the river or I float face down in it.

"I'll sign this, but please do me one favor."

"What would that be?"

"I would like to be a part of whatever team goes in and destroys your disgusting abominations."

Her smile widened with her white teeth baring like a predatory animal. "I believe that can be arranged, Mr. Valheart. Thank you for your cooperation."

I picked up the pen and signed my name. *If I do anything now, I'll need proof. I'll be able to get that the closer I am to the source.*

~ Michaels

They brought me an MRE along with some water. The nasty glob of paste and crackers were not appealing, but it was something I could use. I mixed up all the food into the gross mass and placed the twitching root system into it with some water and the pollen sample in a plastic sandwich bag. I hid it away inside a locker.

A few minutes later I heard the voice of my loving fiance'. "Is the prisoner comfortable?"

Prisoner? What does she mean, prisoner?

"He is as comfortable as can be, ma'am. You are cleared to enter."

The door opened and it was definitely a sight for sore eyes. "Hello Miss Conoly, how may I be of assistance?"

She let out a small laugh and rushed over wrapping her arms around me and kissing me like I had been away at war. Couldn't say I blamed her, I felt the same way. However, the look the guard escorting her gave me spoke volumes about how he was let down.

I stared back with a smile and mouthed the words "she does" as I held her close. His eyes widening as he knew I had heard him talking shit and he had a look of fear as he appeared to understand what that would imply.

Leaning in, I kissed her neck near her ear. "Is everything ready to go?"

"Yes, now we need to gather your things, our transport is waiting. They will be initiating their safety protocol earlier than expected and perimeter bases are being evacuated."

I gave her another squeeze and I followed her down the corridor. With all that had happened, I had to reflect on all the events of the last day. Walking through the halls, I remembered the prison and its draining walls and bars. Passing by all the scurrying soldiers it was like my colleagues at the lab when the specimens were released. The armed escort to our eventual freedom. It all seemed so well organized for an emergency response.

As we stepped into the busy warehouse sized auto depot there was an armored transport with the door open. I stepped up and sat down followed by the two guards. I turned as the door was closing to see my love standing outside. "What's going on?"

She halted the door for a second in order to say something. "I hate to do this, but where I'm going and where you are going are two vastly different places. Enjoy your new lab."

The feeling of betrayal was like a gut punch and I realized now, exactly who was the one who had been playing me from the start, but I smiled through the pain. "Fair play, enjoy your new garden." her smile faded into confusion as the door closed. *I'll have the last laugh, you conniving bitch.*

As the APC pulled out from the depot, I watched through the back window. The sight of jets and massive bombers flew overhead going towards where I could still see the shadow of the beast waving in the distance.

~ Chris

Coming to terms with the loss of my family, I listened to this sweet child describe what all she has witnessed, she still wants to help me find them. Each step we took closed the distance and I didn't know how I was going to be able to react seeing them in the state they were left in. I knew they were gone, but I didn't want to leave them alone in a cell. Maybe we could at least bury them in a way.

She allowed me to see what she saw and I felt the anticipation building as the prison came into view. The sensation of my hand being held helped me relax. I still did not know what was happening with my lack of body, yet I somehow was able to touch in some way. It was the closest feeling of being human I could still enjoy.

Our feet crashed through the walls surrounding the compound. As we stood over the building I felt my hands being guided as huge fleshy vines erupted from our body and plunged them deep into the bricks, flinging them away like plastic blocks. The tips opened to allow us to see inside, each one taking separate paths until the cell was found.

The door was still closed and I knew what was beyond it. One of the vines reached out "Please don't... I have to do this myself." I felt the warmth stammer before it slowly dissipated and I was on my own again.

Slowly, I took control of the limb and I gently maneuvered it to the handle. I tried to open it, but felt a slight resistance before the whole thing tore from the wall. I dropped it to the side and averted the eyes away except for one. As the dust cleared from the broken frames and ground away cinder blocks, I saw them. If I still had my own eyes I would have cried. Seeing the husks that used to be my family, I broke down and wanted to turn away. Another brush of warmth caressed where my cheek would be as if to wipe away a tear before guiding me to look again. I had lost control of the appendage and it rose up and above Beth's head. The vine split open and a viscous fluid dripped onto the melded remains. The dark scene of their rotted corpses began to grow fresh life. I felt something within me grow as well. I watched in wonder as their bodies filled with life. They still didn't move and I couldn't feel them joining the hivemind, but they appeared more vibrant as a soft moss covered the brown dried shell that they had just been. In a way I think it was a way for Tabitha to help me cope with their loss. Even for a child, she seemed to at least understand that me seeing them covered in life was better than the alternative.

I felt the embrace from my new friend and she spoke to me again. "Mr. Chris, the big planes are coming back. They are trying to hurt me. Please, can you hold me, too? I'm scared."

Looking through her eyes I saw the incoming angels of death, their bomb bay doors opening. We waited for the final moment and even though I couldn't feel anything coming from my family. I was just happy that if this is the end, then I could finally hold them one last time.

STEVEN BAZYDLO

Epilogue

"Crows nest this is Thor. We have eyes on the target and the hammer is primed for drop. Permission to engage?"

"One moment Thor, we are waiting for clearance codes."

"Target is green, we are ready to go. What are the orders?"

"Thor this is a crow's nest, engage is affirmative. Drop the hammer."

"Hammer is dropped, I repeat, hammer is dropped."

"... is the target neutralized?"

"We are circling around, crow's nest... dear god no! Crows nest negative, target is still alive I repeat target is sti... Eject! Eject!"

"It's too lat... Ahh! (static)"